* * * * * * *

"I got an anonymous phone call a few minutes ago. It was a man's voice, but he didn't identify himself. He said that there was a body near a slash pile at the end of one of the logging roads near Medicine Mountain," the sheriff said.

"There has to be a dozen or more logging roads in that area. Did he give you any more details as to where the body was located?" Bill asked.

"No. I'm sure there are a lot of logging roads in that area. It may be a crank call, but it might not. I think it would be a good idea if we check it out."

"Yes, sir. I agree."

"I want you to go up there and see if you can find the body. I know it's late and you won't have a lot of time to look for it. If there is a body, we need to find it as soon as possible, before any evidence is lost."

"I understand. I'll get ready and go up there."

* * * * * * *

Other titles by J.E. Terrall available at Amazon

Western Short Stories
- The Old West *
- The Frontier*
- Untamed Land*
- Tales from the Territory*
- Frontier Justice*

Western Novels
- Conflict in Elkhorn Valley*
- Lazy A Ranch (A Modern Western)
- The Story of Joshua Higgins*
- The Valley Ranch War*
- Jake Murdock, Bounty Hunter*

Romance Novels
- Balboa Rendezvous
- Sing for Me*
- Return to Me*
- Forever Yours*

Mystery/Suspense/Thriller
- I Can See Clearly *
- The Return Home*
- The Inheritance

Bill Sparks Mysteries
- Murder in the Backcountry*

Nick McCord Mysteries
- Vol – 1 Murder at Gill's Point
- Vol – 2 Death of a Flower
- Vol – 3 A Dead Man's Treasure
- Vol – 4 Blackjack, A Game to Die For
- Vol – 5 Death on the Lakes
- Vol – 6 Secrets Can Get You Killed
- Vol – 7 Murder on the Racetrack

Peter Blackstone Mysteries
- Murder in the Foothills
- Murder on the Crystal Blue
- Murder of My Love
- Murder in the Dark of Night

Frank Tidsdale Mysteries
- Death by Design
- Death by Assassination

Non-fiction
- Two Brothers Go To War Letters from WWI

*Also available in Large Print Editions

MURDER AND THE GOLD COINS

A BILL SPARKS MYSTERY

by

J.E. Terrall

All rights reserved
Copyright © 2021 by J.E. Terrall

ISBN: 978-09997823-7-8

No part of this book may be reproduced or transmitted in any form or by any means, electronic or mechanical, including photocopying, recording or by any information storage or retrieval system, in whole or in part, without the expressed written consent of the author.

This is a work of fiction. Names, characters, and incidents are either a product of the author's imagination or are used fictitiously, and any resemblance to actual persons, living or dead, is purely coincidental.

Printed in the United States of America
First Printing / 2021 – kdp.com

Cover: Photos for Front and back cover taken by author, J.E Terrall

Book Layout/
Formatting: J.E. Terrall
Custer, South Dakota

MURDER AND THE GOLD COINS

To
My brother-in-law, Dale Luze.
Over the years, we grew to know
each other and became friends.
I miss him.

Interesting facts related to this story:

The Air Force base located outside Rapid City, South Dakota, was known as Rapid City Air Force Base at the time of this story, 1948. It wasn't until 1953 that it was renamed Ellsworth Air Force Base.

A slash pile is a pile of branches, twigs and other small parts of trees left after they have been stripped from trees that have been cut down for use as lumber. Slash piles are usually left to dry, then burned after a year or two or when they are dry enough to burn well. They are usually burned in the winter when it is cold and there is snow on the ground to prevent a forest fire.

Negro Creek was probably named by Spanish missionaries. The word Negro in Spanish means black. There is some information that indicates some of the Spanish missionaries came up as far as the area of the Black Hills and had contact with some Indian tribes in what is now the north central part of the United States.

CHAPTER ONE

It was a quiet late Sunday afternoon in the small town of Hill City in the heart of the Black Hills. Bill Sparks, a Pennington County Deputy Sheriff, was leaning back in his favorite chair. He had been listening to a baseball game on the radio when he fell asleep.

He was suddenly awakened by the sound of someone turning into his driveway. Bill looked at his watch and remembered that Julie Turnquest, his girlfriend, was going to stop by on her way home from work at the hospital in Rapid City.

He got up and walked to the front door. A smile came across his face when he saw Julie getting out of her car. She smiled up at him as she walked toward the house.

"It looks like you might have been napping," she said.

"I guess I dozed off while listening to the ball game," he said as he ran his hand through his hair. "It wasn't that interesting a game, anyway. I heard you drive in."

Julie stepped up on the porch and reached up and put her hands on his shoulders, then raised up on her tiptoes.

Bill wrapped his arms around her narrow waist, pulled her close and kissed her. Just as Bill let go of her to lead her into the house, his phone began to ring.

Bill turned and hurried into the house to answer the phone. Julie followed him into the house and watched him as he hurried across the living room and picked up the receiver.

"Hello."

"Bill, this is Sheriff Henderson."

"Yes, sir."

"We got an anonymous phone call a few minutes ago. It was a man's voice, but he didn't identify himself. He said that there was a body at the end of one of the logging roads near a slash pile. He said the logging road leading to the slash piles was near Medicine Mountain."

"There has to be a dozen or more logging roads in that area. Did he give you any more details like which logging road it might be, or something that would give us some idea as to where the body was located?" Bill asked.

"No, I'm afraid not. I'm sure there are a lot of logging roads in that area. It might be a crank call, but then it might not. I think it would be a good idea if we check it out."

"Yes, sir. I agree."

"I want you to go up there and see if you can find the body. I know it's late and you won't have a lot of time to look for it. If there is a body, we need to find it as soon as possible, before any evidence that still might be there is lost. The evidence will help us determine if the victim died of an accident, or natural causes, or if he was murdered."

"I understand. I'll get ready and go up there right away."

"I'm afraid that's all I have. The desk sergeant tried to get more information, but the guy hung up on him. About all the help I can give you is the desk sergeant said the guy's voice sounded like he might be a young man, but that may not mean anything."

"Okay, I'll get up there as soon as I can."

"Good. I'm sorry if I ruined you evening."

"No problem, sir."

"Call as soon as you have something, and take care. We have no idea what this call is really about, so be prepared for almost anything. It could be a trap."

"I understand. I will be watchful."

"Good luck," the sheriff said then hung up.

Bill hung up the phone. He could hear Julie in the kitchen. Bill went to his bedroom and changed into his uniform, then went to the kitchen. He found Julie in the kitchen making him a sandwich.

"I take it that was the sheriff you were talking to on the phone," Julie said.

"Yes, it was."

"You have to leave, don't you?"

"Yes. He got a report of a body up near Medicine Mountain. I have to go see if I can find it."

"I guessed that from your conversation. I thought you might like some coffee and a sandwich to take with you," Julie said.

"Thanks, Honey. There's no telling how long I'll be out there."

After Julie had filled his Thermos with coffee and put it in his lunchbox with a sandwich and an apple, Bill picked it up. He was ready to leave.

"Is it all right if I wait here for you? I'll worry about you."

"Sure. If you get tired, you can sleep in my bed. You might want to call your grandfather and tell him you're staying here so he won't worry about you."

"I will. Will you wake me when you get home?"

"If you want me too, but I don't have any idea how late it will be."

"I still want you to wake me. I'll want to know you are home safe."

"Okay."

Bill took her in his arms and kissed her. After their kiss, he reluctantly let go of her.

"I better get going."

"Drive safely."

"I will."

Bill walked out of the house and got in his patrol car. He started it, then backed out of his driveway. He turned down the street and immediately headed out of Hill City and into the backcountry toward Medicine Mountain.

As he drove toward Medicine Mountain, Bill's first thoughts were of Julie and the fact the she was going to sleep in his bed tonight. He smiled at the thought of her being in his bed when he got back.

However, it wasn't long and his thoughts turned to the call from the sheriff. Bill would be looking not only for the body, but for any abandoned vehicle that might have been used by the person he was looking for. There was no report about how the body might have gotten there, or if foul play was suspected. There was also no report on if the body was male or female, or the condition of the body. It would be up to Bill to find the body, if there was one, and to determine if it was foul play or not.

With so little to go on, Bill figured it could prove to be a long night. With what information he had, he was sure that if he didn't find the body tonight, he would have to go back into the backcountry again in the morning.

As Bill drove along the dirt and gravel roads, he kept an eye out for any abandoned vehicles. He took the most direct route to the Medicine Mountain area hoping that he might see an abandoned vehicle, but he didn't see any.

It took him almost an hour to reach the area of Medicine Mountain. He slowed down and began to watch for places where a vehicle might be parked, while watching for logging roads.

As soon as he found a logging road, he would turn in and see if there were any tracks from a vehicle. He would then drive back in until he came to the end of the road.

When he reached the end of the logging road, he would check to see if there was a body near the slash piles. If there was not a body, he would then head for the next logging road.

The sun was beginning to drop down over the horizon by the time he covered most of the logging roads around the base of Medicine Mountain. There had to have been at least a dozen logging roads. Most of them were fairly short, but a couple of them went almost all the way around the base of the mountain. Bill didn't find an abandoned vehicle anywhere, or a body.

It was getting almost too dark to continue searching with so little possibility of success. Bill pulled off to the side of the road and called in on his radio.

"Car eight to dispatch."

"Dispatch, go ahead."

"Mary, I'm out near Medicine Mountain searching for the body. I have not found any sign of it, or of an abandoned vehicle. Have you heard anything more about a body near Medicine Mountain?"

"We have not heard anything more about it."

"It looks like I will need to wait until morning to continue the search."

"What's the weather like out there?"

"It's cool and there's a slight breeze out of the northwest. It feels like there's a slight chance of rain, but that's about all."

"The sheriff told me to tell you that if you don't find the body before it's too dark, you should go back up in the morning," Mary said.

"I understand. I saw a couple of logging roads on the other side of the road, on the east side of Medicine Mountain. It looks like they go away from the mountain. I don't know how far back they go in from the road, but I don't think it is too far back into the forest. I haven't checked them out yet. I'll check them out. If I don't find anything there, I'll go home."

"Okay. If you don't find anything, call in when you get home. The sheriff wants a report of your activities. You can tell me and I'll give it to him first thing in the morning."

"I will. Out."

Bill turned his car round and drove back to where he had seen the first logging road. It was located east of Medicine Mountain, and looked like it headed away from the mountain.

He turned his patrol car onto the logging road and stopped. Bill turned his spotlight on and began checking the road for signs of activity. He saw a few tracks in the dirt, but nothing that he thought were important to finding the body. The tracks appeared to have been made by a heavy truck, probably a logging truck. It looked like they had been hauling logs out of the area.

Since Bill had no idea what kind of vehicle might have been used by the dead person, he started to move his spotlight from side to side as he drove slowly along the logging road. He hadn't gone more than about two hundred yards when he came to a wooden bridge across Negro Creek. He drove across the creek. It was only a couple of hundred feet beyond the bridge when he came to the end of the logging road. It opened into an area where he could turn around.

It was clear that logging had been done in the area recently. There were several slash piles waiting to be burned. It looked like the logs had already been picked up and taken to one of the local sawmills.

Since the reporting of the body mentioned that the body was near a slash pile, Bill got out of his car. He turned on his flashlight and walked around the slash piles. He didn't find a body. Bill returned to his patrol car, got in it and started to leave.

As he turned around, he checked out the open area with his headlights and spotlight. He found nothing to indicate there had been any activity in the area in the past few days.

Bill drove back to the main road and headed for another logging road that headed away from the mountain. The second logging road was only a short distance from the previous one. He turned onto the second logging road, stopped and checked for tracks. He found what looked like tracks from a small truck or a car. Bill once again used his spot light as he continued on along the logging road.

It was less than a hundred yards or so before he came to a bridge across Negro Creek. As soon as he crossed the bridge, the road turned from generally east to a southerly direction. He continued along the logging road. It ran fairly close to the creek in a number of places. It crossed back and forth across Negro Creek two or three times.

Bill slowly worked his way to the end of the logging road. It was longer than the other logging road, going back into the forest maybe half a mile or more before it came to the end. At the end, he found several slash piles. From the looks of the ground, the logs had been hauled off sometime ago. There was plenty of room to turn his car around.

He began to turn around when his headlights shined on something lying on the ground near the end of one of the slash piles. Bill stopped and shined his spotlight on what appeared to be something made of cloth lying in a sandy area just off the grass near the end of one of the slash piles.

Bill got out of his car, took his flashlight from his patrol car and turned it on as he walked toward the pile of cloth. When he was only about ten or twelve feet from the pile of cloth, he saw that it was a body lying face down in the sandy area. He moved up to the body. Bill knelt down beside the body to check to see if the person was dead. He was dead.

Bill could not identify the victim because it was lying face down. From the looks of the body, it was clear that it was a male and that he had been dead for possibly a couple of days.

Returning to his patrol car, Bill got his camera. He took several pictures of the body and the area immediately around it. He then knelt down and rolled the body over. Bill quickly discovered that the front of the victim's clothing was covered with dried blood. It was easy to see that the victim had been shot twice in the chest. From the looks of the wounds, he had been shot at fairly close range.

The victim's face looked as if he had been beaten before he was shot. He had a number of cuts and bruises on his face that appeared to have been inflicted sometime before his death. Bill took several pictures of the victim before he continued to look over the body.

As he looked over the body, it was clear that it was the body of a young man with dark brown hair. He appeared to be in his early to mid-twenties, although it was hard to tell with the beating he had taken before he was shot, and the time since his death.

Bill took an interest in what the victim was wearing. The boots on the body were the same type of work boots that were issued to airmen. The boots were in very good shape and laced left over right like most military personnel laced their boots and shoes. The clothes on the body were obviously civilian style clothes very much like most men wore this time of year, and who lived in the area; jeans and a flannel shirt. He had a hunting knife on his belt, but didn't have any other weapons on him.

Bill checked his pockets in the hope of finding some form of identification on the body. If he was a military man, he would have a Military ID card on him, and probably dog tags. He would also have a driver's license. Bill found nothing that would help identify the body, no ID card, no driver's license, no dog tags and no wallet. In fact, he found nothing in any of the victim's pockets, nothing at all.

The victim was a young man who was old enough to be in the service. His hair cut was like that worn by many of the men in military service, fairly short and well-trimmed.

Bill stood up and stepped back away from the body. Using his flashlight, he carefully looked over the body. It quickly became clear that the young man had probably been shot some time ago. Based on Bill's experience in the military, he guessed he had been shot twice, maybe two days ago. The weather had been fairly cool during the past few days. Bill figured that the victim was probably killed on Friday, or possibly on Saturday.

There were some tracks in places where there was no grass or weeds, but none that would be very useful in the sandy soil. They were too scuffed over to get a clear footprint.

Bill continued to look around without moving around the area any more than necessary. The last thing he wanted to do was to destroy any evidence that might be there. He was already afraid that he might have destroyed any possible car tracks that might have been on the logging road into where he found the body.

The only thing that Bill could do now was to call in and report a homicide. Being as careful as possible, he walked back to his car using the same area of ground he had used to get to the body. Once in his car, he called dispatch.

"Car eight to dispatch."

"Dispatch, go ahead."

"Mary, I would like you to call the sheriff and tell him we have a homicide."

"Do you know who it is?"

"No. I don't know who it is. The victim would be about the right age to be a military man, maybe an airman from the Air Force base. His hair cut and boots are like the young men in the service wear."

"I'll notify the sheriff. He'll probably send the coroner out there to get the body."

"It's a little hard to find this place. Tell the sheriff that the coroner should take road T3-1-7 then turn north on 2-9-7 toward Medicine Mountain. He should start looking for me about a mile north of that junction. I'll be standing next to the road with a flashlight."

"Okay, but it will take him awhile to get there."

"I know. I'll go out to the road in about forty-five minutes and wait for him."

"Okay. I'll tell him."

"Thanks, out," Bill said.

Bill looked out the windshield of his patrol car at the body. His thoughts were of the young man and why someone would want to kill him.

Bill's thoughts were suddenly disturbed when a raindrop hit the windshield. Rain was the last thing he wanted right now. If it rained very much at all, it would wipe away almost any tracks that might have been evidence. He couldn't stop the rain, but he could cover the body with a tarp he had in the trunk of his patrol car.

He quickly got out of the car, opened the trunk and took the tarp out of it. He quickly ran over to the body and spread the tarp over the body and as much of the ground around the body as he could. He picked up some rocks and set them around the edge of the tarp to keep it in place.

Bill had just finished securing the tarp over the body when the rain began to increase in intensity. He ran back to his patrol car and got in.

Bill sat in the patrol car and watched it rain. Since there was nothing he could do at the moment, he opened his lunch box. He ate the sandwich and drank some of the coffee while he waited for the coroner. About all he could think about was that any evidence of what had happened there was slowly being washed away.

It wasn't very long before the rain slowed and turned into a light steady rain. He found his rain cover for his hat and his yellow rain coat. He put the rain cover on his hat then slipped into his raincoat.

Bill got out of his car and walked over to where the body laid. He took a couple of rocks off one corner of the tarp and lifted it up. He was glad to see the body was dry as well as the ground close to the body. He replaced the tarp and rocks then returned to his patrol car to wait until it was time to walk to the road and meet the coroner.

Time passed slowly. All Bill could do for now was speculate about what had happened. He hoped that he would be able to find a clue or two on what actually happened there, but the rain wasn't going to help if it washed away all the evidence.

Gradually the rain slowed to a steady light drizzle for about twenty minutes, then it stopped completely. Bill was glad that it had stopped raining since it was time for him to go back to the road and wait for the coroner. He got out of his patrol car, checked his flashlight then began walking back toward the road. When he got to the road, he looked up and down it. He didn't see anything. It was too dark to see more than a few yards in either direction.

At the edge of the road, he saw a large rock. Bill moved over to the rock and sat down on it to wait.

Bill had spent a good deal of time camping in the woods over the years. He was used to the sounds of the night in the forest, but tonight it seemed especially quiet. The only thing he could think of for the night to be so quiet was the recent rainstorm.

It always seemed that immediately after a rainstorm, the forest turned quiet. It was as if the birds were sitting in the shelter of the trees and other animals had found places to stay dry. Often after a rainfall, even the breeze seemed to take a rest. Tonight was no different.

Bill's thoughts about the forest after a rainstorm were suddenly disturbed. The quiet of the night was broken by the sound of a vehicle coming up the road toward him. He stood up and looked toward where the sound was coming from. It was only a minute or so before he saw the glow of headlights coming toward him

He turned on his flashlight and waved it toward the oncoming vehicle. As the vehicle approached him, it slowed down then came to a stop next to him. Bill stepped up to the panel truck and looked in.

The man behind the wheel of the panel truck was Ralph Wickum, the Pennington County Coroner. He was a short stocky man in his late forties. He had thinning brown hair with a little gray in it. He wore heavy glasses that made him look scholarly, something akin to a professor. Bill knew him to be a man who missed very little when it came to investigating the death of a person. He took his job seriously.

"Hi, Bill. What have you got for me?"

"I've got the body of a young man with two bullet holes in his chest."

"Well, get in and let's go take a look," Ralph said with a tone that made it sound pretty routine to him.

Bill got in the panel truck and pointed to where Ralph was to go. It was only a matter of a few minutes before Ralph pulled up behind Bill's patrol car. Bill opened the door and got out. Ralph got out and walked to the front of the truck.

"The body's over here," Bill said as he pointed to the slash pile.

Ralph followed Bill to where the body laid. They carefully removed the rocks from the tarp then lifted it off the body. Ralph then shined his flashlight on the body. He carefully looked over the body while Bill stood back and watched him. Ralph turned and looked at Bill.

"Do we have a name for this guy?"

"No. Someone called the Sheriff's Office and told him there was a body out here," Bill said. "I've never seen this guy before. I don't think he is from around here."

"Well, we'll list him as a John Doe for now," Ralph said. "Have you taken any pictures?"

"Yes. I took several before I turned him over, and several after I turned him over. He was lying face down when I arrived. I didn't know he had been shot until I turned him over in an effort to find out who he was. He didn't have anything in his pockets."

"He didn't have anything in his pockets?" Ralph asked as if he wondered if Bill was speaking literally.

"Not a thing, no ID, no matches, no wallet, no change, no keys, no driver's license, nothing. The only thing he has is the knife on his belt and the clothes he's wearing."

"That's a bit strange," Ralph said thoughtfully. "I would say that someone wanted to make it hard for us to identify him."

"I would have to agree. The only thing I noticed that might not be strange are his boots. That and his hair cut. The boots are military issue and his hair cut is typical of many young military men. The boots are the same kind issued to airmen."

"You think he's from the airbase?"

"He could be, but it's not uncommon for civilians to purchase the same kind of boots at the Army Navy Surplus store in Rapid City," Bill said.

"Do military men still put their name on the inside of their boots?"

"I hadn't thought of that, but they do that in boot camp so they don't grab someone else's boots," Bill said feeling a little dumb for not thinking of it himself.

"However, they don't very often put their names in the boots when they get a new pair of boots after they are out of boot camp. Those boots look pretty new, Bill said."

"I'll take a look when I get him on the ME's table and take his boots off."

"Let me know what you find out."

"I will. Let's get him in the truck before it starts raining again."

Bill and Ralph rolled the body onto the tarp that had covered the victim, then wrapped it up. They lifted the body onto a stretcher then put it in the back of the panel truck.

As soon as the body was in the truck, Ralph walked back to where the body had been. He carefully walked around the place, shining his flashlight on the ground."

"I don't see anything here that will help," Ralph said. "Are you going to come up here tomorrow during the day?"

"I plan to. I need to take a better look at the area when there's some good light."

"Good. It's too dark to see what might be here. Let me know if you find anything in the sand where you found him, especially if it will help identify him."

"I will."

Ralph nodded, then walked back to his truck. He pulled a tarp out and gave it to Bill. It was the same kind and size as Bill's tarp.

"You can have this one," Ralph said. It's just like yours."

"Thanks, I got the one I had from your department."

Ralph smiled then got in the truck and left the scene. Bill stayed behind to cover the area where he found the body with the new tarp. He again secured it by setting rocks around the edge of the tarp. He wanted to make sure that if it rained again, the place where the body had been would not get wet and ruin any possible evidence that might still be there.

Once Bill was sure he had done all he could to secure the scene, he got in his patrol car and headed back to Hill City.

As soon as he arrived home, he called dispatch and reported what he had found, and that the body had been removed by the coroner and taken to the ME's office. He also reported that he was unable to identify the body. As soon as he finished his brief report, he hung up.

Bill yawned then went into his bedroom. As he took off his uniform, he noticed Julie was in his bed. She looked so peaceful he didn't want to disturb her. He did tell her that he would wake her when he got home. He sat down on the edge of the bed, then reached out and touched her lightly on the shoulder.

"Julie," he whispered.

She opened her eyes and smiled.

"Hi. Did you find the body?" Julie asked, sounding half asleep.

"Yes."

"Do you know who it is?"

"No."

"But you found someone?"

"Yes. The young man I found was dead. He had been dead for a day or two."

"Oh. Are you coming to bed?"

"As soon as I shower. You might as well go back to sleep. I'll be back shortly."

"Okay."

Bill went into the bathroom and took a quick shower. When he returned to the bedroom, he found Julie had gone back to sleep. Not wanting to disturb her, Bill carefully climbed into bed. It had been a long day, and it wasn't long before he was fast asleep.

CHAPTER TWO

The sun was just coming up when Bill's phone began to ring. Still half asleep, Bill scrambled out of bed and found his way to the phone.

"Hello," he said, still not fully awake.

"Bill, this is Sheriff Henderson. Did I wake you?"

"Yes, sir."

"I'm sorry about that. I know you had a long night last night."

"Yes, sir. Has the ME been able to identified the man I found near Medicine Mountain?"

"Not yet. The reason I called is I want you to go back where you found him to see what you can find. I know you said that the body had been laying out in the open for a day or two, but I'm sure you know what to look for."

"Yes, sir, I do. I'll get there as soon as I can. I was already planning to go back up there to see if I could find any evidence."

"Good. I might suggest that you take some time to have a good breakfast before you head out. I'm sure you could use one, and a few extra minutes probably will not make any difference."

"Yes, sir. Thank you."

"Call me when you get done."

"Yes, sir," Bill said, then the phone went dead.

As Bill hung up the phone, he turned and looked toward his bedroom. Julie was standing in the doorway looking at him. He just stood there looking at her. Even though she had just gotten out of bed, she looked very sexy wearing one of his shirts. He certainly didn't want to go anywhere at the moment.

"I take it that was Sheriff Henderson?"

"Yes. He wants me to go back up to where I found the body and look for any evidence that might be there."

"That's not going to be easy. It rained last night."

"Yes, I know. I just hope the tarp I laid over the area where the body was is still there."

"Do you have to go now?" she asked.

"He did tell me to take time to have a good breakfast."

"In that case, I guess I'll get dressed. Would you like me to fix you breakfast?"

"That would be nice," Bill said as he walked toward her.

As he stepped up to her, he reached out and pulled her up against him. She wrapped her arms around his neck and kissed him. She looked up at him and smiled.

"I like the way you hold me," she said.

"I like holding you," he said, then kissed her again.

After a few more kisses, she drew back a little and looked up at him.

"I better get dressed," she said breathlessly.

"I'll shave while you get dressed."

Julie returned to the bedroom to dress while Bill went to the bathroom. As soon as Julie was dressed, she went to the kitchen to fix breakfast for them.

As much as Bill would like to stay home and spend the rest of the day with Julie, he knew how important it was to find any evidence that might be at the site as soon as possible. He took a quick shower, mostly to help wake himself up, then shaved. He then put on his uniform and went to the kitchen.

Bill could smell what was cooking as he entered the kitchen. The table was set, the eggs and bacon were ready to eat, and Julie was just setting the toast on their plates.

"Breakfast is served," she said as she set the plates on the table.

They sat down and started to eat. It was obvious that they were both hungry. They didn't talk much at first.

When they were almost done, Julie looked at him across the table.

"I made enough coffee for you to take some with you. I also made a sandwich in case you get hungry."

"Thank you."

"If you don't mind. I'll clean up the kitchen before I go home. I need to make sure grandfather gets something to eat," she said with a smile.

"You don't have to do that. It'll wait tell I get home."

"You won't feel like cleaning up the dishes when you get home. Besides, you need to get going. You have a lot of work to do."

"Okay. Will I see you tonight?"

"I won't be able to get here before ten or a little after. I have to work in receiving from one to nine today. You will probably be pretty tired."

"I'm sure you're right."

"I'll call you in the morning. You better get going."

Bill got up and put his dirty dishes on the counter next to the sink. As soon as Julie stood up from the table, he leaned toward her and gave her a kiss.

"I love you," he said.

"I love you, too."

Bill grabbed his lunch box off the counter and walked out the door. He got in his patrol car and headed out.

As he drove by the Hill City Café, he noticed Rutledge's truck was parked in front of the café. He thought about talking to Rutledge about the area around Medicine Mountain, but decided not to stop and talk to him in the café. Rutledge might not feel like talking to him if anyone was close by, Bill thought. Besides, Bill needed to get up to the site where he found the body and look for any evidence that might still be there. A talk with Rutledge could wait for another time.

Bill headed back to where he found the body. The closer he got to Medicine Mountain, the more his thoughts turned to the body he found last night. He couldn't help but think the body was that of a serviceman, probably an airman from Rapid City Air Force Base. The only problem was he couldn't prove it. He hoped that he would find something that would help identify the victim.

It took Bill almost an hour to get back to where he had found the body. Just as he turned onto the logging road, he stopped. Bill got out of his patrol car, walked around in front of it and looked at the road. What he saw was what he had expected to see. The rain had washed away any signs of anyone who might have driven or walked along the logging road. Even the tracks from where he had driven his patrol car last night, and where Wickum had driven his panel truck were gone. It had obviously rained again after he left the area.

Bill got back in his patrol car and drove to the place where he had parked last night. He got out of his patrol car and walked over to where he had left his tarp.

The tarp was still right where he had left it, and looked as if it had not been disturbed. The tarp was covered with water from the rain. Bill carefully removed the tarp from the area, being very careful not to let the water on the tarp spill onto the area where the body had been covered. He draped the tarp over a couple of branches on a nearby slash pile so it could dry while he looked around.

Being careful not to destroy any possible evidence, he started searching the ground that the tarp had covered. Except around the edges, the ground was dry where the tarp had been. The first thing he noticed was where he had knelt down to check the body and rolled it over in the hope of identifying the body. It was clear that he had knelt down in the dirt on only one side of the body. There was nothing to indicate that anyone else, besides himself and the coroner, had even walked anywhere in the area that had been covered by the tarp, either before or after the tarp had been laid over the body.

Bill used the area where he had knelt down as a starting point. Slowly and carefully, he began searching every inch of ground that had been under the tarp. The area that had been under the body consisted of mostly dirt and sand. There was a fairly large area in the sandy soil that was discolored by the victim's blood. Instead of the sandy soil being a fairly light brown like the surrounding soil, it was a dark reddish brown caused by the mixture of dried blood and the sandy soil.

Such a large area of blood clearly indicated that the victim had probably been shot right where he had laid when Bill found him. Making it clear that this was the murder site.

While slowly and methodically searching the area for clues, he saw something in the bloodstained soil. It looked like it was round. Bill took a picture of it, then carefully removed it. It looked like it might be a fairly large coin, a little bigger around and slightly thicker than a silver dollar. It was hard to tell what kind of coin it was because it was covered in dried blood mixed with the sandy dirt.

He had not seen the coin last night. It had been dark, and with the blood and dirt on it, it would have been hard to see even with a flashlight to help him search the area. It was also half buried in the bloodstained soil.

After picking up the coin, he did notice that it seemed to be fairly heavy. Bill took his handkerchief from his hip pocket. He carefully wrapped the coin in it without wiping it off. He put it in his shirt pocket and buttoned the flat over the pocket.

Once he had the coin secured in his pocket, he continued to search the area. It wasn't very long and he found a second coin in the bloodstained soil. It was about the same size as the first one he found. He picked it up and put it in his pocket with the first coin. Since he had found two coins in the sandy soil, he went to his patrol car and got the mixing spoon from the casting kit he used to make castings of tire tracks.

After getting the spoon, he went back to where he had found the coins and began slowly and carefully shifting through the loose dirt where the body had been. He continued to search the entire area where the body had been in a grid pattern so he could be sure that there was nothing else of importance. There were no more coins in or near where the body had been.

When he had finished looking for more coins, he continued to search the rest of the area that had been under the tarp for any other evidence. At the edge of the area, in the grass just a few inches outside the tarped area, Bill found a .45 caliber shell casing. It didn't look like it had been on the ground very long.

Bill used a stick to pick up the shell casing in order to prevent disturbing any fingerprints that might be on it. He really didn't expect the lab would find any fingerprints since the shell casing had not been under the tarp, and had been in the rain. It had also been there for a day or two.

Bill checked the base of the shell casing for markings showing where and when it was made. The stamping on the base showed that it was military issued ammunition from World War II. After looking the shell casing over, he slipped it into his other shirt pocket leaving the stick in the end of it so he could remove the shell casing from his pocket without touching the outside of it.

He continued to search in the grass for a second shell casing since the victim had obviously been shot twice, but he didn't find a second shell casing. It seemed strange that there wasn't a second shell casing in the area.

Having had experience as a Military Policeman with the .45 caliber Army issued model 1911 semi-automatic Colt pistols used by the military during World War II, he began to think about it. That weapon would automatically eject the spent shell when fired. The question came to mind that whoever had fired the gun must have picked up one of the empty casings. If that was the case, why didn't he pick up both casings? Bill was sure that would be one of those questions that would probably never get answered.

Bill's thoughts turned to the fact that there had to be a lot of men in the service who had such a gun and probably had a good amount of ammo to go with it. In fact, he had one when he was in the service as a Military Policeman, and he still had it. Bill also knew that very few enlisted soldiers had been issued pistols. However, there were a lot of officers who had them.

Bill quickly began to reason that in this case, knowing what was used to kill the man did little to help him figure out who was the shooter. There were any number of people who had that kind of gun because a large number of them had been sold off as surplus after the war. That simply meant that just because it was a military issued gun, didn't mean it was someone in the military who had shot the victim.

Bill continued to search the area around where the body had been. He was looking for anything that might help lead him to the killer. He found nothing more that could even remotely be connected to the murder as evidence.

He walked back to his patrol car and sat down in it. He opened his Thermos and poured some coffee into the cup. As Bill took a sip while staring out the windshield of his patrol car, he thought about what might have happened there.

Suddenly, a thought came to mind. He had not looked around the slash piles. Bill had no idea if there was anything there. If he didn't at least look, he would always wonder if he had missed something important.

Bill quickly finished his coffee, then got out of his patrol car. He began walking around the slash piles. He was surprised when he found a sleeping bag lying behind one of the slash piles with a ground cloth rolled up beside it. Bill got his camera out and took several pictures of it, both back at a distance and up close. Instead of picking up the sleeping bag and ground cloth, Bill took a few minutes to look over the rest of the slash pile.

Even with all the rain last night, Bill discovered a hole in the ground. It was at the opposite end of the slash pile from where he had found the body. It had been dug at the base of the slash pile.

Checking out the hole, it didn't look like a hole that had been dug by an animal looking for something or building a den. It looked more like a hole that had been dug to bury something, or to retrieve something. It had all the markings of being dug by a human with some kind of shovel.

It was hard to see what might be in the hole, or how deep it went since it still had some water from the rain in the bottom of it. Bill returned to his car and got his flashlight. He returned to the hole and shined his flashlight into it. He had to get down on his knees in order to see all the way in. The hole was only about a foot in diameter and about a foot and a half to two feet deep. There didn't appear to be anything in it other than about a quarter of an inch, or so, of rain water.

Since the sides of the hole were fairly solid and smooth, Bill was sure it had been dug with a shovel. Having seen a good many holes that had been dug using a small folding Army shovel, he was sure that it had been dug using such a shovel, or something very similar to it.

The folding shoves, like the one probably used to dig the hole, were issued to, and carried by, soldiers on their backpacks. They were used primarily to dig fox holes and latrines. Bill was sure that anyone could purchase one at the Army Navy surplus store. There was one such store in Rapid City.

It also looked like the hole had been dug recently to bury something, possibly the coins the victim had found, but nothing appeared to have been put in the hole. From the pile of dirt next to the hole, it had probably been dug before it rained. If it had been dug by the dead man, it would have probably been dug just before or at about the time the victim was murdered.

Several questions came to Bill's mind. Thinking that there might have been more than just the two coins he found, three questions immediately came to mind. How many coins were there, where did they come from, and why did someone want to bury them? There was also the question, if there were more coins, who had the rest of them now?

Bill once again started looking over the slash piles in case there was some other place where there had been some digging, or a place where the slash piles might have been disturbed. After looking over the slash piles and walking completely around them, he found nothing to indicate that there had been any more digging in or around the slash piles. It was also clear that nothing had been moved since the slash piles had been stacked up.

As he looked up at the slash pile while thinking, he noticed a small smooth piece of wood sticking out at the top of the slash pile only a couple of feet above his head. It was smooth and didn't look like it belonged there, it certainly wasn't like the rest of the material in the slash pile. It looked more like the handle of a shovel or some garden tools. After looking around, he carefully climbed up on top of the slash pile. Once on top of the slash pile, Bill found a backpack and an Army folding shovel. The shovel was open as if it was ready to use. The shovel had dirt on the blade like the dirt at the base of the slash pile. It was apparently the shovel that had been used to dig the hole.

Bill climbed down taking the backpack and the shovel with him. He then gathered up everything he had found and put them in his patrol car.

Once he had all the evidence gathered that he had been able to find safely secured in his patrol car, Bill began to widen his search of the area. It wasn't until he was about ten to twelve yards back in the woods behind the slash piles that he found anything of interest.

Under a large Pondarosa Pine, Bill found what appeared to be the scratching of a horse's hooves in the ground. The scratch marks had not been washed away by last night's rain. The tree had apparently sheltered the hoof prints from being washed away.

On one of the lower branches, Bill found signs on the bark that something had been tied to the branch, probably the reins of the horse since the cuts in the bark were not round like a rope would make, but flatter like the reins of a bridle. The cuts in the bark were directly above the hoof prints, indicating that a horse had been tied there sometime before it rained.

It was beginning to look like whoever had killed the young man, had used a horse to get there, and possibly to get away. His other thought was, did the horse belong to whoever had called in about the body. There was the possibility that the horse belonged to the person who killed the victim. There was also the possibility that the person who called the sheriff's office was the person who killed the victim, but that didn't seem likely.

Knowing a horse was there didn't help Bill a lot as most of the people in the area had horses. However, the hoof prints might help.

Not wanting to lose any possible evidence, Bill laid a dollar bill next to the clearest hoof print and took several pictures of it, then he took several of the ground at a slight distance to show all the hoof prints and the scratching in the ground. Bill wasn't sure how well the details of the hoof prints would show up in a photo, but he still had to make the effort to get the pictures of what might be evidence.

The idea of making casts of the hoof prints crossed his mind. Since tire tracks could help identify the vehicle that made them, hoof prints might also help identify the horse that made the hoof prints.

Bill returned to his patrol car and got his casting kit from the trunk. He mixed up a small batch of Plaster of

Paris then carefully poured it into a couple of hoof prints that showed good detail.

While he waited for the Plaster of Paris to set, Bill walked down to Negro Creek to wash out his mixing pan and spoon. The creek was about forty feet from where had he found the body. When he knelt down to rinse them off, he noticed something on the other side of the creek. He wasn't sure what it was, or if it had anything to do with the murder, but to fail to check it out could mean that he missed an important clue.

Bill took off his shoes and sox, rolled up his pant legs and wadded into the creek. When he got to the other side, he stepped out of the creek, but couldn't see anything. He knelt down close to the ground where he thought he had seen something shiny.

After searching the area where he thought he saw it, he discovered what looked like a small pocket knife. He picked it up and looked it over. On one side, scratched in the knife's handle was the name, "Sean Carter". Carefully examining the knife, he found it was clean. It was apparent it had not been there very long. There was not a bit of rust on it.

Bill didn't know Sean, in fact he had no idea what he looked like. He did know that his mother lived in Hill City, and he thought he had heard that Sean was in the Air Force. Bill knew that his next move was to find and interview Sean, once he finished at the murder site. It crossed his mind that the body he had found might be that of Sean Carter.

Bill walked back across the creek and put his shoes and sox back on. He then returned to look around for more hoof prints in the hope of finding out where the horse had gone. As soon as the horse had gotten out from under the trees and out into the open, its tracks had been washed away by the rain.

Bill looked around. He was sure that he had found all he was going to find. He took his castings of the horse's hoof prints, marked them as to what hoof had made the print, where they were made and when the castings were made. He then wrapped them in a towel and carefully put them in the trunk of his patrol car.

After making sure all his evidence was secure in the patrol car, he remembered there was a small ranch just a little over a half mile south of his current location. He decided to drive over there and have a talk with the owner. He got into his patrol car and left the scene.

Bill drove about a half mile to a turn off that would take him to the small ranch of Mr. and Mrs. Dieter Schmidt. Bill didn't know Mr. Schmidt personally. He pretty much kept to himself. However, he did know that Mr. Schmidt lived only about a half mile, as the crow flies, from where he found the body. Bill also knew that Mr. Schmidt was married.

From what he had heard from different people in town, Dieter Schmidt and his wife had only lived on the small ranch for about nine or ten years. He had also heard that they had come here from Germany three or four years before the war.

During the war, they had kept to themselves which had caused a lot of rumors to float around that he was a Nazi. Dieter had a few encounters with a couple of local trouble makers because he was a German and had a very strong German accent, but the sheriff at the time put an end to it before it got out of hand.

According to the sheriff, the FBI cleared him of any connection to the Nazi party. Even after the war, Dieter and his wife continued to keep to themselves.

It didn't take long before Bill was at the drive to the Schmidt's ranch. He turned in and almost immediately found himself facing a closed gate with a "No Trespassing" sign printed in large letters hanging on it. There was also a fairly heavy lock on the gate.

Bill could see the log house from the gate. He could also see three horses in the corral next to a barn behind and to the left of the house. Bill didn't want to trespass as he didn't have a warrant, or cause to trespass, but he did want to talk to Mr. Schmidt. He took a minute to think about how he was going to get Mr. Schmidt's attention. He decided that since he was there on official business, he would turn on the red flashing light on the top of the patrol car. He turned the red light on and waited for a couple of minutes, but got no response.

Since the red light didn't work, he hit his siren a couple of times. He saw someone in the cabin pull the curtain back and look out. Whoever it was simply let the curtain fall back over the window, but didn't come to the door. Bill hit the siren again, only this time he held it longer.

Finally, Mr. Schmidt opened the front door and stepped out on the narrow porch with a rifle in his hand. Bill reached down and drew his pistol, then opened the door and stepped out of his patrol car keeping his gun hidden from Schmidt's view behind the car door. He kept the car door between him and Mr. Schmidt.

"Put the rifle down, Mr. Schmidt," Bill called out.

"Go away," he yelled with a heavy German accent.

"I just want to talk to you."

"Go away," he yelled again. "You are not welcome here."

"I just want to talk to you. Leave the rifle on the porch and walk out here to the gate."

"NO!"

"Okay, I'll get a warrant to search your entire ranch and will be back with several more officers to enforce it, is that what you want? All I want is to talk to you for a little bit, and ask you a couple of questions," Bill said.

Just then a woman in a simple cotton dress stepped out on the porch and moved close to Mr. Schmidt side. She took hold of his arm and talked to him while looking at Bill. He could not hear what she was saying to him. Mr. Schmidt looked at her for a moment before he set his rifle down. He stepped off the porch and walked toward the gate. When he got to the gate, he stopped.

Bill slipped his gun back in his holster, then stepped out from behind his patrol car door. He walked up close to the gate.

"Mr. Schmidt, I'm Pennington County Sheriff's Deputy Bill Sparks. I have just a couple of questions to ask you. I would like to know if you heard any gunshots coming from over near the logging road, in the past couple of days?"

"I mind my own business," he said sharply.

"I'm sure you do, but I'm only asking if you heard anything, especially the sound of gunshots anytime in the past couple of days?"

Mr. Schmidt looked at Bill for a minute.

"Dieter, answer the officer," Mrs. Schmidt said as she walked up next to her husband.

Dieter glanced at his wife then looked back at Bill.

"Yes," he said.

"About when was that?"

"About two days ago. I think it was Saturday, but I'm not sure."

"What time of the day did you hear the shots?"

Dieter looked as his wife. She nodded indicating that he should answer the deputy.

"About one or one-thirty in the afternoon. Right after our dinner."

"How many shots did you hear?"

"I heard two shots."

"Only two shots?"

"That is what I said. Two shots," he said rather sharply.

"Did you see anyone around here about that time? Maybe someone drove by in a hurry, or maybe you saw someone on a horse about that time."

"No. I did not see anyone."

"Did you hear anything else, other than the shots?"

"I heard a horse," he said. "Is that what you mean?"

"Yes. Did you see the horse?"

"No, but it made my horses nervous."

"Why was that?"

"The horse didn't like something that was going on. It sounded like it was trying to get away, but I don't know what from."

"Maybe the sound of gunshots?"

"Maybe. It was about the same time."

"Thank you, Mr. Schmidt. I may want to talk to you again. And thank you for your cooperation. And thank you, Mrs. Schmidt," Bill said as he looked at her then touched the brim of his hat.

Mrs. Schmidt nodded then Bill turned around and walked back to his patrol car. He had gotten as much information as he was going to get, at least for now. If he left now on something close to pleasant terms with the Schmidts, it might be easier to get them to talk if he had to call on them again.

Bill got in his patrol car, turned around and drove back to the road. Once he was out on the road, he headed for Rapid City to share his findings with Sheriff Henderson.

CHAPTER THREE

Bill arrived in Rapid City at a few minutes before one. A look at his watch showed him that there was little chance of finding the sheriff in his office. He would probably be out to lunch. Since Bill was feeling a bit hungry, he decided he would stop and get something to eat before going to the office.

He knew there was a café only a couple of blocks from the sheriff's office. He drove to the café, went inside and looked around. He saw Officer Douglas Thomas sitting in a booth. Bill walked up to the officer.

"Hi, Doug. Do you mind if I join you?"

"No, not at all. How's it going with your investigation?" Doug asked.

"It's hard to tell. I've got a few pieces of evidence, but nothing to connect the murder to anyone."

"It's early. You'll figure it out. Those things take time."

"Yeah. I know."

The two officers chatted while they ate their lunches. There was very little said about Bill's investigation. Doug had been out that morning issuing summons to court, a job that most of the officers didn't care to do, but it was part of the job.

After they finished eating their lunches, Doug went on his way while Bill drove to the sheriff's office. When he walked in the door, he saw the sheriff standing in front of the officer on duty at the front desk.

"I want to know when Deputy Sparks calls in," the sheriff told the sergeant on duty at the front desk.

"Is it all right if I talk to you in person?" Bill asked with a big grin.

The sheriff turned around and saw Bill standing there. He immediately noticed the backpack, sleeping bag and a ground cloth Bill was holding.

"I didn't expect to see you here. What do you have there, anything interesting?" Sheriff Henderson asked as he glanced at the backpack and sleeping bag. "Or are you planning on staying the night?"

"No. Actually, I'm not sure what I have. I haven't opened the backpack yet."

"Let's go to my office," Sheriff Henderson said.

The sheriff turned and walked down the hall to his office. Bill followed the sheriff into the office and waited for the sheriff to sit down at his desk. He then sat down in front of the sheriff's desk.

"I take it the backpack and sleeping bag have something to do with what you found last night."

"I'm not sure if it has anything to do with anything. I found the sleeping bag and ground cloth behind a slash pile near where I found the body. I found the backpack and the Army folding shovel on top of one of the slash piles. The folding shovel had dirt on it. It was apparently the shovel used to dig a hole near the back of the slash pile that might have been intended to be used to bury the coins I found this morning."

"What coins?" the sheriff asked as he straightened up in his chair and leaned forward.

"I found a couple of coins where the body had been. They would have been under the body before I turned the victim over. I found the coins in the bloodstained soil this morning. I couldn't see them last night." Bill said.

Bill reached into his shirt pocket and pulled the handkerchief out and carefully opened it on the edge of the sheriff's desk. Sheriff Henderson leaned forward and looked at the coins. Bill also pulled the stick with the .45 caliber shell casing from his pocket and set it on the desk.

"What are the coins?"

"I don't know, sir. I thought I should let the lab remove the blood and dirt from them. The lab might want to check the blood type to see if it was from the victim, or from someone else."

"Good thinking. What's with the shell casing?"

"I found this shell casing from a .45 caliber bullet. The victim was shot twice, but I didn't find a second shell casing anywhere around there," Bill said. "I thought the lab might be able to get fingerprints off the shell casing.

"As for the backpack and sleeping bag, I have no idea who they belong to, or why the backpack was up on top of the slash pile. The backpack appeared to have been tossed up on top of the slash pile with the folding shovel. I don't have any idea what is in the backpack. I haven't looked inside."

"Well, let's see what's in it. You can empty it out on the table," Sheriff Henderson suggested as he stood up.

Bill took the backpack to a table along the wall across from the sheriff's desk. He opened the backpack and started taking out everything that was in it. It contained a pair of pants, two shirts, socks, a light jacket, an Army poncho and a cook kit. There were also two cans, one was canned meat and the other a can of mixed vegetables."

"Is that all?" Sheriff Henderson asked.

Bill checked the small side pocket.

"Apparently not," Bill said.

Bill tipped the backpack upside down. A gold coin fell out and started to roll toward the edge of the table. He caught the coin before it could roll off the table. Bill held it up and looked at it. He was surprised to see it.

"What is it?" Sheriff Henderson asked. "I've never seen a coin like that before."

"If I'm not mistaken, it is a German gold coin. I've seen a coin very much like this one before."

Bill handed the coin to the sheriff. The sheriff examined the coin, then looked at Bill.

"Where did you see it?"

"When I was in Europe, we caught a couple of German officers who had them. They each had five of them. It looks like it might be the same kind of coin as the two I found covered with blood. Although it seems a little smaller."

"That might be because the others were covered with blood and dirt," Sheriff Henderson suggested as he looked at it.

"You might be right."

"Do you have your camera? I want pictures of this," the sheriff said.

"Yes, I have it with me. I took a lot of pictures, both last evening and this morning," Bill said.

The sheriff laid the coin on the table. Bill put the camera up to his face, aimed it at the coin then took a picture of the coin. He then turned the coin over and took a picture of the other side of the coin.

"Take the film over to the lab along with the bloody coins. Tell them I want a copy of every picture you took as soon as possible. I'll keep this coin here for now."

"Yes, sir."

Bill picked up the gold coins covered with the bloodstained dirt, then wrapped them in his handkerchief and put them back in his pocket.

"Anything else?"

"Yes, sir. I found a hole in the ground on the backside of the slash piles, but the only thing in it was water, probably from last night's rain. I have no idea if it has anything to do with the murder, but it might have been where someone, possibly the victim, was going to bury the coins, maybe a large number of them. It had been dug within the past two or three days."

"It doesn't seem to me that burying the coins next to a slash pile is a very good idea. The place where they buried them would be out in the open when they burned the slash pile."

"True, but not if the person who planned to bury them knew that the slash pile is fairly new, and that the forestry guys don't burn them while the wood is green. They wait a couple of years for the wood to dry, then burn them in the winter when there is snow on the ground."

"So, they had recently been cutting down trees in that area?"

"Yes, sir."

"If whoever dug the hole knew that the slash piles would be there for a couple of years, he might have planned to bury the coins, then dig them up sometime in the future before the slash pile was burned."

"That would be my guess," Bill said. "However, the coins could have been buried and left there until after the slash pile was burned. With the coins covered with dirt and the fire on top, it would not hurt the coins. The location of the fire would take several years before the ground would be reclaimed enough by mother nature to make the hiding place hard to find. Whoever buried the coins would have four, maybe five years, before where they were buried would be hard to find."

The sheriff took a minute to think about what Bill had said.

"That's true," he agreed. "Do you have anything more?"

"Yes, sir. I also took a casting of a horse's hoof prints that were back in the woods only a few yards from where the victim was killed," Bill explained. "I have no idea whose horse made the hoof prints. I don't even know for sure when they were made and if they have anything to do with the murder. What I do know is the hoof prints were fairly fresh."

"I take it you took pictures of everything?"

"Yes, sir."

"Good work."

"I have a witness, well, sort of a witness. He said he heard the sound of two shots being fired about two days ago. He wasn't sure if it was Friday or Saturday, but he was sure that it was about one or one-thirty in the afternoon. It may have been about the time our victim was killed. If nothing else, it gives us an approximate day, and a time of the murder."

"Who was this witness?"

"Dieter Schmidt."

"Do you think he is a reliable witness?"

"Yes, I think he is reliable. He lives less than a half mile south of where I found the body. There are no hills between where he lives and where I found the body to deaden the sounds of the shots."

"I've heard of Schmidt. If I remember correctly, he's a German fella who came here just before the war."

"That's him. He wasn't very cooperative until his wife insisted that he talk to me and answer my questions."

"Good work. Do you have any leads as to who might have killed the young man?"

"Maybe one, so far. I was thinking I would try to contact Sean Carter. I think he is in the Air Force and stationed at Rapid City Air Force Base."

"I don't think I know him. What's your interest in him?"

"Sean might know who the victim is. I found a small pocket knife with his name scratched on it just across Negro Creek from where I found the body."

"Why do you think he might know something about what happened there?"

Bill handed the pocket knife to the sheriff.

"As you can see the knife is fairly clean. There's no rust on it. That would indicate that it had not been there very long. He might have been around there about the time our victim was murdered. He may have seen something, or heard something."

"I see your point. Okay. Take this stuff over to the lab and have them go over it to see what they can come up with. Also have them develop the film. I want to know everything there is to know about all of this, and I want those pictures as soon as possible. Get a new roll or two of film from the lab while you're there. And while the lab is working on that, go out to the air base and see what you can find out from Sean Carter."

"Yes, sir," Bill said as he stood up.

"By the way, good work, Bill."

"Thank you, sir."

Bill turned and left the sheriff's office.

Bill walked out to his patrol car, left the parking lot and drove over to the lab. He dropped off everything, and told the head of the lab what Sheriff Henderson had instructed him to tell them at the lab. However, Bill requested two sets of the pictures. He was told it would be a couple of hours before the pictures would be developed. Bill thanked the man in the lab. He left the lab after telling the head of the lab that he would be back in a couple of hours to pick up the pictures. He then headed out to the Rapid City Air Force Base.

Bill arrived at the main entrance to the Rapid City Air Force Base about twenty-five minutes later. He was stopped by the guard on duty at the gate. He rolled down his window and looked up at the guard.

"May I help you, sir?" the guard asked.

"I would like to talk to whoever is in charge of your Military Police force on the base?" Bill asked.

"That would be Captain Butler. He is in charge of the Air Police here. Does Captain Butler know you are coming to see him?"

"No."

"Just a moment," the guard said, then stepped back into the guard house.

Bill couldn't hear what the guard was saying on the phone, but it was clear he called the Air Police Station on the base. While the guard was on the phone, he often looked at Bill. Bill guessed it was to make sure that he didn't just drive onto the base without permission. It was only a couple of minutes before the guard hung up the phone and returned to the side of Bill's patrol car.

"Captain Butler will see you. You need to drive down this street to the next street. Take a left. It's the first building on the left. There will be an airman waiting for you to take you to the captain's office."

Bill repeated the guard's instructions, then thanked him. He put his car in gear and followed the guard's instructions. When he turned the corner, he saw an airman standing in front of the building. Bill pulled in front of the building, parked his patrol car in a space that was designated for visitors, then got out.

"Right this way, sir," the airman said.

The airman turned around and went into the building. Bill followed the airman.

Once inside, the airman led him to a door across the large room. The name on the door was Captain M. R. Butler. The airman knocked on the door.

"Come in," a voice said.

The airman opened the door then stepped aside. He motioned for Bill to enter. Bill stepped into the office, then the airman closed the door behind him.

"I'm Captain Butler," he said as he stood up.

"Deputy Bill Sparks of the Pennington County Sheriff's Office."

"Welcome, Deputy Sparks, what can I do for you?" he said as he motioned for Bill to sit down.

As soon as Bill sat down, Captain Butler sat down behind his desk.

“I would like to know if you have an airman by the name of Sean Carter stationed here?”

“What is your interest in Airman Carter?”

“I take it you have an Airman Sean Carter stationed here?”

“Yes, we do. Sean Carter is an airplane mechanic. What is your purpose for wanting to talk to him?”

“It is possible that he might know the name of a man who was found dead in the backcountry, west of Hill City. We received an anonymous call that the body of a young man was found in the area of Medicine Mountain. I went up there and found the body. In my investigation, I found a small pocket knife with Sean Carter’s name scratched on it in the immediate area of the body. I would like to talk to him to see if he was in the area at the approximant time that we believe the victim was murdered.”

“Do you think he might have killed the man?” the captain asked.

“We have nothing to indicate that he did, or that he had anything to do with it. The only thing we are interested in is to find out what he might know about it. If he heard or saw anything around the time we believe the murder took place.”

“So, this is a murder investigation.”

“That would be correct.”

“It might take me a little while to locate Airman Carter.”

“I’ll wait, if you don’t mind.”

The captain smiled at Bill as he reached for the intercom on his desk. He pressed the button on an intercom and ask someone in the outer office to locate Airman Sean Carter and get his supervisor on the phone. It took a moment or two before the phone began to ring. He picked up the receiver.

“This is Captain Butler of the Air Police. Is Airman Sean Carter there today?”

There was a moment of silence before the captain spoke again.

"I would like you to send him to my office, on the double."

After another moment of silence, the captain said, "He can come as he is. I need him here as soon as he can get here."

A moment passed before the captain said "Thank you," then hung up.

"Airman Carter will be here shortly. I would like to be in on any questioning of him, if you don't mind."

"I have no problem with that. I can talk to him right here, if you wish." Bill said.

"The man that was murdered, do you have some idea why he was murdered?" the captain asked.

"Not at this time. It's very early in the investigation. At this point, all we know is we have the body of a male in his early to mid-twenties, as best we can determine. We have no idea who he is. He took two rounds to the chest from a .45 caliber pistol. Based on the shell casing found at the scene, it was a .45 auto, most likely a gun often used by the military.

"I notice that you carry one, that's not to say that you shot him," Bill said with a grin. "There are hundreds, if not thousands of those guns around. I even own one myself."

"That is all you have?" the captain said with a look of surprise.

"Yes, sir. That, and Airman Carter's knife found very close to the scene. We only found the body late last night and have not been able to identify him, yet. I'm hoping Airman Carter can tell us something helpful."

Just then there was a knock on the captain's door.

"Come in," the captain said.

Bill turned around and saw a young man who was not very big, maybe five feet nine inches tall and weighing about a hundred and sixty pounds. He was wearing coveralls and looked as if he had been working on an engine, probably an aircraft engine since that was his specialty.

"I'm sorry for my appearance, sir. I was told to get over here on the double, sir," the young man said to the captain as he stood at attention.

"It's all right, airman. At ease. Are you Sean Carter?"

"Yes, sir."

"This is Deputy Sparks from the Pennington County Sheriff's Office. He would like to talk to you."

"Yes, sir," Carter said then turned and looked at Bill.

"You can relax, Sean," Bill said. "I have just a few questions I would like to ask you."

"Yes, sir."

"Sean, were you up around Medicine Mountain about three or four days ago?"

"Yes, sir"

"When were you there, what day of the week?"

"We were there on - - Sunday."

Bill noticed the slight hesitation in answering the day he was in the backcountry. He decided to press him a little.

"What time on Sunday were you there. In other words, when did you get there and when did you leave?"

"Ah - - we got there about nine or nine-thirty in the morning, I think."

"When did you leave?"

"I think about four, no, it was closer to four-thirty."

"You said 'we". Were you with someone else?"

"Yes, sir."

"Who were you with?"

"I was with James Goodman, - - Chuck Smart, and - - ah - - Robert Hood."

Bill wrote the names in his pocket notebook.

"What were you doing?"

Sean glanced over toward the captain before he answered. Bill wasn't sure why he was looking at the captain except maybe to figure out if he was in trouble.

"We were exploring around Medicine Mountain," he said after a minute or so.

"Were the four of you always together?"

"Yes. Well, we were at first," he said then looked at the captain, again.

"Why did you break up?"

"James and I got tired of panning for gold, so we went off to see what was up on Medicine Mountain."

"If you were panning for gold, then you were not on Medicine Mountain. The mountain is across the road from Negro Creek. Were you panning for gold in Negro Creek?"

"Yes, but we were near where a logging road goes back in the woods. Next to the bridge."

"When you and James went to explore Medicine Mountain, what did Robert and Chuck do?"

Bill could see he was getting nervous. He also noticed that he kept looking at the captain.

"Robert wanted to stay and continue to pan for gold in the creek. James and I decided to hike back up on Medicine Mountain for a little while. Chuck decided to stay with Robert and continue to pan for gold in Negro Creek."

Bill watched Sean closely in the hope of telling if he was being truthful. The more he questioned Sean, the more nervous he seemed to be. Even though Carter tried to look relaxed, a little twitch in the corner of his left eye gave him away. He wasn't as relaxed as he might have wanted Bill and the captain to believe.

"Did you find any gold?" Bill asked with a grin.

"No, just a little fool's gold, and I'm not sure about that, sir."

"Did the others find any gold?"

"I don't know, but I don't think so. At least they didn't say they had."

"Did you see anyone else in the area?"

"No, sir."

"Are the others also Airmen?"

"James Goodman is, but Chuck is from Hill City. We went to school together, although we were not all that close. We only had a couple of classes together." Sean said.

"Do you wish to talk to Goodman?" Captain Butler asked.

"No. I don't think so. I might later," Bill said, then turned back to Carter.

"Robert Hood. What can you tell me about him?" Bill asked.

"He's a friend of Chuck's. I think he lives in Rapid City, but I'm not sure. This was the first time I've ever seen him."

"Does Chuck still live in Hill City, or was he visiting someone," Bill asked.

"He still lives there. He works for the lumber mill just outside of town."

"Just one more thing and then you can return to work. While you were in the backcountry, did you hear or see anything unusual?"

"Like what?"

"Like maybe gun shots around one in the afternoon, maybe a little after one, or see anyone on horseback in the area about that time?"

Bill noticed a slight change in his stance. That question caught him off guard.

"No," he said looking first at Bill, then at the captain.

"Thank you, Sean. Unless the captain has anything, I would think you could go back to work," Bill said. "However, I may need to talk to you again."

Sean looked at Bill for a second, then at the captain. Bill got the feeling that he was hoping the captain didn't want to ask him anything.

"You may return to your duties, Airman," Captain Butler said.

"Yes, sir," Sean said.

Sean did an about-face and left the captain's office.

Bill and Captain Butler watched as Sean left the captain's office. As soon as he was gone, Bill turned back and looked at the captain.

"What do you think?" Captain Butler asked.

"I think he was a little nervous, but then it might have been simply because he was called to the principal's office, so to speak. I also think he knows more than he is telling us. He is either not sure he should tell us, or he's afraid to tell us." Bill said.

"You might be right," the captain said with a grin. "I got the feeling that he might know something, too. Yet, it could have been that he was a little nervous about being called to this office, and being questioned. Is there anything else I can do for you?"

"I don't think so. I may want to talk to Goodman later if my investigation leads in that direction."

"I have a question for you. Why didn't you ask Carter about the knife you found?"

"First of all, I'm not sure that it has anything to do with the murder. Secondly, I'm holding that piece of information back, for now."

Captain Butler looked at Bill for a moment, then smiled.

"Well, if I can be of help, just let me know," Captain Butler said as he stood up. "I'll make sure Airman Carter will still be around, and Goodman, too."

"Thank you," Bill said as he stood up.

Bill reached across the captain's desk and shook hands with Captain Butler.

"And thanks for your cooperation, Captain."

Bill turned and walked out of the captain's office. He left the building, got in his patrol car and returned to Rapid City.

It was close to four in the afternoon by the time Bill arrived back at the lab. He went into the lab's office and requested the photos from the film he had brought in earlier.

The lab tech didn't seem to know what Bill was talking about, and said they didn't have any film to be developed for the Sheriff's Office. Since the lab tech didn't seem to know anything, Bill requested the lab tech get his supervisor.

"I would like to talk to your supervisor," Bill said.

At that moment the lab supervisor came in. He had heard Bill's request for the lab tech to get his supervisor.

"What's going on here? Oh, hi, Deputy Sparks. Are you here for the photos?

"Yes, sir."

"Just a minute. I did them myself."

The supervisor turned and walked back to his office. Within a few minutes he came back carrying a yellow envelope.

"Here you go. There are two sets of all the pictures on the rolls of film you left. Let me know if you want blowups of any of them. I still have the negatives."

"Thank you."

"Is there anything else, deputy?" the supervisor asked seeing that Bill didn't look like he was ready to leave.

"Yes. First of all, I would like a couple of rolls of film. Secondly, I was also wondering if you have had a chance to clean up the gold coins, I brought in with the film earlier this afternoon?" Bill asked.

"Yes, we have. We do not have the result of the test for blood type, yet. But the coins are definitely from Germany. No one here has ever seen coins like them, but they are solid gold."

"I have seen coins like them when I was in Germany during the war, but I don't know anything about them. Is there anything you can tell me about them?"

"We know that they are molded, not stamped. When looked at under a magnifying glass, we could tell from the coins they were made using a mold, and by that, I mean the mold used was probably handmade. In other words, it had tiny flaws in the engraving of the mold that were consistent with using hand tools to make the mold, and most likely made by someone with some skills working on very little things, but probably an amateur at making molds.

"The flaws on the coins were caused by flaws in the mold that was used to make them, and each coin has the same flaws, which tells me that both coins were made from the same mold, and they were made one at a time. That's very time consuming.

"We also weighed each one of them. Their weights are not consistent which helps reinforce my belief they were made by pouring the gold in a liquid state into the mold by hand, then letting it cool and harden."

"How much gold is contained in each coin?" Bill asked.

"Approximately three ounces, but like I said, they are not the same weight. Each coin varies in weight by a couple of grams."

"I find that interesting. It would appear that someone melted down some gold and made it into coins," Bill said thoughtfully.

"I would agree with that, deputy," the supervisor said while grinning.

"But, why?" Bill said thinking out loud.

"That, deputy, is something for you to find out," he said with a grin. "I have no idea why someone would melt down gold unless it was to make it smaller and easier to sneak into this country, or out of Germany. Maybe both."

"You just might have hit on why it was melted down," Bill said with a grin.

"Which was it?" the supervisor asked.

"Since the coins were apparently made in Germany and found here in the United States, I would think that the gold was melted down to get it out of Germany and into the U.S. undetected. It would not be difficult to bring in gold coins a few at a time."

"I agree," the supervisor said. "Well, is there anything else we can help you with today?"

“Were you able to get any fingerprints off the .45 caliber shell casing I brought in?”

“Yes, but they were pretty badly smudged. I doubt we will be able to connect it to a person. All the reports on the items you brought in are in the envelope, except for the blood type. I will get the report on the blood type over to the sheriff as soon as it is done.”

“Thank you. I’ve taken up enough of your time.”

“Anytime we can be of help, deputy.”

Just then a lab assistant stuck out his hand and gave Bill two fresh rolls of film.

Bill nodded a ‘thanks’ then turned and left the lab.

Bill drove to the sheriff’s office and went inside. Sheriff Henderson was not in his office. Bill sat down at a desk in the outer office and wrote out his report about his activities for the day and his interview with Sean Carter at Captain Butler’s office. He also put in his report what he had found out from the lab supervisor. He clipped his report to the envelope after taking a set of the pictures out of the envelope.

On the outside of the envelope, Bill scribbled a brief note that he was headed back to Hill City. He then laid the envelope on the sheriff’s desk. He left the sheriff’s office and went out to his patrol car. He got in and left Rapid City to return to Hill City.

It was a few minutes after six by the time he returned home. He had just walked in the door to his house when his girlfriend, Julie, pulled into the drive. Bill waited at the door for her to step up on the porch.

“I’m sorry that I’m so late,” Julie said.

“It’s okay, I just got home. You have time for a cup of coffee?”

"No. I think I better get home. Grandfather will be worried about me. He probably hasn't eaten since he expected me to be home earlier."

"In that case, you best be going. Besides, I doubt I would be very good company this evening. I'm pretty tired. I had a long day yesterday, a short night last night, and a busy day today."

"What happened?"

"I had to search the area where I found the body, talk to some people, then I went to Rapid City. After taking the evidence to the sheriff, I went out to the air base to interview an airman who had been in the area around the time when the victim was shot."

"Oh. I guess you have had a busy day."

"We still have not identified the victim. He didn't have any identification on him."

"I better get going. You can tell me about it later. Try and get some rest."

"Okay."

"Can I have a kiss before I go?"

"I'm not too tired to kiss you," Bill said as reached out and pulled her up against him.

It was not a real passionate kiss, but it was one that told her he loved her. After a moment, she drew back and looked up at him.

"That was nice. Will I see you tomorrow?" Julie asked.

"I will be busy during the day, but hope to be home in the evening. Oh, would you like me to call your grandfather and tell him you are on your way?"

"I would like that. I have tomorrow off. I work nights in Rapid City for a couple of days after that."

"I'll try to come out tomorrow evening."

"Good," she said with a smile then kissed him lightly. "Get some rest."

Julie gave him a quick kiss, then turned and walked back to her car. She waved at him as she left his drive.

Bill waved back then went into the house as soon as she was out of sight. He took a minute to call Julie's grandfather before he took a quick shower. After his shower, he got something to eat before going to bed. It didn't take him long to fall asleep.

CHAPTER FOUR

Bill was awakened by his alarm clock going off. He had been sleeping so soundly that it startled him. After finding his alarm clock and finally getting it shut off, he flopped back down and looked up at the ceiling. He laid there for several minutes while his head cleared.

It wasn't long before he began thinking about the body he had found in the backcountry. What was the reason for someone shooting the victim? Who felt it necessary to kill him?

Bill knew he was not going to get the answers lying in bed. He sat up and swung his legs over the side of the bed. He looked around the room as he thought about what he needed to do today.

The first thing that came to mind was he wished that he had kept one of the gold coins. Bill would like to have one of the coins to show to Mr. Schmidt to see what his reaction would be. Maybe just telling him about the coin would be enough to get a reaction from him, Bill thought.

Another thing he thought about was where did the tracks left by the horse go? Why had the horse been tied to the tree only a short distance from one of the slash piles, and only a few yards from where the body was located? Tracking the horse might lead him to someone who had been at the scene of the murder. At the very least, it might lead him to someone who had heard or had seen something important in the area.

Tracking the horse could also prove to be a fruitless effort since most, if not all, of the tracks had probably been washed away by the rain. He would still have to try to find tracks left by the horse in the hope of finding out where the horse went, and who owned the horse. Bill had his doubts about finding the horse. He knew it was a long shot when he made the castings.

The thoughts that ran through Bill's mind were enough to get him up and get him moving. He went into the bathroom and took a short wake-up shower, shaved, then got dressed in his uniform.

Bill had just walked out the door when he remembered that he had pictures of one of the gold coins. He turned around and went back inside to his desk. Bill searched through the photos he had gotten from the lab yesterday. He quickly found the pictures of the gold coin that had been in the backpack. He picked out one of the pictures and slipped it into his shirt pocket. Bill left his house, got in his patrol car and went to the Hill City Café for breakfast.

When Bill arrived at the Hill City Café, he picked a booth where he could see almost everyone who was in the café. There were four other customers when he entered the café. Two of the men in the café were sitting alone. One of the men who was sitting alone, he didn't know. The other one was Martin Cannon.

Cannon was well known to be somewhat of a bully and a hot head with a very short and nasty temper. He had been arrested several times for fighting with people who simply didn't agree with him. Most recently, he had beat up a man who Cannon claimed was trespassing on his property. It was quickly proved that the man was actually a good half mile from his property, and he was on U.S Forest land.

Fortunately for Cannon, but not for justice, the man refused to press charges. The man would have won the case easily since he had several reliable witnesses.

Bill had tried to get the man to press charges, but he refused. Bill was sure Cannon either paid the guy off to get him to drop the charges, or threatened him in some way if he didn't drop all charges. Whatever the reason for dropping the charges, it apparently had had a profound effect on Cannon's disposition.

Cannon spent just a few nights in jail, and was told that he was facing a very long prison sentence if he was found guilty. Even his attorney told him it didn't look good for him if it went to trial. The thought of spending years in a prison must have caused Cannon to think about the way he dealt with people who didn't agree or upset him. His time in a jail cell might have had something to do with him thinking about it, too. Cannon had not been in any kind of trouble since that incident, and it had been a little over a year ago.

Bill knew Cannon owned a small mountain ranch somewhere near Medicine Mountain, not far from Spring Creek. Bill wasn't really sure where his ranch was located, but didn't think it would be too hard to find. If it was on the southside of Medicine Mountain, Cannon might have heard something. Bill was reasonably sure Cannon lived fairly close to where the body had been found, probably less than a mile. Cannon might have heard the shots or seen someone near his place who was not from the area.

The others in the café were Mr. Joseph Reynolds and his wife, Margret. They were a quiet couple who kept pretty much to themselves. They had a small ranch where they raised draft horses. Most of their horses were Morgans, but he also had a matched pair of Percherons. Mr. Reynolds was known for his ability to train the large work horses well. According to the local newspaper, he had won a good number of ribbons, including several blue ribbons, at the annual stock show in Rapid City with his Morgan draft horses.

Mr. Reynolds was also known for using his draft horses to drag trees out of the woods to where they were stacked. The horses could pull the logs out of the woods when tractors could not get to them. When there were enough logs in the stack, the lumber mill would load them on trucks and take them to the saw mill just outside of Hill City.

Bill knew where the Reynolds lived. It was several miles from where the shooting took place. The hoof prints

Bill had found would be way too small to have been made by any of Reynold's large draft horses. Bill also knew that Reynolds had not been working in an area close to where he found the body.

Sandy, a short, stocky, middle aged woman with tired eyes walked up to Bill and set a cup of black coffee in front of him.

"What'll it be this morning?"

"I'll have the breakfast special. Eggs over easy."

"I have fresh whole wheat bread this morning. Would you like toast with that?"

"Sure, and with a little of your apple butter?"

"Sure," she said with a smile.

Sandy turned and walked back to the kitchen.

Bill didn't often eat breakfast at the café, but he ate there often enough that Sandy had gotten to know him. She always brought him black coffee whenever he came in and sat down.

It wasn't long before Sandy brought him a plate with a thick slice of ham, two eggs over easy, fried potatoes, and a small plate with two slices of wheat toast with apple butter on it. She set the meal in front of him then returned to the kitchen.

As Bill began to eat, he noticed that Cannon was sitting across the room looking at him over the top of his cup of coffee. From the look in his eyes, Bill wondered what he was thinking about. Cannon was squinting as if he really hated Bill, which could very well be the case. After all, Bill had arrested Cannon a couple of times. Usually, he just ignored Bill and didn't even talk to him.

Bill watched as Cannon got up and left the café. He thought about how Cannon had looked at him, but then he looked at half the people in Hill City like he hated them. It was understandable because Bill knew that very few people in town, if any, liked the man, and there were a number of them who would have nothing to do with him.

When Bill finished his breakfast, Mr. and Mrs. Reynolds were still sitting at the table sipping on their coffee and talking quietly to each other. Their plates were empty so Bill was sure they were in no hurry. He smiled to himself thinking that they seemed happy just being together.

As soon as Bill finished his breakfast, he got up, dropped a couple of quarters on the table and went to the counter to pay for his breakfast. While Sandy was making change, he looked out the window. He could see Cannon standing across the street leaning against the building near his patrol car. Bill wasn't sure, but he thought that Cannon might want to talk to him, although he couldn't think why.

Bill got his change, thanked Sandy, then walked out of the café. He looked both ways then walked across the street to his patrol car. When he stepped up on the curb, he looked at Cannon.

"You want to talk to me?" Bill asked.

"Yeah."

"Okay, talk."

"I heard you was investigating a murder up by Medicine Mountain."

"That's correct," Bill said then waited for Cannon to talk.

"I know you don't think much of me, and I've been in a lot of trouble around here. But I want you to know that I had nothing to do with it."

"Okay. If you had nothing to do with it, would you mind if I come out to your place and talk to you? I have a few questions I'd like to ask you."

"No, I don't mind. In fact, it might be best if we talk at my place where others can't see us talking," he said as he looked around.

Bill didn't respond to the last part of his comment, but it caused him to think about it. Bill didn't think Cannon was worried about "others" seeing them talking. Why would he?

He never seemed to care what others thought of him in the past.

"I'll be out your way later today."

"Okay. I'll be home all day. I'm on my way home now."

"See you later. I have other things to attend to before I come out there," Bill said then turned and got into his patrol car and drove away.

Bill could see Cannon in his rearview mirror as he drove off. Cannon was watching him as he drove away. He could see a slight grin on Cannon's face. It caused Bill to wonder what Cannon wanted to talk to him about, but at the moment he had other things to think about.

One was to pay a visit to Mr. Schmidt. He was interested in seeing what kind of a reaction he might get when he showed him the photo of the gold coin.

Second was to track the horse from the slash piles at the end of the logging road where the body was found. He wanted to know where the horse had gone.

Bill would go to Cannon's farm last. He knew Cannon had a number of horses. With all the trouble Bill had had with Cannon, it crossed his mind that maybe, just maybe, the horse tracks might just lead him right to Cannon's farm. It certainly would not surprise him if they did.

Bill drove out of Hill City and headed for Schmidt's ranch. His ranch was about a half mile west of the place where the body was found.

It took Bill a little over a half hour to get to the Schmidt's ranch from Hill City. He was surprised when he drove in the drive to find the gate wide open and the "no trespassing" sign had been removed from the gate. It seemed obvious that Mr. Schmidt was expecting him, although he had not told Schmidt if or when he might be coming back.

Bill followed the drive up to the house and stopped. Mr. and Mrs. Schmidt immediately stepped out on the porch and waited for Bill to get out of his patrol car. This time, Mr. Schmidt did not have a rifle in his hands.

"What brings you out here this morning?" Mr. Schmidt asked, his voice more cordial than the last time Bill had talked to him.

"Are you expecting someone? I noticed that the gate was open."

"My wife thought that if the gate was open, it might be more welcoming to people, maybe even invite people to visit. Since I don't have any livestock here in the yard, the gate didn't need to be closed."

"You have a very smart wife," Bill said with a grin.

"Yes, I do."

Dieter grinned a little for a moment, but the look on face turned serious.

"I should apologize for the way I talked to you the last time you were here, and for having a rifle that I held in a threating way."

"Apology accepted."

"Thank you. Now, what is it that brings you out here this morning?"

"What brings me out here is I have a picture of something that you might be able to help me by identifying it for me."

"Okay. I will try. Let's go inside and sit at the table," Dieter suggested, then turned and went inside.

Bill followed Dieter into the house. His wife was just getting cups of coffee. Dieter and Bill sat down while Mrs. Schmidt set the cups on the table. She then sat down next to her husband.

"What is it you want me to see?" Dieter asked.

Bill reached into his shirt pocket and pulled out the photograph. He handed it to Dieter, then watched his face for some kind of reaction. He didn't have to wait long.

From the look on Dieter's face, he was surprised to see what was in the picture. In fact, it almost took his breath way. He looked at Bill for a second before he said anything.

"Where did you get this photograph?" he asked, his voice quivering a little.

"It's not the photograph that interests me. It's the gold coin. I would like to know something about it. I take it from the look on your face, you know something about the coin. What do you know about it?"

Dieter looked at the photograph again then slowly turned his head and looked at Bill. His hands were shaking.

"That is a coin that was made in Germany in 1935 by a small group of men who were getting ready to escape Germany."

"How is it you know about the coin?"

"My father was one of those men. There were one hundred and forty of the coins made. They were made one at a time in the basement of my father's clock shop. The coins were to be divided evenly among seven men, and were to be used to buy their way out of the country," Dieter explained.

"That would mean that each man had twenty of the coins."

"That is correct."

"Were you one of those men?" Bill asked.

"No. We were able to get out of Germany with the help of one of my father's friends. My father told me about what he was doing in the basement. He told us to leave because we knew about what my father was doing. We left Germany before the coins were actually made."

"How is it you can recognize the coin if they had not been made yet?"

"My father showed me his drawing of what the coins would look like. I recognize the writing on the coin in the picture."

"Can you tell me anything about the men who were to receive the coins."

"Of the seven men who were to receive the coins, as far as I know only two managed to get out of Germany. You see, the seven men were engineers, designers, chemist, and others that were needed to build the weapons of war for Germany. They did not want to build weapons for a man like Hitler."

"So, you never actually saw any of the coins?"

"That is right. How did you get this photograph?"

"I took it."

"You have seen this coin?" Dieter said with surprise.

"Yes. Do you know where the two men who got out of Germany went?"

"I only know about one of them. He got to England where he worked with the English in their fight against Germany during the war. He was a chemist."

"What about the other one?"

"He got out of Germany, but I don't know what happened to him after he got out. I heard he went to Switzerland, but that is only what I heard. I do not know for sure."

"Any idea how the coins got here?"

"No," Dieter replied while looking at the photograph.

"Do you know the names of the seven men who had the coins?"

"I only know the name of one of the men. That would be my father, Adolph Schmidt," Dieter said with a sad look in his eyes. "My father didn't want me to know their names. I think it was for fear that if I got caught, I might be tortured and tell the Germans their names."

"Did your father make it to the United States?" Bill asked.

"No. He was captured by the Germans in 1937. It was just as he was about to cross the border into Switzerland. He was taken, with my mother, to a prison camp. I was informed after the war that they died while in prison. Based on the information I was given by your War Department, they were killed shortly after they arrived at the prison camp. They murdered them," he said with a hint of sadness in his voice, mixed with a good deal of anger.

"What makes you think that?"

"First of all, my father was a clock maker. His skills were not needed in the war effort. Those who were not of value to the war effort, and caught while trying to escape Germany, were most often killed."

"I'm sorry," Bill said, not knowing what else to say.

"Thank you." Dieter said.

"Do you know what happened to his coins?"

"No, but I would guess that some German officer ended up with them. German officers often took anything of value away from prisoners, and most of the time kept it for themselves.

"How many of the coins did you find?" Dieter asked.

"I found three of them," Bill said.

"Can I ask where you found them?"

"For now, I would rather not say. They are part of my investigation."

"I understand," Dieter said with obvious disappointment showing on his face.

"I will tell you when my investigation is over. Do you think your folks were killed so they could not tell anyone about the coins?"

"I had not thought of that, but I guess it would be possible. It might explain why they were killed so soon after they were imprisoned."

"It would be interesting to find out how the coins got to the United States," Bill said thoughtfully.

"Yes, it would be interesting, very interesting," Dieter agreed. "If you should find out how they got here, I would like to know."

"When my investigation is over, I will let you know, if I can. I should be going. Thank you for the information. If you think of anything else, I would appreciate it if you would get in touch with me," Bill said as he stood up.

"I will," Dieter said as he stood up.

"I would also appreciate it if you would not tell anyone about our conversation, and about the coins."

"We will not tell anyone," Dieter said as he looked at his wife.

"Thank you, and thank you for the coffee, Mrs. Schmidt," Bill said then turned and walked to the door.

Dieter followed Bill as far as the porch then watched as Bill walked to his patrol car. As he got in his patrol car, he looked up at the porch. Mrs. Schmidt stepped out onto the porch and took Dieter's arm as she watched Bill start his patrol car.

Bill could see Dieter standing on the porch watching him leave. He found what Dieter had told him very interesting. He wondered what Dieter had not told him. If he came up with more information on the coins, he might want to talk to Dieter again.

The questions that came to Bill's mind were who brought the coins to the United States? Did any of the other men who had coins get to the United States? If one of the men got to the United States, how many of the coins made it to the United States? There was also the question of how did the dead man get his hands on the gold coins found under his body and in his backpack?

Bill had a lot on his mind as he left Dieter Schmidt's ranch. His talk with Dieter caused more questions than it answered.

It wasn't long when his thoughts turned to where he had seen the hoof prints near the slash piles. He headed for the logging road that led to the murder site.

CHAPTER FIVE

A number of questions ran through Bill's mind as he drove toward the logging road that led back into the place where the body had been found. He couldn't help but think about the dead man and the gold coins. Bill wondered how the dead man had come to have the coins? Had he found them, or did he steal them from someone? If he found them, where did he find them? If he stole them from someone, who did he steal them from?

It didn't take Bill very long to get to the logging road. When he turned onto the logging road, he stopped and got out of his patrol car. The first thing he did was look for tracks that led toward the slash piles.

Bill found two sets of tire tracks, one going toward the slash piles and one that was headed away from the slash piles. A closer look at the tire tracks showed that the two sets of tire tracks were made by the same vehicle. It looked like the tire tracks were made by a car, or a small truck, such as a pickup truck.

For the first time, Bill was glad it rained the other night. It cleared all the old tracks from the road making the new tracks very clear.

Before Bill went any further down the logging road, he took time to make casts of the new tire tracks. He had no idea what they would prove, but it seemed like a good idea at the time.

Once the casts of the tire tracks had dried enough, Bill wrote on the casts where and when he made them. He wrapped them in an old towel and put them in the trunk of his patrol car. He got in the patrol car and proceeded along the logging road to where the slash piles had been. Bill parked his patrol car where he had parked before. He got out and looked at the new tire tracks. He could clearly see where the vehicle had stopped, and where it had turned around to leave.

Bill walked over to where the vehicle had stopped. There was some indication that whoever had driven there and stopped and gotten out of the vehicle. Bill moved closer to where the vehicle had stopped and stood about where a person inside the vehicle would have gotten out. He looked around. He quickly discovered that the vehicle had stopped where anyone inside could look out at where the body had been found and would be able to see it clearly.

Bill looked down at the tire tracks and carefully examined the ground. It became clear that the tire tracks of the vehicle showed it had suddenly taken off leaving skid marks in the wet grass. It seemed to Bill that the vehicle left in a hurry. The tire tracks indicated that the vehicle was probably a pickup truck. Bill photographed the tire tracks in several different places.

When he finished photographing the tire tracks, he started looking for footprints of the person who had gotten out of the vehicle. He found some indentation in the ground, but with the grass, he was unable to identify them.

Why did the person get out of the vehicle? Was it to make sure the victim was dead, or was it simply to check to see if any evidence had been left there? Was he looking for the gold coins? The few partial footprints showed where someone had walked over toward where the body had been, then quickly returned to the vehicle.

The footprints close to where the body had been were not clear enough to be identifiable. Bill could not tell if they were made by shoes or boots, or what size they might have been. He wasn't sure, but it looked like whoever had been there had pushed around the bloodstained dirt close to where the body had been.

The first thought that crossed Bill's mind was everything seemed to point to the person probably looking for the gold coins. If he was the person who killed the victim, what caused him to leave the site before he had been able to search the victim for the coins at the time the victim was killed? How did he know the dead man had the coins in the first place? Did he find a coin at the time he killed the young man and came back to see if he could find more?

While looking around, Bill noticed that the footprints showed signs of the person turning around sharply, then running back toward the pickup truck. Had he heard something or someone and didn't want to be seen there? Bill had a lot of questions, but darn few answers.

Since there was nothing Bill could do to get useable photos, or casts of the footprints, he turned his attention to where the horse had been tied. As Bill moved back into the woods to where the horse had been, he studied the ground looking for shoe or boot prints. He found none.

When he got to where the horse had been tied, he studied the horse's tracks under the tree very carefully. He wanted to be able to distinguish them from any other tracks he might come across.

Outside the protection of the trees, the tracks had almost completely disappeared due to the rain with only an occasional hint of the direction the horse had gone. The tracks made by the horse left an impression showing that the horse might have gone directly away from the slash piles, and that it had headed north.

Bill started to walk north away from the trees. When he was about twelve feet away, he lost the tracks. Bill began to walk in a circle hoping to find tracks which would give him some idea of where the horse had gone.

Within a few minutes, Bill was able to find the tracks under a tree the horse had passed under. They indicated that the horse had turned and headed northeast.

Bill continued in the direction he thought the horse had gone. He was able to follow the tracks as the horse passed under trees every few yards or so, or left an occasional indentation in the soft earth that the rain had not completely washed away.

He managed to follow the horse for about half a mile before he came to an open field surrounded by a barbed wire fence. Bill had no idea who owned the open field.

Bill looked at the fence to see if had been cut so the horse could pass through, or if there was a gate to the other side. He didn't find any of the wires cut, nor did he see a gate. He looked up and down the fence line but couldn't see any place where a horse could cross over to the other side of the fence, nor could he see any tracks along the fence line to show him which way the horse might have gone. It appeared that the horse had just vanished or had jumped the fence.

Bill stood there and studied the fence and the field. He had lost the tracks of the horse, but he noticed a place in the fence where the top rung of the barbed wire fence looked like it might be missing. He walked along the fence until he came to the place where the top wire was missing. There was little doubt that a horse would be able to jump the fence with little difficulty, even with a rider on its back.

Bill carefully looked for tracks on the other side of the fence. He found tracks in the ground that made it look like the horse had jumped the fence. With no way to follow the horse, it was time for Bill to return to his patrol car.

Once Bill arrived back at his patrol car, he sat down in the car and opened his Forest Service map of the Black Hills. It took him only a few minutes to figure out where he had been when he saw the field. The map did not tell him who owned the field, but it showed a road that probably went by the other side of the field. Bill quickly figured out the way he would have to go to get there, then started his patrol car. He left the murder site and headed to where he thought he would find a farm or small ranch that was part of the field.

Bill drove down the road until he came to a crossroad. He was pretty sure the crossroad would take him where he wanted to go. Bill turned and drove along the road that he was sure would go past the other side of the field, but all he could see was the forest. It wasn't until he drove almost a mile along the road that he suddenly came into a clearing. He pulled to a stop and looked out across the open field. It took him a few minutes of looking at the field before he was sure it was the same field he had seen earlier.

Bill took a minute to look down the road. He could see what looked like the top of a barn. He put the patrol car in gear and drove down the road. As he topped the hill, he could see a house just off the road with a barn behind it. He could make out three horses in the small corral on the side of the barn. He had no idea who owned the farm, but he was about to find out. He continued to drive down the hill toward a driveway.

Bill turned into the drive. The first thing he saw was a mailbox with the name "Martin Cannon" on the side. He was surprised because he thought Cannon lived about three miles further south.

He followed the drive up as far as the house. Bill stopped and got out of his patrol car.

As he got out of his patrol car, a young woman stepped out onto the porch. She was wearing a light blue cotton dress with a white apron over it. Her black hair was pulled up in a bun. She was drying her hands on a towel as she watched Bill walk toward the porch.

"Good afternoon," Bill said as he approached the porch.

"Good afternoon, deputy," she replied cautiously.

"I'm Bill Sparks, a Pennington County Deputy Sheriff. Might I ask your name?

"Martha Cannon," she replied.

"Well, I guess I'm in the right place," he said with a smile. "Is Martin home?"

"What do you want with Martin? Is he in trouble again?"

"No. I saw him in town this morning and he wanted me to stop by. He wanted to talk to me about something, but didn't say what it was about."

"He's out in the barn," she said flatly.

"Do you mind if I go out there and talk to him?"

"Suit yourself," she said.

Bill watched her as she went back into the house. He wondered if there was something wrong. Mrs. Cannon seemed uninterested or indifferent about Bill being there. It was almost as if she didn't care why he was there, or if he was there at all. It crossed his mind that she might have had a fight with her husband, but he knew of nothing that would support that thought.

Bill turned and walked out to the barn. The barn door was opened halfway. He stepped inside and called out.

"Martin? Deputy Bill Sparks here."

"I'm up here," Martin replied.

Bill looked up at the hay loft. Martin was looking down at him.

"I'll be down in a second. I'm going to drop a couple of bales of hay down. You might want to step back. I don't want to get you dirty."

Bill stepped back away from the edge of the loft and watched as Martin dropped two bales of hay down on the barn floor. It was only a minute or so before Martin came down from the loft.

"I'm glad you came out," Martin said.

"You said you wanted to talk to me. What about?"

"I'm not sure if this means anything or not," he said, then hesitated.

"Why don't you tell me what's on your mind. I'll decide if it means anything to me."

"Okay. I know you are investigating a murder over on the logging road near Negro Creek."

"How is it you know that?"

"People talk. There are very few secrets around here. You hear things in the café and in the stores in town."

"Okay, you heard things. What did you hear?"

"The day of the murder, I heard the report of two shots from over that way," he said as he pointed out across the field behind his barn."

"What day and time was that?"

"It was a little after dinner on Saturday. It was about one or one-fifteen in the afternoon."

"Where were you when you heard the shots?"

"I was in the corral at the back of the barn. I had just started working with a new colt."

"How far is it from here to the end of the logging road, as the crow flies?

"I would guess it's about a mile, maybe a bit more, but not much."

Bill thought about what he was saying.

"Are you sure you heard just two shots?" Bill asked.

"Yes, just two shots."

"Did you see anyone about that time on the other side of your field?"

"No. It's hard to see that side of the field from here because the slop of the land."

"Did you go to investigate the shots?"

"No. I figured it was just someone hunting. When I found out about the murder, I thought you would like to know about the shots."

Bill took a moment or two to think about what Cannon had told him. Schmidt only told him about the sound of shots when he was questioned. Bill doubted that anyone in town would have known about it this morning when Cannon was in town. He knew that he had not told anyone about it.

As far he knew, the only people in Hill City or in the area who knew about the murder were Julie and possibly her grandfather, if she had told him about it. As far as he knew Julie's grandfather, Wilbur, had not been in town. There was also the fact that he had not told Julie how many times the victim was shot, or how many shots had been fired.

Bill turned and walked out of the barn and into the corral behind the barn. He stood just inside the corral and looked off toward where the body had been found, then turned and looked at the ground for a moment as if the was thinking.

He was thinking, but he was also looking at the hoof prints in the soft dirt of the ground in the corral. He wasn't sure, but the hoof prints in the corral looked like the ones he had seen at the murder site. He could not be sure without comparing them to the castings he had made.

Cannon had followed Bill out into the corral. He stood next to Bill wondering what he was thinking.

"What are you looking at?" Cannon asked.

"I was just thinking," Bill replied as he looked up at Cannon.

Cannon's barn was more than a mile away from the end of the logging road. Would it be possible to hear a gunshot at that distance? The real question was would he be able to hear a gunshot at that distance with the corral being located down behind the hill? With the trees between them and the logging road, plus the contour of the land, would the sound of gunshots travel that far and still be recognized as gunshots, especially since it was a pistol that had fired the shots?

There was also the fact that the shots were fired from the other side of the slash piles which would reduce the sound of the shots toward the barn considerably. Then there was the fact that the shooter would have had his back toward Cannon's place.

With all those factors taken into consideration, Bill had his doubts that Martin would have heard anything. If that was the case, how is it that he knew just how many shots were fired?

"What's on your mind?" Martin asked, disturbing Bill's thoughts.

"I was just thinking. I guess I don't have any other questions for you at this time. I might want to talk to you again, later."

"Sure thing. Come out anytime."

"Thank you for the information," Bill said then turned and walked out of the corral.

Bill walked out to the front of the house and got in his patrol car. As he reached to turn the ignition key to start the car, he looked up at the house. Mrs. Cannon was looking out the window at him. He wondered what she was thinking, but he wasn't going to go ask her, not yet anyway.

Bill started his patrol car and drove out to the road. He turned and headed back to the murder site. When he got back to the logging road, he didn't turn in. Instead, he just stopped and looked down the logging road. He was thinking about what he had seen and heard today. He was also wondering how he could get a better look at the hoof prints in Cannon's corral.

He had also seen a pickup truck parked next to the barn. It had some mud on it that was like the mud on the logging road, not like the mud from the gravel roads.

It had been a long day. Bill decided that he would head for home. He had a lot to report to the sheriff, and a lot to think about. He would go home and write his report while it was all fresh in his mind. As far as he was concerned, he had at least one good suspect, Martin Cannon. If he could get a warrant to search Cannon's farm, it might prove interesting. The problem was, he didn't have anything solid that he could use to get a search warrant.

When Bill arrived home, he got something to eat and sat down at his desk. He filled out his report of his day's activities in great detail. When he was finished with his reports, he remembered that he had told Julie that he would come out to her grandfather's farm. He was tired. He decided to call her. He picked up the phone and called Julie.

"Hello."

"Hi."

"Hi. Are you coming out?"

"I've had a long day and I'm tired. Would you be too upset with me if I don't come out tonight?"

"No, of course not. Is everything okay?"

"Yes. it's just that I'm beat. These past couple of days have been hectic with a lot of long hours."

"I understand," Julie said.

"You have to go to work tomorrow night, right?"

"Yes."

"Would you like to have dinner with me, here, before you go to work?"

"I'd like that. I'll see you tomorrow evening. Get some rest. I love you."

"I love you, too."

As soon as Bill hung up the phone, he went into the bathroom, took a shower and got ready for bed. Within minutes of his head hitting the pillow, he was sound asleep.

CHAPTER SIX

Bill's alarm clock went off waking him out of a deep sleep. He rolled over, reached out and slapped the clock shutting off the alarm. He flopped back down and looked up at the ceiling.

As his mind cleared from being awakened suddenly, Bill began to think about what he had learned so far. He had noticed that Sean had been rather nervous when he questioned him about his trip into the backcountry with his friends. It caused Bill to wonder what it was that made Sean so nervous. He also remembered that Sean had mentioned Chuck Smart as one of the men who had gone into the backcountry with him.

Sean had told him that Chuck Smart lived in Hill City and worked at the lumber mill just outside of town. Bill thought it might be a good idea to have a talk with him. He wondered if what Chuck might tell him would agree with what Sean had said.

Bill rolled out of bed and went into the bathroom. He took a quick cool shower in the hope it would wake him up. As soon as he was out of the shower, he got ready to leave for work. Deciding that he didn't want to fix his own breakfast, his first stop would be the Hill City Café for breakfast. It had also crossed his mind that he might be able to pick up a little information about Chuck at the café.

When Bill walked into the café, the first person he noticed was old man Rutledge. Rutledge was well known as a scavenger of old deserted mines and quarries in the area, or anyplace else he thought he could find something he could use or sell without getting caught.

Bill decided that he didn't want to talk to Rutledge about Chuck Smart. He doubted that Rutledge would know much about Chuck anyway. Bill had had run-ins with Rutledge on several occasions, most of them unpleasant. Rutledge looked at Bill, but quickly looked away when he saw Bill looking at him.

Bill found an empty booth. He sat down and waited for Sandy to wait on him. It was only a minute or so before Sandy brought him a cup of hot black coffee and set it down in front of him.

"What will it be this morning?" Sandy asked.

"I'll have the morning special, eggs over easy. Oh, do you still have some of your Apple Butter?"

"Yes," Sandy said with a smile. "Would you like that on some fresh whole wheat bread, lightly toasted?"

"All the better," Bill replied with a smile.

Sandy smiled then turned and went to the kitchen.

While Bill waited for his breakfast, he looked around the room. There were only a few people in the café. Most of them he knew, but not well.

His thoughts turned to Sean. Bill went over in his mind what Sean had told him, and his reactions to Bill's questions. There was little doubt in Bill's mind that Sean knew something. The question was what did he know that made him so nervous?

Bill also needed to question Robert Hood and James Goodman. First of all, he wanted to know if Goodman would tell the same story as Sean had told him. Goodman would be easy to find since he was an airman and lived on the air base. Plus, Captain Butler had assured Bill that Goodman would be available for questioning.

Robert Hood would be a little harder to find. Bill had been told by Sean that Robert lived in Rapid City, but he didn't know where in Rapid City.

Bill's thoughts were interrupted when Sandy brought his breakfast to the table. Bill leaned back while she set his breakfast on the table in front of him.

"Sandy, do you know the Smart family?"

"Sure."

"Do you have a minute?"

Sandy looked around the café. Seeing that it was not very busy, she sat down in the booth across from him.

"What can I do for you?"

"Tell me a little about the Smarts. I don't know the family very well. Do you know them?"

"I guess I know them about as well as anyone around here."

"Good. What can you tell me about them?"

"Well, Floyd Smart died about nine or ten years ago in a logging accident. He was a lumberjack and a good family man. Alice Smart works at the school as a cook in the cafeteria during the school year. She's been working there for years, even before Floyd died. During the summer, she works in Custer State Park as a cook at one of the restaurants. I think at Blue Bell Lodge, but I'm not sure. She started working there shortly after Floyd died."

"What can you tell me about Chuck?"

"Chuck is a little different. He didn't really have a father in his life during the time a boy really needs a father, at least in the last nine or ten years. After his father died, he was raised by his mother.

"Chuck didn't do all that well in school, but he did manage to get accepted into the Army. Book wise, he wasn't a very good student, but he is good with cars and trucks. He is a pretty good mechanic."

"Did he ever get into any kind of trouble that you know of?"

"Yes. He had several scrapes with the law, but nothing very serious. If I remember correctly, he did get into something that was a bit serious, at least it went before a judge. I don't know any of this firsthand, or any of the details, but I was told that the judge didn't want to give Chuck a record that might affect his future. The judge apparently felt Chuck needed some discipline in his life, and since his mother couldn't seem to do it, maybe the military could," Sandy explained.

"Chuck joined the Army. As far as I know, he cleaned up his act. After he was discharged, he moved back here and went to work at the mill."

"Do you know what kind of trouble he got into?"

"No. I never heard, and the judge that handled his case died a year or so ago."

"Do you know anything about a Robert Hood?"

"Now there's one for you. He was always in trouble. I heard that he joined the Army to keep from going to jail, too. I think it was kind of like what happened to Chuck.

"What I heard was mostly rumors. Chuck and Robert went in front of the judge at the same time. They also went into the Army about the same time. If it was something they did together, it would be my guess that Robert was the instigator in all of it. He was always in trouble. Chuck was more of a follower in those days.

"After Robert was in the Army, he apparently got into some kind of trouble and they discharged him. It was an 'Undesirable Discharge', I heard.

"After his discharge, he worked at the lumber mill for a short time, but they fired him, too. I heard he got into a fight with his foreman. He didn't like being told what he was to do by his foreman.

"The last I heard was he lives in Rapid City. I did see him in here about a week ago. He was with two other guys. One of them was Chuck, I don't know the other one. That's about all I can tell you about them."

"Thanks. You've been a big help," Bill said.

"By the way, Robert Hood's mother still lives in the Hill City area. She divorced Robert's father and married a man a couple of years back. He has a small ranch in one of the small valleys about four miles out of town on road 389.

"Robert's mother and stepfather won't have anything to do with him. I heard he stole money from his stepfather.

His stepfather threw him out of the house and told him if he ever came back, he would shoot him as a trespasser."

"That seems pretty harsh, but then I don't know all the circumstances," Bill said.

"The money he stole was for seed for the next planting season, so I'd heard."

"I see. Thanks for the information. By the way, what is his stepfather's name?"

"Lawson, Samuel Lawson."

"Sergeant Sam Lawson of the 101st Airborne division that parachuted into France at night ahead of the D-Day invasion?" Bill asked, knowing that the Sam Lawson he knew about was a well decorated soldier.

"He doesn't talk about it much, but he's the one."

"What about Robert's father? Do you think he might have gone to live with him?

"No. Robert's real father was killed in some kind of accident several years ago. He was living in North Dakota at the time. I believe he worked for the railroad up there."

"Thanks again."

"You're welcome. I best get back to work," Sandy said as she scooted out of the booth.

Bill nodded, then watched her as she walked away. His thoughts were on what he had been told. Based on what Sandy had told him about Robert and Chuck, it was clear that they knew each other, and probably well.

After Bill finished his breakfast, he paid for it then left the café. As he walked to his patrol car, he decided to go to Rapid City Air Force Base to talk to Goodman. On his way, he would stop off at the lumber mill and have a talk with Chuck Smart. The lumber mill was located just outside Hill City on the way to Rapid City.

When Bill got to his patrol car, he called in.

"Car eight to Dispatch."

"Dispatch, go ahead."

"Mary, I'm checking in. My plans are to stop at the lumber mill here in Hill City to question Chuck Smart, then go out to the Rapid City Air Force Base to question James Goodman. Both of them were with Sean Carter, and were in the area about the time the victim I found must have been killed."

"I'll log you in with a note of where you are going and who you are going to see."

"Thanks. I will also try to find Robert Hood, the fourth member of the group. He's supposed to live in Rapid City, but I don't know where. See if anyone there might know where he lives."

"I'll check around. I have you logged in."

"Thanks. I'll call in later."

"Okay. Dispatch out."

Bill put his patrol car in gear and started out of Hill City toward the lumber mill. It didn't take him very long to get to the mill. He parked in front of the office and went inside. There were three people in the office. He stepped up to the counter.

"May I help you?" the middle-aged women asked.

"Yes. I would like to talk to Chuck Smart, please."

"One moment."

The woman turned around and called out to one of the two men in the office.

"John, do you know if Chuck Smart is working today?"

"He was scheduled to work, but didn't show up," John said.

He got up from his desk and walked toward the counter.

"Did he call in?" Bill asked.

"Nope. He just didn't show up," John said as he stepped up to the counter.

"Does he fail to show up very often without calling in?"

"No. In fact, he's been very reliable and a good employee. I can check the records, but to my knowledge this is only the second time he has missed work in the past two years he has worked here. The other time, his mother called in and told us he was sick. He missed two day's work, and I know for a fact that he was sick that time."

"How long has he been missing?"

"Since last Monday. He wasn't scheduled to work the weekend. He had Friday, Saturday and Sunday off. He was due to return to work at six o'clock Monday morning. He didn't show. I called his mother's home, but never got an answer. Is there a problem, officer?"

"I just want to talk to him. Thank you," Bill said then turned and left the mill office.

As Bill got into his patrol car, his thoughts were of Chuck. Was it possible that Chuck Smart was the body he found in the backcountry near Medicine Mountain? Another talk with Sean was definitely in order.

Bill started his patrol car and drove on out to the Rapid City Air Force Base. When he arrived at the gate, he found the same guard was on duty that was there the last time he visited Air Police Office. Bill smiled at the guard as he stopped at the gate.

"I would like to talk to Captain Butler again."

"I'll call him and see if he is in," the guard said.

"Thank you."

Bill watched as the guard called Captain Butler's office. It only took a minute before the guard hung up and stepped up close to Bill's car.

"The Captain will see you. First left, first building on the left."

"Thank you."

Bill drove to the Air Police Office. He was again met by an airman who took him inside and knocked on Captain Butler's door.

"Come in."

The airman opened the door and stepped back so Bill could enter. Bill found Captain Butler sitting at his desk. The captain pointed to a chair and Bill sat down.

"What can I do for you today"

"I would like to talk to James Goodman and Sean Carter. I would like to talk to Goodman first," Bill said. "But before you call them in, I would like to know if they work together?"

"I'll find out."

Captain Butler pressed the button on his intercom and called for the sergeant in the front office to come in and bring his roster. Within a couple of minutes, a sergeant came into the office carrying a large binder.

"Sergeant, I need to know where James Goodman works. I already know where Sean Carter works."

"Yes, sir," the sergeant said.

The sergeant sat down in a chair next to Bill and opened the binder. It took him a minute to find what he was looking for. He looked up at the captain.

"James Goodman works in the division office as a file clerk in the records section," the sergeant said.

"Excuse me," Bill said. "Do Goodman and Carter live in the same quarters?"

The sergeant looked back at the book, then looked up.

"No, sir. Their quarters are in different buildings. The buildings are also in different areas of the base."

"Thanks," Bill said.

"Never mind Carter. I know he works as an airplane mechanic in D hanger. I want you to call the division office and have Goodman report to me here as soon as possible. Don't tell him why, or who is in my office," Captain Butler said looking directly at the sergeant.

"Yes, sir."

The sergeant stood up, turned sharply and left the office. It wasn't but a couple of minutes before the sergeant stuck his head in the door and reported that Airman Goodman was on his way over.

"I take it you have something you wish to find out from Goodman?" Captain Butler said.

"I would like to see if Goodman has the same story that Carter told us. So far, I know of four men who went into the backcountry, apparently together. Since I can account for two of them, there are still two left that I have not found and can't account for," Bill said.

"Do you think that one of the men you can't account for is the dead man?"

"I don't know. It is certainly possible. If neither of them is the victim, there's a chance, a good chance that one, or possibly both, killed the one I found. If nothing else, they probably know who the victim is."

Just as the captain was about to say something, there was a knock on his door.

"That's probably Goodman. Come in," the captain said.

A young airman stepped into the office and stood at attention in front of the captain's desk.

"Airman James Goodman reporting, sir."

"At ease, Goodman. This gentleman is Deputy Sheriff Sparks of the Pennington County Sheriff's Office. He has a couple of questions to ask you."

Goodman turned and looked at Bill. He looked a little nervous to Bill, but then it isn't every day that the airman gets called to the Air Police Office.

"James, I understand that you went into the backcountry around Copper Mountain about three or four days ago, and you were with some other guys. Is that correct?"

"No, sir," he replied looking rather nervous.

"No? Then where did you go?"

"We went to Medicine Mountain instead."

"Sorry. I got the wrong mountain. Whose idea was it to go to Medicine Mountain?"

"I'm not sure, but I think it was Robert, Robert Hood's idea. He wanted to go over to Medicine Mountain and do a little panning for gold in Negro Creek."

"So, it was Robert's idea to go to Medicine Mountain and Negro Creek?"

"Yes, sir," James said showing a little more nervousness than Bill thought he should.

"Who were the men you went with?"

"Ah - - Sean Carter, ah - - Chuck Smart, and Robert Hood."

"Was there anyone else?"

"No, sir."

"Did you do any panning for gold?"

"No, sir. Sean and I went up on the mountain and nosed around a couple of old cabins up there. No one lives in them anymore."

"Just you and Sean?"

"Yes, sir."

"Did Sean do any panning for gold?"

"No, sir."

Bill looked at the captain. He was sure that the captain caught the same thing he remembered Sean had said. Sean had said that he had panned for gold.

"Did Chuck and Robert stay at the creek all the time you were there?"

"To be honest, I can't say that they stayed at the creek all the time. We couldn't see them most of the time we were on the mountain. We were on the mountain for about two hours, maybe a little longer. They were at Negro Creek when we left and they were there when we returned."

"You said that you and Sean went up on the mountain, and Robert and Chuck stayed at Negro Creek, is that right?"

"Yes, sir."

"You said they did a little panning for gold in the creek. Do you know if they found any gold?"

"No, sir. I don't know if they found anything."

"Didn't they tell you if they found gold or didn't find gold?

"No. They didn't say one way or the other."

"Whose idea was it to pan for gold?"

"I'm not sure, but I think it was Robert's, but it could have been Chuck's."

"So, the four of you were not together all the time. Is that correct?"

"No, sir. I mean, yes sir. We were not together all the time." he said.

"Are you sure that Robert and Chuck actually panned for gold?"

"Well," he said as he thought about it. "I guess I can't say for sure. We could not see them once we were in the woods. Medicine Mountain is fairly heavily wooded. And I'm sure they couldn't see us either."

"Was there any time that you might have gone to a place where you could see them and either one or both of them were not at the creek?"

"I don't remember even taking the time to check and see if they were still there."

"So, all the time you were gone, you never checked to see if they were still there?"

"That is true. I guess I didn't think about it."

"I have just two more question for you. Did they find any gold, and did you all come back together?"

"Ah - - I don't think they found any gold. At least, they said they didn't," Goodman said.

"So, you're not sure if they found any gold or not. Is that correct?"

"Yes. I'm not sure."

"You didn't answer my second question. Did you all come back together?"

"Well, yes. Yes, we did."

"You don't sound too sure about that. Please explain."

"Well, we all came back as far as Hill City together," he said, but hesitated for a moment.

"Please explain that."

"Robert and Chuck were sitting in the back seat of the car. I could hear them talking about going back up to do a little more panning for gold."

"Do you know if they did?"

"No, not for sure. Sean and I returned to the base in my car."

"Sean didn't take his car back to the base?'

"No, sir. Sean said his car was in need of repairs, and he had to get the parts before he could fix it."

"So, it was your car that was used by the four of you to go up to the mountain?"

"Yes, sir."

"Do you know if Robert and Chuck went back up to the creek?"

"No, sir. I don't know for sure. I only know that they talked about it."

"If they went back up to the mountain, how would they get there since you and Sean returned to the base in your car?"

"They probably went back up in Robert's car."

"Robert drove up from Rapid City?"

"Yes, sir. He left his car in Hill City. We met at the Hill City Café. We all went up to the mountain in my car."

Bill had a pretty good understanding of how things had played out. Goodman's answers seem to confirm what he had been told by Sean except for one little thing. Sean had told Bill earlier that he had panned for gold. James indicated that neither he nor Sean had panned for gold, but instead had gone up on Medicine Mountain together.

"I guess that will be all, unless the captain has any questions," Bill said, then turned and looked at Captain Butler.

"You may return to your duties, airman," the captain said.

Bill watched as Goodman left the captain's office. He wondered if Chuck and Robert returned to do some more panning for gold. The thought ran through Bill's mind that they may have found some gold, but didn't want anyone to know. It also passed through Bill's mind that the gold coins he had found at the murder site were part of the gold they found in or near Negro Creek at the base of Medicine Mountain and didn't want the others to know about it.

"Well, what do you think?" Captain Butler asked.

"I think his is scared to death, but I don't have any idea why?"

"You think he's not telling you everything?"

"Possible. I do know that at least one of the four men has suddenly disappeared. I found out this morning that Chuck Smart didn't show up for work at the lumber mill in Hill City when he was scheduled to work. There is one other I have not talked to, yet, but that is because I don't know where in Rapid City he lives."

"You think one of them might be the victim?"

"It's certainly a possibility. It's possible that the reason Sean and Goodman are so nervous is they know who was killed, or they have a pretty good idea who killed the victim."

"What now?" Captain Butler asked.

"A stop at the lab to see if they have identified the body. If they have, it might help me figure out what happened in the backcountry."

"Good luck. Let me know if I can help in any way."

"Thanks, Captain."

"I think you can call me, Mike.

"You can call me, Bill."

Bill stood up, shook hands with Mike, then left the office. He went to his patrol car and left the air base.

Bill stopped at the Sheriff's Office and left a report of his interviews. While in the Sheriff's Office, he took a few minutes to see if he could find an address for Robert Hood in the telephone book. He did not find a listing for a Robert Hood, and none of the other officers had any idea where he lived.

Since it was getting late and Julie was going to stop by for dinner, Bill decided to head for home. He had hoped to get home in time to run out and visit Sam Lawson, but that could wait until morning.

Bill arrived home just twenty minutes before Julie drove into the driveway. He had just put the meat loaf in the oven when she came in the door.

"Hi. I hope you are going to be able to stay for a little while. I just put a small meat loaf in the oven. It takes about an hour to cook," Bill said as he stepped in front of her.

"I think we have time," she said as she reached out and put her hands on his shoulders. "I have about three hours before I need to leave for work."

Bill wrapped his arms around her and pulled her up close. He leaned down and kissed her.

The evening passed by quickly. They listened to a little radio, ate a meal together, then cleaned up the kitchen. Once the kitchen was taken care of, they sat on the couch for a little while, just enjoying being close for what little time they would have together. They didn't talk about his investigation.

When it was time for Julie to leave, Bill walked Julie to her car, then took her in his arms. She rose up on her tiptoes and kissed him.

"Will you stop by on your way home in the morning? I could have breakfast for you," Bill said.

"I'd like that, but I can't stay very long. I need to get home to make sure grandfather gets a good breakfast."

"That's okay. I will have a lot to do tomorrow anyway, but we still have to eat."

"I'll be here about eight?"

"I'll be ready," Bill said then kissed her again.

He then reached out and opened the door to her car and held it while Julie got in. Bill closed the car door, then stepped back and watched her drive off.

As soon as she was out of sight, he went inside. He listened to a couple of programs on the radio, but didn't find anything of interest. His mind seemed more focused on his investigation. He reviewed in his mind what he knew and what he planned to do tomorrow. Questioning Hood and Smart were foremost in his mind.

Bill finally gave up on the radio. He went to the bathroom and took a shower, then went to bed. Although he went to bed, it took him some time to get to sleep.

CHAPTER SEVEN

Bill woke early with the anticipation of Julie stopping by on her way home from the hospital where she worked the night shift. He was up, showered, shaved and dressed for work by seven o'clock.

Bill had started preparing a good breakfast for Julie. He had decided on making baked eggs in a muffin tin with cheese on top. Bill had a thick slice of ham in a pan to start as soon as she showed up, and bread in the toaster was ready to go. The coffee pot was already brewing coffee, and orange juice was poured and set on the table. He even had the table set. Everything was ready. All he had to do now was wait for her.

It wasn't long before Bill's attention was directed toward outside when he heard a car pull into the drive. He went to the door and looked out. Julie was just getting out of her car.

"You're right on time. Breakfast will be ready by the time you get inside and sit down," Bill said.

"Do I get a kiss first?" Julie asked with a grin.

"There's always time for that," he said as she stepped up on the porch.

Julie stepped up close to Bill, put her hands on his shoulders, rose up on her toes and kissed him. She then looked up at him.

"I'm starving."

"Come in and sit down. Breakfast is ready."

Bill held the door for her, then followed her into the kitchen. He went to the oven and took out the muffin tin, then slid the eggs out onto a platter. He added the slices of ham and set the platter on the table. After getting the coffee and the toast, he sat down at the table.

"Dig in."

She didn't respond. She put two eggs and a slice of ham on her plate. Not much was said while they ate. As soon as they were finished, Julie leaned back in the chair and sipped on her coffee.

"I didn't think to ask you about your investigation yesterday. How is it going?"

"Slow would be the best way to describe it. I have four suspects, but either one of the two I have not questioned could be the victim. They still have not identified the victim. I have not been able to find two of my suspects. I'm hoping to find them today."

"Do you think the victim might be someone other than one of the four?"

"That's certainly a possibility, and is still very much on my mind. At this point almost anything is possible."

"Well, I should get home and fix grandfather his breakfast. He won't fix something for himself if he thinks I will be there shortly to fix it for him," Julie said with a smile as she stood up.

Bill walked her out to her car and gave her a kiss, then opened the door for her. Once she was in the car, he closed the door. He stepped back as she started the car. He watched her as she drove away.

As soon as she was gone, he returned to the kitchen and cleaned it up. He then went out to his patrol car and left. Bill had decided that he would drive out to Sergeant Sam Lawson's ranch. He knew where Sam lived even though he had never visited the ranch.

Bill arrived at Samuel Lawson's ranch shortly before ten in the morning. It was a fairly long drive from the road to the house. When Bill pulled up in front of the house, he saw Samuel Lawson step out on the porch. He waited on the porch for Bill to get out of his patrol car and walk up to him.

"Good morning, Deputy. What brings you all the way out here?"

"Good morning, Mr. Lawson. I'd like to talk to you about your stepson, Robert."

"Okay. What's he done now?" Sam asked with a strong note of disgust in his voice.

"I don't know if he has done anything. Have you seen him lately?"

"No. I haven't seen him for a couple of years."

"Would that be when you ran him off?"

"So, you've heard about that. Yes, I ran him off. Robert is just plain no good. He broke the law, then joined the Army to avoid going to jail. Once in the Army, he socked an officer. He was discharged as an undesirable after serving six months in a military jail at Leavenworth.

"When he returned to Hill City, John at the Hill City Lumber Mill was nice enough to give him a job, and what does he do? He gets in a fight with his foreman and ends up getting fired. Then he stole from me. That was the final straw. He's just no damn good."

"Do you think he would come back here to hide out?"

"I wouldn't think so. He knows how I feel about him."

"Why, because you threatened to shoot him as a trespasser?"

"You heard about that, too."

"Yes. I think almost everyone in town has heard about that. If he didn't come back here, do you have any idea where he might go?"

"He might go to his aunt's place in Rapid City. His mother once told me that she thought he was staying with her."

"Do you have an address for her?"

"Yeah. I'll get it for you," Sam said then turned and walked back into the house.

Bill stood on the porch and looked around. The small ranch seemed to be doing well. The buildings were in nice shape as were the fences around the corral.

It didn't take Sam long before he returned. He handed Bill a slip of paper with an address on it.

"If you don't find him there, I have no idea where he might be," Sam said.

"Thanks for your cooperation. I'm sorry it had to be under these circumstances."

"You're just doing your job, officer. I understand that."

Bill nodded then turned and walked back to his patrol car. He looked toward the porch at Sam while he started the patrol car. Sam was just standing there looking at him. Bill knew that Sam had a reputation for being a demanding person, even being hard on people. He expected a lot from those who worked for him, but he also worked hard right alongside them. Honesty was what Sam expected from everyone, and would tolerate nothing less.

Bill turned his patrol car around and drove back to the road. Once on the road, he headed for Rapid City. His plan was to visit the ME and find out if they had discovered the name of the victim. Just knowing the name of the victim could go a long way toward answering a couple of questions. It could also add to the questions he already had in mind. It might possibly do both. He also hoped to visit Robert Hood at his aunt's home while in Rapid City. Bill decided to stop by the sheriff's office on his way to find Robert.

Bill arrived at the sheriff's office shortly before noon to see if the sheriff had been notified of the identity of the victim. The sheriff was in and told Bill to come to his office. Bill sat down in front the sheriff's desk while the sheriff sat down behind the desk.

"Well, how's it going?"

"I've questioned Sean Carter and James Goodman about where they were and what they did in the backcountry about the time the victim was killed. Both men are in the Air Force and stationed at Rapid City Air Force Base. I got pretty much the same story from both of them. There was a slight discrepancy in their stories, but I'm not sure it makes much difference.

"From what I was told, all four of them went into the backcountry and were in the area where I found the body. By that I mean, they were within a half mile or less from where I found the body. I found a knife with Sean Carter's name on it less than twenty-five feet from the body, but I don't know when it was lost there.

"I was also told that they all came out of the backcountry together. However, there is a possibility that two of them went back to Medicine Mountain."

"Who are the two who went back to the mountain?"

"Chuck Smart and Robert Hood. The two I have not talked to, yet"

"What can you tell me about the two you have not questioned?"

"I stopped by where Chuck Smart worked, but he didn't show up for work and never called in. He had not shown up for work on Monday. However, he had Friday through Sunday off."

"Any idea why Smart disappeared?"

"No. It has crossed my mind that he might be the body we have in the ME's office, but I'm not sure about that.

"Robert is the other possibility. Robert Hood doesn't live with his mother and stepfather. I found out from his stepfather that he might be living with his aunt here in Rapid City. I plan to see if I can find him and hopefully get a chance to talk to him. Robert's stepfather gave me the address of Robert's aunt."

"I'll give the ME a call and see if he has found out who our victim is."

The sheriff reached over and picked up the receiver. He placed a call to the ME's office. The phone was answered. Bill could hear the conversation.

"Pennington County Medical Examiner's Office. How may I help you," the woman asked?

"This is Sheriff Henderson. I would like to speak to Doctor Harrison."

"Yes, sir."

It took a minute or so before Doctor Harrison answered the phone.

"What can I do for you, Sheriff?"

"I'm interested in knowing if you have identified the body you received a couple of days ago with two bullet holes in his chest?"

"I have not identified the young man, yet. I can tell you one thing that is a little strange."

"What's that?"

"He was shot once. I said 'once' with a .45 caliber handgun, and once with a .38 caliber handgun, probably a revolver. He was not shot at real close range, probably over twelve, but no further than twenty feet away. Both slugs were still in the body."

"That explains why my officer found only one .45 caliber casing."

"I would think so. By the way, the .45 caliber slug was military issue."

Bill looked at the sheriff and pointed to his boots. He mouthed the word 'name'.

"Bill would like to know if you found a name in the boots the man was wearing?"

"No name. It looks like they could by surplus from the war. If the victim was in the service, he could have been issued a new pair of boots and didn't put his name in them. The boots looked fairly new. They showed very little wear."

"So, he could be an airman from the base."

"That is a possibility."

"Did you find anything in his clothing?"

"No, nothing. He had nothing in his pockets at all. Did your officer remove anything from his pockets?"

"No. He reported to me that he found it strange that the victim had absolutely nothing in his pockets."

"The only thing I found in his pockets was a very small amount of cigarette tobacco in his shirt pocket, like you might find if he had a loose cigarette in the pocket, but nothing else. His fingers were stained like those of a heavy smoker, but he didn't have any cigarettes, a lighter, or matches on him.

"This is also a little strange. On his body, I found a long wound like a very sharp thin knife blade or straight razor would make if someone slashed him with it. It was not very deep. Just deep enough to cause the wound to bleed. It was approximately eleven inches long and ran diagonally across his chest as if it had been done in a slashing motion"

"You mean as if someone swung a sharp knife at him?"

"That would be correct. The cut was there before the shirt he was wearing had been put on and before he was shot. The wound looked like it might be a couple of days older than when he was shot. It appeared to be healing very well. There were bits of thread in the gunshot wounds confirming that he had been shot through his shirt, and the holes in the shirt confirm that."

"What do you make of the cut across his chest?" the sheriff asked.

"I have no idea. He might have gotten in a fight with someone, but that's only a guess on my part. It would also be my guess that the two are related, but like I said, it's just a guess."

"What makes you think that?"

"The wounds are fairly close together in time. It may have been the same person that cut him, who shot him. Oh, by the way, he had some bruises on his knuckles. My guess was he was in a fight with someone. The bruises on his knuckles could have occurred at the time he was cut across the chest."

"Thanks. Will you give me a call as soon as you find out who he is?"

"Sure thing. I'm sorry that I couldn't be much help, but I'll keep working on it. I'm hoping to get something from his fingerprints within the next few days."

"Thanks, Doc," the sheriff said then hung up the phone.

"Nothing on who the victim is," the sheriff said looking at Bill.

"I heard most of your conversation. It looks like he might have been shot by two people, at or about the same time. The knife wound and bruises indicate that he had been in a fight before he was shot," Bill said thoughtfully.

"That would be my guess, too."

"I think I'll try to find Robert Hood at his aunt's home. I might be able to get a picture of Hood from his aunt, if he's not there."

"Good idea. Let me know how things work out."

"Yes, sir."

Bill stood up then left the sheriff's office. When he got into his patrol car, he just sat there to think. Since the long wound on the victim's chest wasn't very deep, the victim probably didn't go to the hospital. He might have even taken care of the wound himself.

His thoughts turned to the four men he knew had gone into the backcountry together. From what he had learned, all four of his suspects had certainly been in the backcountry long enough to have killed the victim.

Since the victim had been shot only twice, it was possible that after they split up, two of the four that went into the backcountry could have shot the victim. Bill didn't think that all four of them were involved in the actual shooting of the victim. Although, Bill thought that all of them probably knew about it.

The two airmen, Carter and Goodman, had been very nervous when he questioned them. Since they answered his questions without much hesitation, he didn't think they had anything to do with the murder. However, that didn't mean they didn't know about it.

The two men he had not had a chance to talk to might have had something to do with it, but that was yet to be seen. If it turned out that one of the four was the victim, then the other three could be the ones that killed him. If that was the case, why did they kill him? Was it over the gold coins?

Bill could think of a hundred scenarios as he sat in the patrol car thinking. With no answers, he reached down and started his patrol car. The address he had for Hood's aunt was on the other side of town. It was in one of the less affluent parts of town.

It took Bill about twenty minutes to find the house where Hood's aunt was supposed to live. He pulled up in front of the house.

As he shut off the engine of his patrol car, he looked up at the small two-story house. The yard was not well maintained. The grass needed cutting and the small flower bed was overgrown with weeds. The house itself looked like it could use a good coat of paint and some serious repairs.

Looking at the house, Bill noticed a curtain in a second story window move as if someone had been looking out. His first thought was there was someone looking to see if he was going to get out of his patrol car. Bill wondered if Robert's aunt had a husband. He had no information that she did., but he didn't have any information indicating that she lived alone, either.

Bill opened the door and stepped out of the patrol car. He continued to look at the house as he approached the front porch. As he stepped up on the porch, the curtain on the window next to the door moved. He was about to knock on the door when the door opened. A woman in her early fifties opened the door. She was wearing a simple cotton dress with an apron over it.

"May I help you, officer?"

"What is your name, Ma'am?"

"I'm Karen Colton," she replied without comment.

"I'm Officer Bill Sparks with the Pennington County Sheriff's Department. I'm looking for Robert Hood."

"What makes you think I would even know him?"

"You are his aunt, aren't you?"

"I am, but I don't know where he is," she said, but not very convincingly.

"Do you live alone?"

"Yes. I'm not married. Why do you ask?"

"Then who is that in the upstairs front window?"

She looked at Bill as if he knew a lot about her and her nephew. She was trying to think of an answer that would, at the very least, sound reasonable.

"Robert is upstairs, isn't he?"

"Robert, you might as well come down here. The deputy knows you're there." She called out while still looking at Bill.

"I wouldn't try to run," Bill added.

It was quiet for a minute. Bill was beginning to think that he was going to have to go upstairs and get him. It was then that he heard a crash out behind the house. Bill looked at Miss Colton for a second, then pushed her aside as he started running through the house. When he got to the backdoor, he couldn't see anything but a good amount of junk in the backyard. He turned and looked toward where he thought he had heard the crashing sound come from. There was a screen from an upstairs window lying on the ground near the back porch.

There was no sense trying to find Robert in all the junk. There were just too many places for him to hide, or too much cover if he got to the alley to know which way he went.

Bill turned and looked at Miss Colton. She was standing on the back porch looking at him. She had a smile on her face.

"I guess since I can't take Robert in for questioning, I will take you in for questioning."

The smile quickly left her face. She was looking worried that he might do what he said.

"You can't do that."

"I can and I will. Now, why was Robert here?"

"He was visiting since his stepfather won't let him go home."

"Not good enough. He hasn't been able to go home for almost two years. I doubt he would want to go home. I have already talked to his stepfather. I think Robert has been living here for some time, probably since his stepfather wouldn't allow him on his property.

"Where do you think he would go if he can't stay here? Your answer better be good," Bill said sharply as he looked her in the eyes.

Miss Colton looked at Bill. There was little doubt in her mind that he would take her to the sheriff's office to be questioned at length. It could be hours before they would let her go.

"Well?" Bill said sharply while growing impatient.

Miss Colton let out a long sigh before she spoke.

"He has a shack somewhere up near Copper Mountain."

"Are you sure?"

"Yes. He goes up there and stays sometimes for weeks on end."

"Are you sure it's near Copper Mountain and not Medicine Mountain."

"He told me it was at Copper Mountain. He said it's really hard to find."

"Why would he have a shack up there?"

"He is always hiding from someone."

"Who would he be hiding from now?"

"You. He said the police have it in for him."

"I know he has been in trouble a good many times, but I know of no warrants for his arrest. We don't go looking for someone without a warrant except when we want to just talk to him. I think you can do better than that," Bill said.

"One night he told me that he had made an enemy in a bar fight last week. He said he didn't start the fight. I think it was over some girl in the bar, but I'm not sure about that."

"Do you know the name of the bar?"

"I believe it's a little neighborhood bar called Lazy Lounge, or something like that. I know he goes there sometimes. It's just a couple of blocks from here. Are you going to check out his story?"

"Yes, of course. But I still want to talk to Robert."

"If he returns, I'll tell him that he needs to talk to you."

"Do you expect him to return here?" Bill asked, thinking she really didn't expect him to come back.

"He might. He said he was low on food at his shack. That was why he was here," Miss Colton said. "I often give him some canned goods and fresh vegetables to take to his shack."

"Have you ever been to his shack?"

"No. I've never been there."

"I'm going to check out the bar. I hope it proves he was there. If it doesn't, you can expect a visit from the sheriff's department with a warrant for your arrest. So, don't leave town," Bill said. "It won't look good for you if you do."

He turned and walked around to the front of the house. He got in his patrol car and sat there for a minute looking at the house while he thought about what he had been told. He wasn't sure he could believe a word she said, but he had no real evidence that would warrant him dragging Miss Colton into the sheriff's office for questioning about her nephew's activities.

Bill started his patrol car and drove away from the front of the house. When he got to the corner, he turned and drove down the street to the alley that ran behind Miss Colton's house. He stopped and looked down the alley. He saw a car parked in the alley at the back of Miss Colton's house.

As he looked down the alley, Bill was thinking about Robert. According to James, Robert had a car. Since there was only one car behind the house, was that car Robert's, or was it Miss Colton's? Did he use her car and didn't have one of his own? Bill had not heard a car when Robert escaped from the house. If Robert owned a car, then where was his car?

Bill turned into the alley and drove as close to the car as he could without being where Miss Colton could see him from her house, yet close enough to get the license plate number. He wrote it down, then backed out of the alley.

Parking on a side street close to the alley, Bill called the dispatcher. He requested the license number he got from the car behind Miss Colton's home be checked to see who was actually owner of the car. He also requested any information he could get on any vehicles that Robert Hood might own.

While he waited for the information, Bill contacted the sheriff and reported what had happened at Miss Colton's home. He also requested that Karen Colton's house be watched in case Robert returned. The sheriff agreed with his request.

It didn't take long and the dispatcher was on the radio. The dispatcher told Bill that the car belonged to Karen Colton. She also told him that Robert Hood owned a 1940 Ford two door sedan. He also got the license number of the car. Since Bill had not heard a car start when Robert left his aunt's home, he wondered where Robert's car was located.

Once Bill had the information he needed, he left his location and drove around several blocks in the area of Robert's aunt's home. Not finding a car fitting the description of Robert's car, he drove to where the neighborhood bar was located.

CHAPTER EIGHT

Bill arrived at the neighborhood bar. Instead of going inside, Bill drove around the block looking for a 1940 Ford sedan. He checked behind the bar and a two-block area around the bar. Since he didn't see even one 1940 Ford anywhere near the bar, he drove to the front of the bar and parked his patrol car out in front, right next to the front door. He sat looking over the bar before getting out of his patrol car.

There was a sign in the window telling the world that it was the Lazy Lounge and that it was open for business. The name of the bar seemed appropriate. Whoever owned the bar had apparently been too lazy to take good care of it. Several of the letters in the sign in the window didn't work very well, namely the "z", the "u" and the "e". They would flash off and on randomly.

The neighborhood bar was kind of a dingy looking place. It was old and had not had very good care over the years. The outside needed painting, the windows were dirty and covered with advertisements for several different kinds of beers. The advertising signs were discolored with age, and some were faded making it hard to read them. Most of them had water stains from ice forming on the inside of the window during the winter then melting on warm days.

Bill got out of the car and walked up to the door. He pulled open the door and stepped inside. Once inside, he moved sideways, away from the door, putting the wall at his back.

The bar was fairly dark due to the windows being covered with advertisements, and the fact that there were very few lights on inside. What lights that were on didn't give off much light. It was probably just as well since the inside of the bar had not had any better care than the outside.

It took a moment or two for Bill's eyes to become accustomed to the darkness inside the bar. As soon as he was able to see clearly, he took a moment to look around.

There were several people in the bar. They all turned and looked to see who had come in. Three of the customers got up and walked out as soon as they saw it was "the law" that came in. None of the three were anywhere near the age of Robert Hood. Since Bill had no interest in them, he did nothing but watch them as they left the bar.

Two others in the bar, both fairly young men, picked up their beers and moved away from the bar to a booth along the wall. Bill noticed that they sat in the booth watching him.

Two young women at the bar, simply moved down toward the end of the bar, never taking their eyes off Bill. An older lady simply looked up from the glass of beer in front of her, then turned back to continue to study her glass of beer.

Bill walked up to the bar and waited for the barkeeper to come to him. It didn't take but a moment or so before the barkeeper moved along the bar until he was standing in front of Bill.

The barkeeper was short and stocky with a beer belly. He was in his early fifties and had at least a three day's growth beard. He was wearing a T-shirt that looked like it hadn't been washed for months. The apron around his ample belly looked as dirty as his shirt. He had a number of tattoos on his rather large arms, and he had the stub of a cigar pinched between his yellow teeth.

"What can I do for you?" he asked without expressing any real interest in what Bill wanted.

"You can answer a few questions."

"I mind my own business. I don't get involved in my customers' lives, so I doubt I could tell you much. Besides, you don't have any jurisdiction here."

Bill looked at him for a moment before he replied.

"That's where you're wrong. Rapid City is in Pennington County. Therefore, I have all the jurisdiction I need. But if you prefer, I'll run everyone out of here, then shut down your bar while we wait for the Rapid City police to come so they can tell you that I have all the jurisdiction I need. Feel free to call them," Bill said with a grin while looking the barkeeper in the eyes.

"Okay. What do you want?" the barkeeper asked.

"I want to know if there was a fight in your bar in the last week or so involving a couple of young men. One of those involved in the fight used a very sharp knife or a razor on the other. Do you recall such a fight?"

The barkeeper looked at Bill. He was wondering just how much the deputy knew, and how much he should tell him.

"Yeah," the barkeeper said reluctantly.

"When was the fight?"

"Ah, last Friday, late afternoon."

"You want to tell me about it?"

"Not much to tell. Two young guys had a few words, then it turned into a pushin' match."

"It was a lot more than that. One pulled a knife or razor and cut the other one across the chest."

"Not while they were in here," the barkeeper said sharply.

"Did they continue the fight outside?"

"They might have. They left the bar shortly after they started pushin' each other around and yellin' at each other. I reached under the bar and pulled out my club, then told them to take it outside."

"Did they both leave?"

"Yeah."

"You're sure about that?"

"Pretty sure."

"Did you hear what they were yelling about?"

"Not really. It was mostly callin' each other names and swearin' at each other. I didn't pay any attention to what they were sayin' 'till they started pushin' each other."

"Do you know the name of either of the two men?"

"I know only one of them, Robert Hood. He lives just down the street a block or two, I think."

"Did either of them come back into the bar after you told them to take it outside?"

"Yeah."

"Who came back inside?"

"Hood."

"The one who had waited for Hood, didn't come back in?"

"Nope."

"Did Hood look like he had been in a fight?'

"He didn't look all messed up? If that's what you mean. He came in holdin' his arm and went to the restroom."

"Did you check to see if he was injured?"

"Nope. It weren't none of my business. Besides, he left by the backdoor as soon as he came out of the restroom."

"Does Hood come in often?"

"He's a fairly regular customer. He would come in a couple of times a week. Come to think about it, I haven't seen him for four or five days, maybe a week," the barkeeper said thoughtfully. "Come to think about it, I haven't seen him since that night."

"You don't know who the other man was?"

"Nope. I only saw him that one time. He came in about two or two-thirty in the afternoon. He sat around drinkin' beer, more like sippin' on the beer. I doubt he was much of a drinker. He had a hamburger and a coke here around three-thirty."

"I take it he was waiting for someone?"

"It sure looked that way to me. He sorta kept watchin' the front door. He was apparently waitin' for Hood."

"What makes you think that?"

"The guy started in on Hood within a second or two after Hood come in the door. There was little doubt that he was lookin' for a fight with Hood."

"From what you said, I'd say he got his fight."

"Yeah, he got what he wanted."

"Do you think there is anyone in here now who would know the name of the man that got in the fight with Hood?"

The barkeeper looked around the bar, then looked back at Bill. He simply shook his head.

"Can you describe the man Hood got in the fight with?"

"Yeah, sure. He was about five nine or ten, weighed - ah - about a hundred and sixty to seventy pounds. He had dark brown hair. It was cut short like the military guys wear, you know?"

"I know."

"He was wearin' jeans and a red plaid shirt, and work boots. Looked to be about twenty-five years old, maybe a bit older or maybe a bit younger. It's hard to tell these days."

Bill thought about what he had been told. The body Bill had found near Medicine Mountain fit the description pretty well, except for the color of the shirt he was wearing. The problem with the barkeep's description was it would fit a lot of other young men in the military. There was also the fact that the barkeeper didn't know his name, making the information almost useless. However, a check with the Air Force base might give him a name if they had someone who didn't show up for roll call or work, Bill thought.

"Thanks for the information. If Hood should show up, call the sheriff's department."

"I will," the barkeeper said.

Bill looked at the barkeeper for a moment wondering if he would call the sheriff's department if Hood showed up. He doubted that the barkeeper would call the sheriff's department for anything other than to stop someone from breaking up his bar. He was more likely to tell Hood the law was looking for him.

Bill turned and walked out of the bar. He got in his patrol car and drove away.

It wasn't long before Bill arrived at the sheriff's department. He stopped by the sheriff's office. The sheriff was in.

"You got a minute?" Bill asked sticking his head in the sheriff's office.

"Sure. Come on in."

Bill walked into the sheriff's office and sat down. He gave the sheriff a full accounting of his day's activities. His interview with Hood's aunt, and his interview with the barkeeper.

He requested that an APB be put out on Robert Hood, and for his car. The sheriff agreed.

"What are your thoughts? You think this guy at the bar is our victim?" Sheriff Henderson asked.

"I'm not sure, but he could be. I don't have any witnesses that saw the fight, so I don't know, and the barkeeper didn't seem to know what the fight was about. The description of the man fits the guy the ME has on his table except for the color of his shirt. However, his description could fit a lot of men in the area.

"I planned to contact Captain Butler of the Air Police on the base, he might be able to find out if someone is missing. It might provide the name of someone who fits the description I got from the barkeeper."

"That's probably a good idea. Where do you think Hood might be?"

"He could be staying with a friend, or he could head for the mountains."

"Do you think Hood went into the mountains?" the sheriff asked.

"From what his aunt said, it would seem to be a strong possibility. According to his aunt, he has a shack somewhere around Copper Mountain. I got the impression from her that he feels safe there. From what she said, it could be up near the top of the mountain, not near the base of it.

"I'm going to try to talk to Mrs. Lawson about her son, Robert, without Sam being present. That may not be easy."

"What's your thoughts on that?"

"I didn't see her when I visited with Sam. However, I think she was there."

"Do you think she is hiding Robert?"

"I don't know, but I don't think so. I'm sure Sam Lawson, Robert's stepfather, would not allow him in the house. However, I think there is a good chance that she might know where Robert is hiding. At the very least, she might be helping him by giving him food or a little money so he could stay in the mountains out of sight."

"What are your plans for now," Sheriff Henderson asked.

"I thought I would give Captain Butler a call at the air base and talk to him in the hope he might be able to find out if someone is missing that fits the description I got from the barkeeper. Captain Butler is the Air Police chief, so to speak.

"Tomorrow, I'm planning on going into the backcountry. I figured I would go up to Copper Mountain and see if I can find where Hood is hiding. He may or may not be where his aunt said he would be, that is on Copper Mountain. I'll be looking for his 1940 Ford two door sedan. If I find that, I'm sure I will find him. I got a feeling that he wouldn't want to be too far from it. I also think he might have a place to hide it which would make it hard to find him."

"That sounds good. You be careful. He might resist if he feels threatened."

"I will. I also would like to find Chuck's mother. His mother might know where Chuck is hiding. He's one of the those who went into the mountains with Sean. His mother works for the school in Hill City during the school year."

"Okay. Keep me posted on what is going on. If you need any help, call me. I'll do what I can to help. You can make your call to the air base out at the officers' desks."

"Thanks," Bill said then turned and left the sheriff's office.

Bill went out to the officers' desks and sat down at one of the desks. He placed a call to the Air Police Office on the Rapid City Air Force Base. It was immediately answered by the sergeant on duty. After telling the sergeant who he was and then requesting to talk to Captain Butler, his call was transferred to the captain.

"Bill, what is it I can do for you?"

"Mike, I would like to know if you have any airmen who are missing from duty? Maybe someone who is AWOL."

"May I ask why you want to know?"

"I admit, I'm clutching at straws, but there is a slim possibility that our victim may be an airman. I'll give you a description of the man I'm looking for."

Bill told Captain Butler the description of the man who had been in the fight with Hood.

"What I'm hoping for is a name. If you are missing an airman that fits that general description, I would like to have someone who knows him to come to the morgue here in Rapid City and see if he can identify the victim for us. Right now, we have no idea who he is."

"It might take me awhile to find who is missing and what they look like, but I'll give it a try. I usually get notice of anyone who doesn't report to his work station, or fails to return from leave. So far, I have not been notified of anyone missing from his duty station."

"It might be someone on leave who isn't due back yet. Could you check and see if you have someone on leave from the base that fits the description?

"Sure. I'll find out who is currently on leave and see if any of them fit your description."

"Thanks a lot. If you should find someone who might be able to identify the victim, the sheriff's office will provide transportation to the morgue and back to the base."

"I'll keep that in mind. If I find someone is missing, I'll do what I can to find someone who can identify the missing person, then give the sheriff's office a call and let them know."

"Great. I hope you don't have anyone missing, but like I said, it's a long shot at best. I'll talk to you later," Bill said then hung up.

After Bill's call, he left the sheriff's office and drove home to Hill City. He decided to stop by his house and grab something to eat before going to talk to Chuck's mother.

It was getting on toward dinner time when Bill got back to Hill City. He decided he would try to see if he could visit with Mrs. Smart before he had his dinner. He thought his best chances of catching Mrs. Smart at home would be around dinner time.

It didn't take him long to find out where Chuck Smart's mother lived. He drove to her address and arrived just as she had pulled into the driveway. He pulled in behind her car and stepped out of his patrol car.

"Mrs. Smart?" he called out to her.

She stood next to her car and looked at Bill. From the look on her face, Bill got the feeling that he was the last person she hoped to see, or have to answer any questions.

"Yes," she said as he walked up to her.

"I'm Deputy Sheriff Bill Sparks."

"I know who you are."

"I would like to talk to you for a few minutes if I may."

"I don't know what you want with me."

"I would like to know if you know where your son, Chuck, is?

"His is at work. He works at the lumber mill."

"I'm sorry, but he hasn't been to work since this past Monday, and he didn't call in sick."

"Then I don't know where he is," she said, showing little concern.

Bill got the idea that she didn't have any interest in why he was looking for her son. He also noticed that she was not going to be very cooperative.

"You don't seem very concerned about him. It is my understanding that he lives with you."

"He does most of the time, but I don't keep tabs on him. He's an adult. Where he goes and what is does is his business."

"In that case, when was the last time you saw your son?"

"The last time I saw him was several days ago when he left to meet with some other young men to go exploring in the backcountry," she said with no sign of any real concern.

"Did he tell you when he would be back?"

"No. And before you ask, I didn't ask him when he would be back, who he was going with, or where he was going. The only reason I know that he was going exploring in the backcountry was because he voluntarily told me.

"I know better than to stick my nose into his business. I'm not like a lot of mothers who have to know what their children are doing every minute of every day even when they are grown up and responsible for what they do."

Bill was a little surprised by her tone and attitude. He was also curious about her comment of knowing better than to stick her nose in his business, and what had caused her to become that way. He had gotten the impression from information he received from interviews with others that she and Chuck were rather close. Her comment indicated that it might not be the case.

"Do you know if he returned home that evening?"

"No, I don't know when he came home."

"Was he here in the morning?"

"I don't know. I left for work early."

It was obvious to Bill that he was not going to get anything of interest out of her. He was not sure if she really knew anything. It was clear that she was not going to get mixed up in anything that was her son's business.

"I'm sorry that I bothered you. If you should hear from him, would you please give me a call? I would like to talk to him."

"If I see him," she replied flatly.

Bill looked at her for a second, then turned and walked back to his patrol car. He got in and reached for the key to start the patrol car. As he turned the key to start the patrol car, he looked out the windshield and noticed that Mrs. Smart was standing there watching him.

Bill started his patrol car and backed out of the drive. He noticed that the garage door was open and that the garage was empty. His first thought was to call in and see if he could find out if Chuck had a car. If he did, Bill wanted to know what kind and what the license plate number was on the car.

Bill turned out on the road and drove away. It had been a long day. On his way home, he stopped by the local grocery store and the gas station. After getting a few things from the store and fueling his patrol car, he drove home. He planned to give Julie a call as soon as he got home.

When Bill pulled into the drive at his home and stopped. He saw a car that he didn't recognize in his drive. There was a young man standing next to the car with his arms crossed. He was leaning against the front fender. Bill thought it might be Chuck Smart waiting for him. Bill stepped out of his patrol car and walked toward the young man.

"I'm Chuck Smart," the young man said sharply. "My mother told me you were looking for me."

"That is correct. I have a few questions I would like to ask you."

"Okay, ask."

"Why didn't you show up for work the past few days, and where did you go?"

"I didn't feel like it, and where I went is none of your business."

"It is my business if you had something to do with the dead man we found near Medicine Mountain."

The look on Chuck's face gave him away. Bill was sure that Chuck knew something about it. What and how much he knew was what Bill wanted to know.

"Don't know anything about any dead man."

"I think you do."

"You police are always looking at me when you don't have anyone else to pin some trumped-up problem you can't solve yourself."

"That's a strange thing to say. I don't recall ever having any contact with you before now. And I don't think the Sheriff's Office has ever talked to you. What are you afraid of?"

"I'm not afraid of anything. Just leave my mother alone. And leave me alone."

Bill watched as Chuck turned and got into his car. Chuck backed out of the drive and turned out onto the street, then sped away.

Bill just stood there and watched him leave. What was he afraid of, Bill wondered? Maybe it wasn't what was he afraid of, but who was he afraid of. He acted tough, but he was scared to death, Bill thought.

Since Bill didn't have anything to hold him on, and he wasn't prepared to question him at length, he let him go without attempting to stop him.

As soon as Chuck was out of sight, Bill got his groceries out of his patrol car and went inside the house. He immediately wrote down the license number of the car Chuck had been driving.

It was time to put his investigation up for the night. He went to the phone and called Julie. They talked for almost fifteen minutes before they said their goodnights and hung up.

Bill fixed his dinner and took it into the living room. He sat down and listened to the few innings of a baseball game on the radio while he ate his dinner. He couldn't seem to get interested in the game with so many thoughts about his investigation running through his mind.

As soon as he finished eating, he took his dishes to the kitchen, then went to the bathroom. He took a shower, then decided he would go to bed. With all that had happened, it took Bill awhile to get to sleep.

CHAPTER NINE

Bill woke early the next morning, even before his alarm clock went off. He still had a lot on his mind. He took a quick wake-up shower in the hope of clearing his head. After the shower, he got dressed and went to the kitchen.

He fixed his breakfast, all the time thinking about the victim. Why had it been so hard to identify him? He couldn't help but think that at least one of the four young men who went into the mountains knew the victim, and one or more of them probably played a part in killing him. Bill was convinced of it. His only problem was he couldn't prove it.

The question that came to Bill's mind, was there possibly someone else involved? Someone that he might not have considered? That thought brought to mind Martin Cannon, probably because of what Martin had told him when he talked to him at his farm.

Bill remembered that Cannon told him he had heard two shots while he was at his ranch training a horse in the corral next to the barn. Bill was sure that he could not have heard the two shots if he was where he said he was. The lay of the land, plus the conditions surrounding the murder scene would not have allowed the sound to travel that far.

That gave Bill an additional suspect, but what was the motive? Was it the gold coins? Were there more than the three coins Bill had found? If there were more, where was the rest of the coins? More importantly, who had the rest of the coins? The bigger question was where did the gold coins come from. In other words, who had the gold coins in the first place. Bill had all those questions and more running through his mind.

Bill knew that he was not going to get any answers to any of the questions at home. He set his breakfast on the table then sat down to eat.

While eating, he reviewed what he had learned so far. He quickly discovered that he really hadn't learned much of anything. He also wondered if the death of the young man was over the gold coins, or if there was something else involved, such as jealousy? Jealous of what or who? Bill didn't know.

If he knew who the victim was and where he was from, it might shine some light on what had happened. It could go a long way in finding a motive and how the gold coins came to bc in the Black Hills.

Just as he finished his breakfast, the thought of Robert Hood having a place in the mountains came to mind again. He had planned to go to Copper Mountain to see if he could find Hood's hideout. If he was not there, he would try Medicine Mountain only a mile or so away. If he could find him, he might get some answers to his questions.

With that thought in mind, Bill took his dirty dishes to the sink. As soon as he cleaned up the kitchen, he left the house. He got into his patrol car and started to leave for Copper Mountain.

As he drove by the Hill City Café, he noticed old man Rutledge's pickup was parked in front to the café. Bill knew their relationship was not very good. He also knew that Rutledge knew a lot about the hills in the backcountry as well as what was going on in the hills.

Bill pulled over and parked his patrol car. He sat there for a moment and thought about what might happen if he tried to talk to Rutledge in the café where others close by might hear what was said between them.

Rutledge was not a very nice, nor was he a very likeable man. Bill had had several run-ins with him over the past couple of years that were, to say the best, not very pleasant, and to say the least, downright confrontational.

Bill decided that he might be able to build some kind of positive relationship with Rutledge if he asked him for a little help and not press him about what he was doing in the backcountry. It might even help if he talked to him in the café. Having people around might tend to keep Rutledge from getting too loud, or too nasty. The worst thing that could happen was Rutledge would refuse to talk to him, and maybe cause a scene. Bill decided that it was worth a try.

He took a deep breath, then got out of his patrol car and walked over to the Hill City Café. He looked in the window and saw Rutledge sitting by himself in a booth.

Bill hesitated for a moment before he opened the door and went inside. Once inside, he stopped and looked at Rutledge. Once Bill made eye contact with him, he walked over to the booth where Rutledge was sitting.

"Do you mind if I sit down with you?" Bill asked.

Rutledge looked around the café, then looked up at Bill.

"There's plenty of other places you can sit."

It was obvious that he did not want Bill to sit down with him. Bill was not about to let that discourage him from talking to Rutledge.

"Yes, there are, but I would like to talk to you for a few minutes."

Rutledge looked at Bill, then looked around the room again to see who might be watching them. When he saw several people looking at them, he turned and looked up at Bill again. After a couple of seconds, he reluctantly motioned for Bill to sit down.

Just as Bill sat down, Sandy brought Bill a cup of black coffee. Bill looked up at her and smiled.

"Can I get you something?" Sandy asked.

"Just the coffee. Thank you," Bill said with a smile.

Sandy glanced at Rutledge, then turned and looked at Bill. She smiled before she turned and walked back toward the kitchen.

Bill turned and looked at Rutledge.

"What is it you want to talk to me about?" Rutledge asked.

"I want to talk to you about the backcountry."

"Okay, what about it?"

"Are you familiar with the areas in the backcountry around Medicine Mountain and Copper Mountain?"

Bill kept his voice low so others could not hear him.

"Yeah. What about them?"

"Do you know if there are any deserted cabins or buildings on either of the mountains?"

"Yeah. So what?"

"Which one?"

"Both of them."

"There are deserted cabins or buildings on both mountains?"

"That's what I said."

Bill was beginning to think that getting any information out of Rutledge was going to be like pulling teeth from a mule. But if he could provide anything that might help, it would be worth the effort.

"Would any of them be useable for a place for someone to use as a hideout?"

"Sure. Why?" Rutledge asked.

Rutledge seemed to be relaxing a little, even a little more willing to talk.

"Please explain that?"

"What's there to explain?"

"Okay. Let me put it this way. On Copper Mountain, how many deserted cabins do you think someone could live in with little or no serious work having to be done to make them livable?"

"Let me think. There might be two on Copper Mountain."

"Do you know where the cabins are located?"

"Sure."

"Have you seen them, or been in either of them?"

"I didn't steal anything from them." Rutledge said sharply, then looked around the room to see if anyone might have heard him. He looked back at Bill then leaned forward."

"I didn't steal anything from them," he said quietly.

"I don't care about that. Let me ask you this. Have you ever seen anyone in or around either of the two cabins?"

Rutledge looked at Bill. He didn't answer for several minutes. Bill gave him time to think about what he was really asking him.

"Yeah," Rutledge finally said.

"When was this? How long ago?"

"A couple of days ago, maybe a bit longer. Maybe three or four days ago."

"Tell me what you saw."

"Well, there was a young fella up there. I was on the east side of the mountain lookin' for things."

Rutledge stopped and looked at Bill. He was thinking that he might have said too much already."

"I don't care about what you were doing there. I want to know what you saw."

Rutledge thought for a moment before he spoke again.

"Well, I saw a young fella. He was carryin' a bag. It looked like it was a grocery bag, you know. It looked pretty full. He had a backpack on that looked full, too. It looked ta me like he was plannin' on movin' in and stayin' awhile."

"Did he see you?"

"Nah. He was lookin' around as if he was afraid someone might see him, but he didn't see me," he said with a slight grin.

"On which mountain did you see this young man?"

"Copper Mountain."

"Did you stick around to see what he was doing there?"

"Nah. I weren't interested in what he was doin'."

"Do you know who the young man was?"

"Nah. I'd seen him around town once or twice, but that was some time ago. I don't know his name."

Bill thought about what Rutledge had told him. He remembered that Robert Hood had a car.

"Did you happen to see a car somewhere close to the Cooper Mountain?"

"Yeah, but it was kinda hidden in some trees so's no one could see it. I saw it, though."

"Do you know what kind of car it was, or who it belonged to?"

"It belonged to the fella I'd seen, I guess. As for the car, it was a 1940 Ford two door sedan."

"How do you know it belonged to the young man?"

"Well, I seen him drivin' it, and where he parked it. He parked it very careful like. You know, like he didn't want anyone seein' it."

"How far up the mountain was the car."

"Not far from the top. There's two fire lanes up that mountain. One goes up the north side of the mountain. That's the one he used. His car is parked about fifty feet from the cabin, just off the fire lane in amongst a bunch of trees."

"Where does the second fire lane go?"

"It comes up the mountain on the east side just off the road that runs in front of the mountain. It wraps around a bit, but ends near the cabin."

Bill sat there looking at the cup of coffee in front of him. He was thinking about what Rutledge had told him. He looked up at Rutledge.

"What about Medicine Mountain? How many cabins are there on that mountain?"

"There's three, but only one anyone could live in. The other two are in pretty bad shape, rotten floors and roofs ready to fall in, yah know."

"Did you see anyone around the cabin on Medicine Mountain?"

"Nah, but one of them had been used recently."

"How do you know that?" Bill asked.

"It looked like somebody had cleaned it up a mite. You know, swept out the cobwebs and the dirt a bit."

"Did you see who was using that cabin?"

"Nah. It had been awhile since anyone was in it. Didn't see no one around."

Bill took a moment to think about what he had been told, then looked at Rutledge.

"Thank you very much for the information," Bill said.

"You going up there?"

"I plan to. Why? Is there something I should know?"

Rutledge looked around, then leaned toward Bill.

"You might want to be careful. It's easy for someone to see yah comin' if yah come from the South or from the road that runs in front of the cabin. The cabin faces the road. It sorta overlooks the road that goes past the mountain. It's easy to see the road from the cabin's front porch, but hard to see the cabin from the road.

"Comin' up from the west or north side of the mountain, you can get real close without bein' seen, if you're careful." Rutledge said. "It's a bit of hike up there. That side of the mountain has a lot of rocky places and some areas with heavy woods."

"Thanks. That's good to know. You have a nice day, Mr. Rutledge."

Rutledge nodded as he watched Bill slide out of the booth. Bill went up to the front counter. Sandy came over to the counter.

"I saw you talking to old man Rutledge. I thought he didn't like you."

"He's not so bad. What did Rutledge have this morning?" Bill asked Sandy.

"Just a cup of coffee. That's about all he ever has when he comes in alone."

"I'll pay for his coffee and mine, and take him a roll on me."

"Okay," Sandy said with a smile.

Bill paid for the coffee and the roll, then left the café. He went to his patrol car, got in, then reached down to start it. He stopped, then turned and looked at the café. He smiled as he thought about his conversation with Rutledge. Rutledge was not so hard to deal with as long as you didn't talk about his scavenging.

He started his car and drove out of Hill City. Bill headed for Copper Mountain.

It didn't take Bill very long to get close to Copper Mountain, just short of an hour. He took Rutledge's warning seriously. Instead of approaching the mountain from the road that went around the south and east side of the mountain, Bill drove past the road leading to Copper Mountain as if he was going to Four Corners that was located several miles west of Copper Mountain.

When Bill got to the Copper Mountain Quarry, he turned in. The Copper Mountain Quarry had been pretty much deserted over the past couple of years. The quarry put him behind and on the west side of Copper Mountain. He drove into the quarry and parked his patrol car in a place where it could not be seen from Copper Mountain, or from the road that went in front of the quarry.

The area just outside of the quarry had a lot of trees. Bill had no idea how hard it might be to get up to the cabin. He also had no idea what Robert Hood might do if confronted by him out there where he was all alone, and without backup.

Bill went to the back of his patrol car, opened the trunk and took out his rifle. After checking it to make sure it was ready to use, he started out the back of the quarry on foot.

Once out of the quarry, it was hard to see very far because of the thick forest. Bill was careful as he moved through the forest toward the mountain. It was slow going as Bill worked his way up the mountain, but Bill was in no hurry. He picked his way closer and closer to the cabin, being very careful not to make any noise.

He wasn't sure how far he had gone when he heard a vehicle start up. Bill quickly moved toward where he had heard the vehicle, again being careful not to be seen.

When Bill came around an outcropping of rocks, he stopped. Just a few feet in front of him was a small clearing. Keeping down behind some bushes at the end of the outcropping of rocks, he looked into the clearing and saw a car slowly coming down from the mountain on an old fire lane.

At first, he thought it was Robert Hood's Ford. It was a black two door sedan. He was sure that Robert Hood was going to leave the area. When the car moved on by him, Bill got a better look at it. It wasn't a Ford, but a 1947 Plymouth. He had seen that car around town, but didn't know who owned it.

Just as it went by, he got a good look at the driver. It was Mrs. Lawson, Robert Hood's mother. It quickly became obvious that she was helping her son to hide. Bill doubted that Sam Lawson, Robert's stepfather, had any idea what his wife was doing. If he ever found out, Bill was sure he would hit the roof.

Bill did not see Robert Hood in the car. He had not seen Robert's car either. He could only conclude that Robert was still in the cabin, or he was not there now.

Once Mrs. Lawson had driven away, Bill started moving cautiously through the forest again. He avoided moving out onto the fire lane that Mrs. Lawson had used to get to the cabin. Instead, he stayed far enough inside the forest to make it hard for anyone to see him.

After working his way along the side of the fire lane, he came to a place where he could see the back of a small cabin. He still didn't see Robert's car. He remembered that

Rutledge had told him it was parked just off a fire lane on the north side of the mountain, about fifty feet from the cabin.

Bill hunkered down behind some thick bushes and looked over the cabin. There were only two small windows in the back of the cabin, and one small window on the only other part of the cabin he could see. There wasn't a door on the two sides of the cabin he could see from his present location.

Bill watched the cabin while he tried to decide what he was going to do. It became clear that the only way he was going to get to Robert was from the front of the cabin. He wasn't sure if there was a door on the far side of it. Since it was a small cabin, he doubted that there would be a second door.

Once Bill committed himself to capturing Robert, he had to make sure Robert could not just run off into the forest and possibly get to his car. If that happened, Robert could get away; and Bill would probably have a very difficult time finding him again.

He moved far enough around toward the front of the cabin to be able to see the front door. Checking out the area in front of the cabin, he discovered that there was no place to hide. The area in front of the cabin was open for a good twenty feet or more. There was no place to hide in front of the cabin to protect himself if Robert had a gun. There was little doubt in Bill's mind that Robert would have a gun.

Bill slowly moved as close to the cabin as possible while staying in the cover of the trees. He took a deep breath, then quickly ran to the side of the cabin. He then moved to the corner of the cabin. Bill didn't hear anything that would make him think Robert might know someone was there. Bill carefully looked around the corner. He could hear someone moving around inside the cabin.

Moving as carefully and quietly as possible, Bill stepped up onto the wooden porch. Leaning against the cabin, he moved next to the window. Peeking inside from the edge of the window, he could see Robert putting cans of food in a cupboard.

Bill quickly and quietly moved in front of the door. He then kicked the door in and entered quickly, holding his rifle on Robert. From the look on Robert's face, Bill had caught him by surprise.

"Put your hands up and don't do anything stupid."

Robert just stood there looking at Bill.

"Drop the can and put your hands up. I don't want to shoot you, but I will if you try anything."

Robert thought about throwing the can at Bill, but the rifle was pointed right at him, and the deputy had his finger on the trigger. He carefully set the can on the counter, then raised his hands in the air.

"Very slowly move over to the wall."

Robert did what he was told, very slowly.

"Now, lean against the wall. Put your hands on the wall and spread your feet apart."

As soon as Robert was up against the wall, Bill set his rifle down and quickly drew his pistol. He moved up behind Robert and stuck the barrel of his gun in Robert's back. With his free hand he slapped a handcuff on one of Robert's wrists. He pulled his hand around behind his back.

"Carefully, bring your other hand behind you back. I would hate to have to shoot you."

Robert again did as he was told. As soon as his hand was behind his back, Bill put the other handcuff on him. Since he was secure, Bill holstered his gun then frisked him. Finding no weapons on Robert, Bill turned him around and pointed at a chair. Robert moved across the room and sat down on the chair. Bill pulled another chair up in front of Robert and sat down on it.

"You sure make it hard to have a talk with you."

Robert didn't say anything. He just sat there looking at Bill.

"You want to tell me why you are hiding here?"

"So people like you can't pick on me."

"Why would I want to pick on you?"

"You guys always pick on me when you need someone to arrest ever since my stepfather reported that I stole money from him."

"As far as I know, he never reported the missing money to the Sherriff's Office."

"He didn't?"

Robert seemed surprised.

"Nope. All I wanted to do was to talk to you. The fact you ran from your aunt's house gave me reason to think you are guilty of something. Are you guilty of something?"

"NO!"

"I just wanted to ask you a few questions, but you decided to run."

"You weren't going to arrest me?"

"No. There isn't a warrant out for you that I know of. There would have been one if your stepfather had reported the theft of his money. However, I have a pretty good idea why you might be hiding."

"Why?" Robert asked. "Is my stepfather looking for me?"

"No, I don't think so. What makes you think your stepfather is looking for you?"

"He said I stole his seed money?"

"Did you?"

"NO! I didn't steal the money he had been hoarding. He said it was for seeds."

"What do you mean by that? He wasn't saving the money for seeds?"

"No. He was keeping it from my mother."

"Did you tell him that you didn't take it?"

"Yes, but he wouldn't believe me."

"With your record before, during and after you were in the Army, can you blame him?"

Robert just sat there looking at Bill and didn't answer.

"Tell me, why are you hiding out here?"

"You don't know?"

"Not really, but I have an idea why you might be. I would rather hear from you why you are hiding out."

"Okay. I figured you wanted me because of the fight I got into at the bar a couple of blocks from my aunt's house."

"That's part of it, but I didn't know about the fight until after I talked to your aunt. You want to tell me about the fight?"

"There's not much to tell."

"Tell me anyway, but first tell me the name of the guy you fought with."

"His name is Frank Parker."

"Okay. When did this fight take place?"

"Friday, late afternoon."

"Let's get this clear. You fought with Parker Friday, late afternoon?"

"Yes."

"That was the day before the four of you were panning for gold in Negro Creek?"

"No. The four of us were panning for gold on Sunday."

"Were you at your cabin before Sunday?"

"Yeah. I was here Friday morning."

"Why were you at the cabin on Friday morning?"

"I was fixing it up so I could come up here and pan for gold. I wanted a place where I could go where no one could find me. I'd been staying at my aunt's place since my stepfather threw me out of the house. Since I didn't have a job, and wasn't likely to get one around Hill City or in Rapid City, I decided that I would do a little panning for gold here in the hills. Maybe make a few bucks so I didn't have to get a regular job."

"Where did you pan for gold?"

"In several of the creeks around here."

"Okay. Did you find any gold?"

"That's the interesting part. I did find some gold, but not in any of the creeks."

"You'll have to explain that to me."

"I found two gold coins," Robert said.

That came as a surprise to Bill, but he didn't let on.

"Where did you find the gold coins?"

"I found them near Negro Creek. It looked like someone might have tried to buried them in a hurry, but it had rained the night before I found them. I think the rain washed some of the loose dirt away from them exposing just a small bit of one of the coins. I almost didn't see it. They were close to a bush about ten feet back from the creek. When I dug it out of the dirt, I found a second coin."

"You found the two gold coins on Friday morning?"

"Yes. After I worked on the cabin, I went down to the creek before noon to do a little panning. I found the coins that morning. I took them to my cabin and hid them."

"Do you still have the coins?"

"No."

"What happened to the coins?"

"I hid them here in the cabin, but someone broke in, found them, and stole them while I was at my aunt's. I went to get some supplies from her. When I returned to the cabin, they were gone."

"Do you know who stole them?"

"I didn't until I stopped off at the bar Friday late afternoon. That's when I ran into Frank Parker. He was at the bar waiting for me. That was the first time I had seen him. He wanted the rest of the coins back. That was what the fight was about.

"Parker drew a knife on me. He cut me with it when I tried to defend myself. I got the knife away from him and slashed at him. He backed off and looked at the cut on his chest. When I saw that he was bleeding, I dropped the knife and ran. I hid out at my aunt's that night."

"What happened then?"

"I figured that he might have died from the knife wound I caused, so I went back to the cabin to hide there, figuring the cops would be looking for me."

"You said he asked for the rest of the coins? Did he tell you how many coins there were?" Bill asked.

"He demanded that I give him the other six coins."

"So, if he wanted six more coins, that would mean there were at least eight coins."

"Yeah, I guess."

"On Sunday, you met up with Sean Carter, Chuck Smart, and James Goodman in Hill City, then went up to Medicine Mountain? Is that right?"

"Yeah. Chuck and I spent most of the time panning for gold in the creek. Sean and James got tired of panning. They went exploring up on Medicine Mountain.

"Did you stay behind to pan for gold, or to look for more gold coins?"

"To pan for gold."

"Tell me about the coins you found."

"I'd never seen coins like them. They were gold coins with some writing on them, but I couldn't read it. I don't know what language it was. They were pretty heavy compared to any of our coins. I was sure that they were solid gold."

"Did you ever see Parker again?"

"No. I never saw him after I cut him at the bar. That's why I thought he was dead. From what you say, I get the idea that he might not be dead?"

"Do you have a gun here?" Bill asked, ignoring Robert's question.

"Yes," he admitted reluctantly.

"What kind is it?"

"It's an Army pistol."

"A .45 caliber pistol?"

"Yeah."

"Do you have any other guns?"

"No."

"I want the pistol. Where is it?" Bill asked.

"It's in the top dresser drawer in the bedroom."

Bill stood up and went into the bedroom. He opened the top dresser drawer and found a .45 caliber model 1911 Colt pistol under a shirt. He wrapped it in his handkerchief, then returned to the where Robert was sitting.

"I'm going to take you in."

"You're arresting me? What for?"

"I'm taking you in for questioning. We'll see where it goes from there."

Robert was not sure what was going to happen to him. Was he being arrested for knifing Parker? That thought caused him to think that Parker must have died.

Bill helped Robert out of the chair and took him outside. He locked up the cabin, then lead Robert through the forest to his patrol car. After putting Robert in his patrol car, he drove to Rapid City.

CHAPTER TEN

When Bill arrived at the county building, he took Robert out of his patrol car and led him into the sheriff's office. He stepped up to the desk sergeant.

"Who do we have here?" the sergeant asked.

"This is Robert Hood. I think the sheriff would like to have a little talk with him."

Without further comment, the desk sergeant called the sheriff. After a brief talk on the phone, the desk sergeant hung up, then looked up at Bill.

"The sheriff will see you. Take him into his office."

Bill nodded, then led Robert by the arm down the hall to the sheriff's office. He knocked on the door.

"Come in."

Bill opened the door and led Robert into the sheriff's office. The sheriff pointed to a couple of chairs in front of his desk. Bill sat Robert down on one of the chairs, then sat down on another chair beside him.

"You want to fill me in?" Sheriff Henderson asked Bill.

"Yes, sir. This is Robert Hood. Robert was one of the four who were in the mountains together on or about the day we think the victim I found was murdered."

"I knew you were looking for him. Has he talked to you?"

"Yes, sir. He was hiding from us. According to him, it was because he thought he might have killed a man by the name of Frank Parker in a fight in front of a bar near his aunt's house. Maybe it is better if he tells you what happened."

"Well, Robert, what have you got to say for yourself?" the sheriff asked.

Robert looked from Bill to the sheriff. He was worried about what might happen to him.

"Well?"

Robert took a deep breath before hc spoke.

"I didn't mean to kill him. He pulled a knife on me. He cut me with it, but I managed to get it away from him. When he came at me again, I swung the knife at him, hoping he would back off, but he didn't." Robert said, then he took another deep breath before he continued.

"He came at me again. I swung the knife at him to get him to back off, but he kept coming. I swung it again, only this time I cut him across his chest. I didn't mean to cut him. That's how it happened, and that's just what I told your deputy. That's how it happened. I swear."

He stopped and looked at the sheriff, then turned and looked at Bill.

"Tell him the rest," Bill said.

"Okay. When I looked at the front of Parker's shirt, I saw the blood on his shirt. He staggered back and looked down at his chest. He turned and ran away. He seemed to be staggering. I didn't mean to kill him. Honest, I didn't."

"Where did he cut you?" Sheriff Henderson asked.

"On my left arm," Robert said.

"Bill, let's see his left arm," the sheriff said.

Bill stood up, took the handcuffs off Robert. He rolled up the sleeve on Robert's left arm. There was a bandage wrapped around the lower part of Robert's arm. Robert held his arm out as he looked at Bill.

Bill carefully unwrapped the bandage. There was a thin cut about three inches long that looked like it was healing well. From the look of the cut, it had been done by a very sharp and thin blade. Bill looked at the sheriff.

"The cut on his arm seems to be supported by the barkeeper. The barkeeper said he saw Robert come into the bar holding his arm as he went to the restroom." Bill said.

"Bandage him back up," the sheriff said.

Sheriff Henderson looked at the pistol Bill had laid on his desk when they first came in. He looked up at Bill just as he finished rewrapping Robert's arm.

"I take it you found this in his possession?" the sheriff asked Bill.

"Yes, sir. It was in the top drawer of the dresser in the cabin he was using for a place to hide it."

"How did you find it?"

"I asked him if he had any guns. He told me he had one and that it was in the dresser in the bedroom. He didn't hesitate to tell me that he had it, and where it was."

"So, it is his gun?"

"Yes, sir. It smelled like it had been fired recently. It had apparently not been cleaned since the last time it was fired."

"What does my gun have to do with Parker dying from a knife wound," Robert asked with a look of confusion on his face.

"We are not sure, but if the dead man we have in the ME's office is Frank Parker, he wasn't killed by a knife wound. He was killed by two gunshots to the chest. One of the guns used to shoot him was a U.S. Army .45 caliber pistol, just like this one," Sheriff Henderson said looking right at Robert.

"You can't blame that on me," Robert yelled as he jumped up. "I didn't shoot anyone. I didn't shoot anyone."

Bill quickly jumped up. He grabbed Robert before he could do anything and pushed him back in the chair.

"Settle down and stay seated. We are not saying you shot anyone," the sheriff said.

Robert looked at Bill like he was looking for a little help from Bill.

"It sure sounds like you're blaming me for Parker's death. If he was shot, I didn't do it," Robert yelled.

Settle down. I need you to describe what Frank Parker looks like," the sheriff said. "I also need to know what he was wearing the last time you saw him."

Robert looked at Bill, then at the sheriff. It took a minute or two before he settled down to catch his breath before he spoke.

"Parker was about my height, about five-ten. He was a little heavier than me. He was wearing jeans and a red plaid flannel shirt."

"What about his hair and eyes?" the sheriff asked.

"Brown hair, cut short and brown eyes. Oh, he was wearing boots," Robert said.

"What kind of boots?"

"Boots. You know, boots."

"Were they work boots, cowboy boots, what kind of boots?

"They were a kind of work boots, you know, boots like the air force guys wear."

The Sheriff looked at Bill. He was thinking about what had been said. Everything he had said was correct except for the color of the victim's shirt. The only difference was the victim was wearing a blue plaid flannel shirt, and the shirt didn't have a cut across the front of it. However, it did have two bullet holes in it. That would indicate that if the victim was Frank Parker, he must have changed his shirt some time before he was shot.

"One more thing." Sheriff Henderson said. "When was the last time you fired this pistol?"

"I've never fired that gun."

"You never fired this gun? It has been fired recently."

"No, sir. I've never fired that gun."

"Where did you get it?"

"I found it in a deserted cabin on Medicine Mountain."

"How long ago?"

"I found it last Sunday afternoon. The same Sunday that Sean, James, Chuck and I went up there together."

"So, all four of you were together when you found the gun?"

"Well, no. I went back up there after we took Sean and James back to Hill City."

"Sean said that you and Chuck went back up to Medicine Mountain after you left Sean and James in Hill City. Is that correct?"

"Yeah."

"So, you and Chuck found the gun. Is that correct?"

"No."

"Let me see if I understand you. You and Chuck went up to Medicine Mountain together, but you didn't find the gun together. Is that what you're saying?" the sheriff asked.

"Yes. Chuck Smart and I went back up to Medicine Mountain to pan for gold, after we left Sean and James in Hill City. I got tired of panning for gold with no results. I decided to go exploring on the mountain. I knew that there had been some old mines in the area."

"How did you know that?" the sheriff asked.

"I had heard about it somewhere a long time ago. Chuck didn't want to go exploring for mines. He wanted to stay at the creek, so I left him there," Robert said.

"Did you find any mines on the mountain?"

"No. I did find a couple of old cabins. One of them looked like it might have been lived in not too long ago."

"What gave you that idea?" the sheriff asked.

"The place was old and looked deserted, but it looked like someone might have used it for a place to spend a night or two. I looked around the place but didn't find anything that wasn't covered with dust except for a couple of places where it looked like someone had laid a sleeping bag or blanket on the floor.

"I started looking in cupboards and drawers to see if anything had been left there that I might be able to use. That was when I found the gun. It was in one of the drawers."

"Did you find anything else?" the sheriff asked.

"I found a couple of blankets in a drawer, a couple of cans of vegetables, a cook kit, but that was about it. Oh, and the gun."

"What did you do with the gun. Did you fire it to see if it worked?"

"No, I left it there."

"Why did you leave it there?"

"I didn't want Chuck to see it, or even know that I found it."

"What did you do from there?"

"I went back to where Chuck was panning for gold. He didn't find anything so we went back to Hill City. I dropped Chuck off and went back to Rapid City."

"What did you do with the gun?"

"Nothing. Like I said, I left it there."

"Did you tell Chuck about the gun?"

"No."

"Why didn't you tell him about it?"

"You have to know Chuck to know the answer to that question."

"Tell me about Chuck," the sheriff said.

"Chuck would want to go get it. He would want to shoot it. Anyone within a mile would hear it. He would probably shoot off his mouth about having it. You can ask anyone. Chuck can't keep his mouth shut. He'd be bragging about finding the gun and shooting it."

"So, you left the gun there?"

"Yes. I didn't have any use for it, and I certainly didn't want Chuck to know about the gun."

"Then explain to me how it got from the cabin on Medicine Mountain to the cabin on Copper Mountain, where Deputy Sparks found you?" the sheriff asked.

"When I left my aunt's home on the day after the four of us went to the mountain, I went to the cabin where I found the gun and it was still there. I took it and went to the cabin where I was hiding and put it in the dresser where Deputy Sparks found it."

Robert turned and looked at Bill as if he was hoping for some sign that Bill believed him. The look on Bill's face gave him no indication if Bill believed him or not. He turned back and looked at the sheriff.

"That would have been on Monday that you went back and got the gun, is that right?"

"No. I returned to the cabin alone on Sunday evening, then went back to my aunt's."

"Which is it. Did you return to the cabin on Sunday evening or on Monday?"

Robert was nervous. He had to think about what he said. He knew his mistake didn't help him.

"I'm sorry. It was Monday. Yes, it was the day after I had been in the mountains with the others. I spent Sunday night at my aunt's. I went back up to Medicine Mountain on Monday morning. I got the gun and took it to my cabin on Cooper Mountain and put it in the dresser drawer," Robert explained carefully.

"What were you going to do with the gun?"

"I was going to use it for protection. There are a few mountain lions up there."

The sheriff thought about what he had been told. It made a good story. He had to admit, it even made a certain degree of sense, but he wasn't sure he was being told the truth. He decided that he should hold Robert until he could look into it a little more.

Bill had been listening very closely to what had been said. If it was true, then someone had shot Parker and tried to hide the gun in the cabin.

Bill began to think about what had been said. He put together in his mind a possible scenario based on what Robert had told them.

If the killer was any of the four who had gone to the mountain early Sunday, at least one of them went back up to the mountain without the others knowing about it. That person got the gun and shot Parker, then put the gun back in the cabin. Robert came back to the mountain after Parker was shot. He took the gun to his cabin and put it in the dresser. That would explain how the gun got in the dresser drawer after it was fired.

Bill was having a little trouble with the time line of events. There was something wrong with it. Suddenly, Bill's thoughts were interrupted by the sheriff.

"Bill, I want you to put Robert in the holding cell, then come back here."

"You're locking me up?" Robert said sharply.

"We are keeping you here for now. We need to check out a few things before we decide if we are going to charge you with something. We don't want you running off. For now, we are charging you with assault, but that may change. We are keeping you while we check out your story. If you're telling the truth, we will probably be letting you go. We're only keeping you because you have shown us that you might run if we let you go," the sheriff explained.

The look on Robert's face showed that he had resigned himself to being locked up. After all, he didn't have a choice.

Bill took Robert by the arm and led him out of the sheriff's office. He took him to the holding cell and locked him in. Bill noticed that Robert looked like he had almost resigned himself to being tried for murder.

Once he was in the holding cell, Bill looked at him. He wondered just how much Robert was involved in the death of Frank Parker, and how much he really knew about the gold coins.

Bill left and returned to the sheriff's office. When he walked into the sheriff's office, he saw the sheriff was on the phone. The sheriff motioned for him to sit down in front of his desk. Bill sat down while the sheriff finish with his phone call.

"Thank you, Captain. Your information should help."

There was a moment of silence as the sheriff listened.

"Yes. He will be retained as a suspect here until we can verify his story. If what he told us turns out to be true, we will turn him loose."

The sheriff looked at Bill while he listened.

"I understand. We will keep you informed. And thanks for your cooperation."

After a brief moment, the sheriff hung up the phone.

"I was talking to Captain Butler. He told me that they have a Franklin J. Parker. Apparently, Parker is on leave and isn't due back to the base for another week."

"What did Captain Butler have to say about us having Robert?"

"Nothing much. He did say that Parker had been disciplined for fighting a couple of times, but they didn't amount to much. Mostly ended with restriction to base for three months, and loss of a stripe and half pay for three months."

"Did he know where Parker was going while on leave?"

"He didn't know where he planned to go. It was not required when he requested leave. He had been on leave before and returned as scheduled. He said that Parker had family in Montana. Captain Butler said he hasn't been in any trouble for the last year and a half.

"I want you to go out to the air base and take a look at the picture of Parker. If the victim we have at the ME's office is Parker, let Captain Butler know. And on your way back, let the ME know that we have identified the victim. If it's not Parker, I guess we are back to square one."

"Okay. I'll get going."

"Take the gun to the lab and have them do a ballistics test on the bullets. If I'm not here when you get back, leave a note on my desk of the results of your visit to the captain."

"Yes, sir."

Bill left the sheriff's office and went directly to his patrol car.

Bill drove out to the air base and was cleared at the gate. He parked in front of the Air Police Station, got out and went inside. The sergeant on duty, escorted him into the captain's office.

"It didn't take you long to get here. I hear you might have one of our airmen on the ME's table."

"Yes, we believe we have one of yours, Mike."

"The sheriff told me you might be out to see a picture of him. I had my sergeant pull his file. I have it right here."

Mike pulled a picture out of a file folder laying on his desk. He handed it to Bill. Bill looked at the picture for a moment or two, then looked up at Mike.

"I'm sorry, but the dead man we have in the ME's office is Franklin J. Parker. He is one of your airmen."

"Can you tell me what happened?"

"I can't tell you what took place that got him killed because we don't know all the details, yet. However, I can tell you that he was shot twice in the chest in the backcountry near Medicine Mountain. One shot from a Military .45 caliber pistol, and a second shot from a .38 caliber pistol. We think we have recovered the .45, but have not found the .38, yet."

"Tell me, Bill. Do you think he might have been killed by two people? Two different guns would certainly indicate that, don't you think?"

"It certainly would, and we have not ruled that out. At this point in our investigation, we found no evidence of two people being involved, but that doesn't mean we have ruled out the possibility that there were two involved."

"I understand you have arrested a young man. Do you think he is involved in the killing of Parker?"

"Right now, we are not sure what his involvement in the death of Parker might be, if any. He had a .45 caliber pistol at the cabin he was hiding in. I'm taking it to the lab to have ballistic tests done to compare bullets. If there is a match, we have one of the murder weapons. If not, we don't have much to hold our suspect on, and will probably have to turn him loose." Bill said.

"Will you be notifying Parker's parents?"

"I don't know for sure, but I would think so since this is really a civil matter."

"On the off chance that your victim was Parker, I wrote down the name and address of his next of kin. I hope this is of help," Mike said as he handed the paper to Bill.

"Thanks. It will help."

"Okay. Keep me posted on your investigation. If I can be of any help, let me know."

"I will, on both counts."

"Bill, take care out there," Mike said.

"I will. Thanks for your help."

"You are welcome."

Bill left the captain's office and left the base. He drove back to Rapid City to the lab. He told the ME the young man that was found in the backcountry was Franklin J. Parker, an airman from the air base. Bill gave the piece of paper with the name and address of the victim's next of kin to the ME.

Bill also visited with the ballistics specialist and told him that the Sheriff was requesting a ballistics test done on the gun with the bullet being compared to the one found in the body of Franklin Parker. He requested that the results of the bullet comparison test be sent to the sheriff's office as soon as it was completed.

Bill thanked the ballistics specialist then returned to the sheriff's office. When he arrived at the sheriff's office, the sheriff was not in. He wrote out a report on his visit to see Captain Butler at the air force base, and on his visit to the lab.

It had been a full day, and there was nothing else he could do for now. He went to his patrol car and headed back to Hill City.

When Bill turned into his driveway, he found Julie's car parked there. He parked his car and walked toward the house. As he stepped up on the back porch, Julie stepped out the door.

"Hi. I was afraid I was going to miss you."

Julie smiled at him as she stepped in front of him. She put her hands on his shoulders as Bill slipped his arms around her.

"Did I forget something? I didn't know you were coming here. I thought you had to work tonight."

"I do. I just wanted to spend a little time with you before I go to work."

Bill kissed her then he turned her and walked back into the house with her.

"What is it I smell. It sure smells good."

"I thought you might like something you didn't have to cook for a change. I made a chicken casserole. It should be ready in about fifteen minutes."

I'll get out of my uniform."

"Okay. You have time to take a quick shower if you want."

"Good idea. I'll be back in a few minutes."

Bill went to the bathroom, took off his uniform and stepped into the shower. After he showered, he got dressed then went out to the kitchen. He could see Julie setting the table.

"Would you like a little help?" Bill asked.

"No. Everything is ready. All you have to do is sit down."

Bill sat down and watched Julie as she dished up the casserole. He thought she looked good in an apron, and comfortable in the kitchen.

"What are you looking at," she said as she smiled at him.

"I was just thinking how nice you look in an apron."

"Thank you, I guess."

"You look nice in almost anything, but especially in one of my shirts."

"I'm glad you think so. Are you ready to eat, or do you want me to just stand here so you can look at me?"

"I can look at you while we eat."

"In other words, you're hungry."

"Yes. I'm starving."

Julie smiled at him, then set a plate in front of him with a healthy serving of her casserole and a serving of vegetables. She sat down across from him after setting her plate on the table. She watched him as he took a fork and sampled the casserole.

"This is very good. You can cook for me anytime."

She smiled at him as he started to eat. It was clear that they were both hungry.

After dinner, Bill helped Julie clean up the kitchen. When they were done, they sat down in the living room on the sofa.

Bill drew her close to him and kissed her. They spent the next hour or so in each other's arms. It didn't seem like it was very long when Julie looked at her watch.

"Oh, I have to go."

"Will you stop by on the way home in the morning. I'll have breakfast for you."

"I'd like that. I get off about seven in the morning. It will be about eight by the time I get here."

"I'll have breakfast waiting for you."

Bill walked her out to her car. He kissed her as they stood beside her car. After several kisses, he reached out and open the car door for her. She got in and started the car, then looked up at him.

"I love you," she said.

"I love you, too. Drive carefully."

"I will."

Bill stepped back away from the car and watched her as she backed out of the drive. He continued to watch her until she drove out of sight around the corner.

Bill went back in the house. He sat down and listened to the news on the radio, then went into his bedroom and went to bed.

Bill had a hard time getting to sleep. There was something running around in his head that didn't seem to make sense. He finally drifted off to sleep, but it was a restless sort of sleep.

CHAPTER ELEVEN

Bill suddenly woke up. He sat up and looked off across the room. He wasn't really looking at anything. Something he had heard had awakened him. It wasn't a noise in his room, or even outside his house, but something he had heard yesterday while interviewing Robert Hood.

"That's it," he said out loud.

What had been bothering him and making it so difficult for him to get anything close to a restful sleep finally became clear. If what Robert Hood had told him and the sheriff was true, he could not have killed Parker. Someone else had to be the one who killed him.

Bill swung his legs over the side of his bed. He rubbed his eyes in an effort to wake himself up so he could think clearly.

Robert had told the sheriff that he found the gun Sunday afternoon when he was in the mountains with Chuck. He left the gun there because Chuck would want to play with it, and Chuck couldn't keep his mouth shut. He dropped Chuck off in Hill City, then went to Rapid City and stayed overnight at his aunt's house. Robert did not return to the cabin on Medicine Mountain until Monday morning. He then took the gun from the cabin on Medicine Mountain to his cabin on Copper Mountain. After taking the gun to his cabin, he returned to Rapid City to stay with his aunt. He was there until Bill had stopped by his aunt's home.

If what Robert said was true, he could not have killed Parker. If Robert didn't find the gun until Sunday, and Parker was killed on Saturday, then who killed Parker?

It was becoming clear that Bill was no closer to finding out who killed Parker than when he started. Bill had a ton of questions running over and over through his head. The main one was who killed Parker? He began to think about the other three who had been in the mountains that weekend. Had one or more of them been up on Medicine Mountain on Saturday, or at least in that area? His thoughts turned to his interview with each of the three who had been up on the mountain.

His thoughts turned to Sean Carter first. His interview was done in front of Captain Butler, which could explain why he was so nervous. The question was, is that what made Sean nervous, or was it something else? Did Sean participate in the shooting of Parker, or did he just know about it and was afraid to tell anyone, or did he have no knowledge of it at all? All good questions, but without a single answer.

What about James Goodman? He was also interviewed in Captain Butler's office and had pretty much the same results as with Sean. He appeared to be nervous, too. What was his reason for being so nervous, and did the slight difference in their stories mean something?

Chuck Smart was the one he really didn't interview. After just a brief talk with him in front of Bill's house, he appeared to be more than a little nervous, and he seemed to be scared half to death. Why? What did he know? Was he involved in the death of Parker, or did he just know something about it?

Bill couldn't answer any of the questions that came to mind. The one thing that he thought he needed to do was drag each one of them into the sheriff's office and question them at length, one at a time.

The thought that Robert had not told the truth was still a strong possibility. Did Robert go to Medicine Mountain on Saturday looking for Parker to try to find out if he had any of the gold coins like the ones Robert found and then had been stolen from him. Maybe he not only wanted the few more, but maybe the six additional coins Parker thought Robert had?

If Robert confronted Parker on Saturday, did something happen and Robert killed him? A good thing to find out was where had Robert been on Saturday.

There was also the problem of who had the second gun? Did Robert have the second gun hidden in the cabin, or did Parker have the second gun and Robert took it away from him and shot him with it and with the .45?

It crossed Bill's mind that there was still the possibility that someone else, unknown to him, who had killed Parker. If that was the case, why was he killed? Was he killed for the gold coins? In Bill's mind, the gold coins seemed to have something to do with everything that had happened resulting in Parker's death.

Bill couldn't help all the questions that ran through his mind. He sat down at his desk and began writing things down. He first wrote out a time table as best he could figure it based on what he had been told by each of his suspects, and each of his witnesses to hearing the gunshots. Bill would be looking for differences in statements made by each individual, and how their stories matched up with others. He would also be looking for any clues that might come out of the interviews.

He also wrote out a list of those he thought might be involved, in short, his suspect list. Bill decided that his suspects were Sean Carter, James Goodman, Chuck Smart, Robert Hood and one, possibly two unknown suspects.

Bill also wrote down as many questions as he could think of to ask when he interviewed each of his suspects. Once he had all the questions written out, he was sure that he was now better prepared to question each of his suspects.

In questioning his suspects, Bill would be looking for differences in statements made by each individual, and how their stories matched up with others. He would also be looking for any clues that might come out of the interviews.

As he was writing down his questions, Martin Cannon came to mind. Bill decided he should include Martin

Cannon as a suspect. He was not totally convinced that Cannon was involved in some way, but he did seem to know a lot about the murder. He also said he heard two shots when he was at his barn. Bill was sure it would have been almost impossible to hear the shots due to the contour of surrounding land, the distance from where they had been fired, and the slash piles that were between the shooter and Cannon's farm.

Bill thought about bringing Dieter Schmidt in, but didn't think he would be able to add much. He could always change his mind and talk to him again.

Bill looked at the clock and found it was four o'clock in the morning. Now that he had everything on paper that had kept him from getting any sleep, he was beginning to feel tired. He walked over to the sofa and laid down hoping that he could get a few hours of sleep. Now that his mind was cleared and he had a plan of action in mind, it didn't take him long to fall asleep.

Bill was awakened by the sound of a car pulling into the drive. He remembered that Julie was going to stop by for breakfast on her way home. Still in his pajamas, he walked to the door to greet Julie.

"Did I wake you?"

"Well, sort of. I had a full night last night."

"Would you prefer I go on home?"

"No. It won't take but a few minutes to fix breakfast."

"Okay, if you're sure."

After a kiss, they went to the kitchen. Bill quickly put together a breakfast of scrambled eggs, bacon and toast with butter and jelly. He had it on the table in just a few minutes. They sat down together to eat.

"How come the rough night?"

"After an interview with a suspect in the case I'm working on, something he said stuck in my mind. I had trouble getting to sleep. I woke up after only an hour or two of sleep and remembered what he said. It got me to thinking. I came to realize that I need to questions a couple of my suspects again, only this time in a better location."

"Where did you interview them before?"

"Two of them in Captain Butler's office on the air base. I think if I have them where it might be in - ah – a more serious surrounding, I might get one or more of them to talk, or at least say something he didn't intend to say."

"Do you think that will work?"

"I don't know, but I'd be willing to bet the sheriff would like the idea."

They didn't talk any more about Bill's investigation. When they finished breakfast, they set the dirty dishes in the sink.

"I'll take care of these," Bill said as he put his coffee cup on the counter next to the sink.

"I can stay and help you."

"You should probably get going. Your grandfather might be getting worried about you. You know he won't eat if he thinks you are going to be there to fix something for him."

"You're right," Julie said with a grin.

Bill walked her to the backdoor. He pulled her to him and wrapped his arms around her.

Julie rose up on her tiptoes as she wrapped her arms around his neck. She then kissed him. It wasn't a long kiss, but it was a very pleasant one.

"I'd better get going before I decide to stay here," she said.

"I wouldn't mind, but I have things to do, too. Will I see you tonight?"

"Sure. I'll stop by after I fix grandfather's dinner."

"I'd like that.

"It would be about seven-thirty or eight before I could get here. We wouldn't have much time together."

"I would still like to have you stop by."

"Okay, but I better be going."

Bill walked with her as far as the back porch. He kissed her then watched her as she walked to her car.

As soon as she drovc out of the driveway, he went inside. He took a minute to call her grandfather and tell him that she was on her way home.

Bill returned to the kitchen. After cleaning up the kitchen, he took a shower, then got ready for work. He picked up the lists he had made during the night, then went to his patrol car. He headed for Rapid City to talk to the sheriff.

Bill arrived at the sheriff's office at about nine-thirty. The desk sergeant told him the sheriff was in. Bill walked down the hall to the sheriff's office and knocked on the door.

"Come in."

Bill opened the door and walked into the sheriff's office.

"Morning, Bill. What can I do for you?"

Bill told him what he wanted to do and why he wanted to interview each of his suspects in the integration room at the station.

"You think if you have them here you might get one or more of them to talk?"

"Frankly, I don't know if I would get anything new or different from any of them. All I know, or should say, I think I know, is that someone is lying to me. I have no idea who it is, or why."

"Okay. If we drag all of them in here, what's your plan?"

"I was thinking that we could bring all of them in here, or as many as we can find, and sit them in the hall, or in a room where they can see each other. Then take them one at a time into the interrogation room and question them. Having to wait while the others are questioned could make the ones waiting get nervous. "We would have to make sure that they don't talk to each other while we're interviewing one. Once they are interviewed, they would not go back to the waiting room. We would either let them go, or hold them in a cell."

Sheriff tipped back in his chair and looked across his desk at Bill. He didn't say anything for a minute or so. Bill wasn't sure the sheriff would be willing to go along with his plan.

"How are you going to get them all here at the same time?"

"I thought we could have Officer Doug Thomas pick up the ones at the air base and bring them in. I've worked with Doug before. Maybe, you could have one of the other officers pick up Martin Cannon while I pick up Chuck Smart."

"What happens if we can't get all of them at the same time?" the sheriff asked.

"We might just have to question those we can get and interview the ones we can't get later."

"Do you think Captain Butler will cooperate with Thomas?"

"I think so. Doug has had dealings with Captain Butler, and the captain has been cooperative with me. He also knows a little about the case from working with me. He certainly has been willing to cooperate so far."

"Do you think Captain Butler would bring them in for us?" the sheriff asked.

"I don't know, but he might. It certainly wouldn't hurt to ask him. He seems like someone who is willing to work with us," Bill said.

"Okay. I'll call Captain Butler and see if he will bring Carter and Goodman in for questioning. I'll have Officer Thomas pick up Cannon. You get Smart. We already have Hood. Let's shoot for two o'clock this afternoon. You think you can get Smart by then?"

"I think so."

"Good. I'll call Captain Butler now. I want you to wait until I clear it with him, just in case he can't do it by two o'clock."

Bill nodded as he watched the sheriff pick up the phone and call the air force base. It wasn't but a couple of minutes before Captain Butler was on the phone with the sheriff.

"Good morning, Sheriff Henderson. What is it I can do for you?"

"You know from working with Deputy Sparks that we are working to find the killer or killers of Franklin J. Parker."

"Yes. Are you making any progress in that effort?"

"We think so, but we could use your help."

"What can I do for you?"

"Let me tell you our plan. We are going to bring all our suspects in for questioning at the same time. We hope it will put a little pressure on the guilty party, or parties, when he sees the others."

"That sounds like a good idea to me. How can I help?"

"I would like to know if you could bring Sean Carter and James Goodman to my office for questioning. If that is not possible, I would like to send an officer out there to pick them up."

"First, I have a question. Would I be able to stay and observe? I wouldn't need to take part in it, just be there as an observer," Captain Butler asked.

"Yes, of course. Neither Deputy Sparks or I have a problem with that."

"Okay. What time do you want me to bring them?"

"Does two o'clock this afternoon work for you?"

"Give a moment."

It was only a couple of minutes before Captain Butler came back on the phone.

"Both of them are here. I'll see you at two this afternoon. In the meantime, I'll get them to my office. I'll be bringing a couple of Air Policemen with me to keep watch on them."

"Thank you for your cooperation. I'll see you here at two, or a few minutes before two. I look forward to meeting you in person."

"1400 hours," the captain said.

"Right," the sheriff said, then hung up.

The sheriff turned and looked at Bill. He smiled.

"Captain Butler will bring them in at two with a couple of Air Policemen with them. Now all you have to do is get the rest of your suspects in here."

"Yes, sir. I would like another officer to help me."

"Since Thomas will not need to go to the air base, you can use him to help you pick up the others."

"Thanks. I best get at it," Bill said.

Bill left the sheriff's office, then went to the officer's lounge. Officer Doug Thomas was sitting at a table writing something. Bill walked up to him. He stood near Doug and simply waited for him to finish what he was doing. Doug looked up at Bill.

Hi, Bill. Do you want to talk to me?" Doug asked.

"Yes. If you're not busy, I could use your help. The sheriff told me to ask for your help."

"Sure, what do you need?"

"I have to pick up a couple of suspects and bring them here for questioning. Since I have more than one, I could use a little help."

"Right now?"

"Yes, if you're available."

I'm free. Do I go with you, or are we taking two patrol cars?"

"I think it would be best for each of us to take our own patrol car. The men we are picking up are not together. However, I think we should go together to pick them up, and bring them back here in separate cars. I don't want them talking to each other."

"Got it, when do we leave?"

"Right now?"

"Sure."

Doug got up and followed Bill out of the sheriff's office. When they got to their patrol cars, Bill stopped. Doug walked up to him.

"I'll give you a heads up. The first one lives outside of Hill City. He has a temper and has been in a lot of trouble over the years. I think we should pick him up together. His name is Martin Cannon."

"I know Cannon. I've arrested him a couple of times. He can be hard to handle."

"Then you know what he is like."

"Yeah. Who is the other?"

"He's a smartass young man who has been in trouble a number of times. His name is Chuck Smart. Do you know him."

"No, but I've heard of him."

"We should probably get him together, too. There's no telling what he might do when we try to arrest him," Bill said.

"Okay, works for me."

"Well, let's get going."

"I'll follow you to Cannon's place. I know about where he lives, but I've never been to his farm. I've only had dealings with him in town," Doug said.

"Okay."

Bill and Doug went to their patrol cars. Doug followed Bill as they headed toward Hill City.

CHAPTER TWELVE

When the two sheriff's deputies arrived at Cannon's farm, they drove into the farmyard and up to the front of the house. Bill got out of his patrol car and headed for the house while Doug got out of his patrol car. Doug stood behind the door of his patrol car with his hand on his gun while he kept an eye out for trouble.

Bill stepped up on the porch and knocked on the door. Cannon's wife came to the door and looked at Bill.

"Is Martin here?" Bill asked.

Mrs. Cannon looked over Bill's shoulder and saw two patrol cars with another sheriff's deputy standing by one of the patrol cars.

"Yes," she said then turned and called to Martin.

Martin came out of another room and saw Bill.

"Deputy Sparks, it's nice to see you," Martin said.

When he saw the two patrol cars out in front of his house, the smile on his face changed to an expression of concern. He looked at Bill.

"I take it this is not a social call?"

"That would be correct. We are taking you into Rapid City to get a statement about what you heard and know about the death of Franklin J. Parker."

"I don't know any Parker. What's this all about?"

"We want a statement about the shooting you claimed to have heard."

"What do you mean by 'claimed to have heard?'"

"We are taking you in for a formal statement that will become part of a formal record. We don't believe you heard the shots you claimed to have heard. If you did hear the shots, we think you were a lot closer than in the corral behind your barn."

"What, my word isn't good enough?"

"I don't really need to answer that, do I? You've lied to us before."

Bill noticed that Cannon looked at his wife. He didn't like the look on her face. He then looked out the front of the house at the other officer.

"I don't want any trouble from you," Bill said interrupting Cannon's thoughts. "Am I going to have trouble with you?"

Cannon again looked at his wife. She had a disgusted look on her face.

"I didn't have anything to do with his death."

"Do you own a .38 caliber pistol?" Bill asked.

Cannon looked at Bill, then at his wife. He didn't like the way she looked at him. He remembered what she had told him the last time he was arrested. He let out a sigh, then looked at Bill.

"Yes."

"Turn around and put your hands behind your back."

Reluctantly, Cannon did as he was told, all the time looking at his wife. Bill put handcuffs on him, then turned him around.

"Where is the gun?"

"It's in the bottom drawer of the desk in the corner," Mrs. Cannon volunteered as she pointed at the desk.

Bill walked over to the desk and pulled open the drawer. Lying there in the drawer was a .38 caliber revolver. Bill took his handkerchief from his pocket and picked it up. He checked to see if it was loaded. It was loaded. He took all the cartridges out of the gun. There were five loaded cartridges in the cylinder and one cartridge that had been fired.

"Thank you," Bill said looking at Mrs. Cannon. "We will bring him back home, if we release him."

"Don't bother. I told him that if he got into trouble one more time, any trouble at all, I would throw him off my farm. You see, he doesn't own this farm. I own it along with my father."

"Yes, Ma'am. I understand," Bill said.

Bill took Cannon by the arm and led him out of the house. He led Cannon out to his patrol car and put him in the back seat. He then got in his patrol car and headed back to Hill City.

As he pulled out onto the road, he glanced in his rearview mirror. He could see the look of defeat on Cannon's face. He could also see Doug was following right behind him.

Once they got back to Hill City, Bill pulled over to the side of the street. He got out of his patrol car and walked back to Doug's patrol car.

"It's not far from here to where Smart lives. I seriously doubt that Chuck's mother will be any help in our arresting her son. However, I don't think she will get in the way, either, but she might," Bill said.

"Okay. I have an idea. It's not the best but it might make it easier for us."

"What's on your mind. I'm open to any ideas that might make this easier."

"I think we should make it so we don't have to worry about Cannon doing anything stupid, or causing us any problems if we have trouble getting Smart. Do you have any rope in your car?"

"Sure."

"Good. We'll tie Cannon in the back seat of your car. That way he can't get out, and it will leave us free to work together in getting Smart."

"Good idea," Bill said.

Bill opened the trunk of his car, and got a rope out of the trunk. He opened the backdoor to his patrol car.

"Tie one end through the link in the handcuffs on Cannon, then feed the rope between the back seat cushion and the back of the seat into the trunk," Doug said.

Bill did as Doug suggested, but not without a show of anger from Cannon.

"You can't do this," Cannon protested.

"You going to give me a hard time?"

"You can't do this to me."

"I not only can do it, I will do it. Now, lean forward."

"No."

Bill looked at him for a couple of seconds, then straightened up. He pulled his night stick from his belt and showed it to Cannon.

"I don't have time to mess with you. Do I have to use this on you to get you to cooperate with me?"

Cannon looked at Bill, then at the night stick. Cannon slowly turned so Bill could slip the rope over the links in the handcuffs. Bill pushed the ends of the rope between the back seat cushion and the back of the seat into the trunk.

Once he had the rope fed behind the back of the seat, Doug got into the trunk of the patrol car, took the rope and tied it tightly to the cross frame behind the back seat. He pulled it up tight so Cannon could not move.

"That should hold him," Doug said as he closed the trunk.

"It's time to go get Smart," Bill said. "When we get to his house, if there is a car in the drive, I'll block it off. Park your car in the street so we can get at it if we need it. I'll go to the front door, while you go to the back of the house. I don't want him to get away. I think there is a very good chance he will try to run."

"Okay. Let's get it done," Doug said.

Doug returned to his patrol car while Bill got into his patrol car. As soon as they were ready, they drove to the Smart residence.

When Doug and Bill arrived at the Smart residence, they found two cars parked in the drive, one behind the other. The car closest to the road was the same car Bill had seen when Chuck Smart had been at Bill's home. It was when Chuck stopped by Bill's house to tell him to leave his mother alone.

Bill pulled up behind the car, stopping so close to it that Chuck would be unable to back out of the drive. Bill then turned and looked at Cannon.

"You just sit there and be quiet. You tear up my patrol car trying to get out while I'm getting Chuck Smart, and you will find yourself hogtied and riding to Rapid City in the trunk. Is that clear?"

"It's clear," Cannon said sharply.

As Bill was getting out of his patrol car. he could see that Doug had parked his car in the street and was running around to the back of the house.

Bill went up to the front door of the house and knocked. It was only a few seconds before he heard the door opening. He was sure Mrs. Smart had seen them drive up, and she was standing by the door just waiting for them to knock.

"What do you want?" she said sharply.

"I want your son. He is a suspect in a murder case."

"He's not here," she insisted.

"I don't think you want me to take you into Rapid City and charge you with harboring a criminal, do you. His car is parked right behind yours."

Suddenly, Bill heard a crashing sound from the far side of the house. Bill didn't waste a second, he took off to the corner of the house.

Just when he got to the corner and could see around the side of the house, he saw Chuck jump over a neighbor's fence. He also could see Doug was in pursuit of Chuck. Instead of running down between the houses, Bill ran across the front yard of the neighboring house.

"Get a car," Doug yelled.

Bill turned around and ran back to Doug's patrol car. He jumped in the patrol car, started it, then quickly headed down the street heading in the general direction that Chuck ran. When he got to the corner in the second block, he turned just in time to see Chuck run across the street. Bill stopped, jumped out of the car and ran after Chuck.

Doug jumped into his patrol car and headed around the block. When he got to the corner, he saw Bill standing next to a short fence. Doug turned the corner and pulled up beside Bill.

Bill turned and looked at Doug. Bill was breathing hard after chasing Chuck, but he was smiling.

Doug got out of his patrol car. He didn't see Chuck. He walked toward Bill. He was about to ask Bill what happened, thinking that Chuck had gotten away, when he saw Chuck.

Chuck was lying on the ground tangled up in a loose roll of barbed wire that had been laying on the ground alongside the fence. Every time Chuck tried to move, he got poked by one or more of the barbs.

"I guess that's one way to keep him from running. Maybe he will think twice before he tries to run again," Doug said with a grin.

"I doubt it. He's not that smart. I'm going to let him stay there and think about it while you go get the other patrol car," Bill said.

"You can't leave me like this," Chuck screamed.

Bill ignored Chuck's complaints, then looked at Doug and said, "I rest my case."

"I get it. I'll walk back and get the patrol car," Doug said with grin.

Bill just looked at Doug as he turned and started back to get the other patrol car. He was pretty sure that Doug would be in no hurry and would take his time.

"Get me out of this," Chuck screamed.

"Relax and shut up. I'll get you out of there when I get wire cutters. The less you move the better."

Bill leaned against the fence while he waited for Doug to return. Doug was just coming around the corner when Mr. Wilson came out of the house.

"What's goin' on officer?"

"He just tried to run away from me. When he jumped your fence, he jumped right into that barbed wire and got all tangled up in it. I'm waiting for my partner to bring the other patrol car. I have a tool box in the trunk with wire cutters in it," Bill explained.

"What's he done?"

"I'm not sure," Bill said with a grin.

"I understand that you don't want to say, but he and I have had our moments."

"What do you mean?"

"He's been a lot of trouble in this here neighborhood for some years. Him and one of his friends. I don't know his friend's name. Them two raise hell with loud music, racin' their cars up and down the streets, and teasin' my dog. Stupid kid's things, yah know. Throwin' beer bottles in my yard, yah know. That sort of thing."

"I get the picture. I'll see what I can do to put a stop to it. Oh. I'm sorry that we're going to have to cut up your barbed wire to get him out of it."

"That's okay. I'm glad it helped yah catch him," Mr. Wilson said with a grin.

Bill grinned, and watched as Mr. Wilson returned to his house just as Doug pulled up next to the fence.

Doug got out of the car and walked over to Bill.

"What did old man Wilson want?" Doug asked.

"He just came out of his house to see what was going on. It seems he has had his share of trouble with Chuck and one of his friends."

"How do we get him out of that barbed wire?" Doug asked.

"There's a pair of wire cutters in the tool box in the trunk of my car. We need to get him out of there if we're going to get these two back to Rapid City by two o'clock."

Doug got the wire cutters out of the trunk and gave them to Bill.

"Lay still and this won't hurt as much," Bill said.

Smart didn't comment, he just looked at Bill.

Bill leaned over the roll of barbed wire and began cutting it. When he almost had Chuck cut free of the barbed wire, he turned and looked at Doug.

"If he tries to run, knock him on his ass. I have no desire to chase him again."

"No problem. He won't get ten feet."

"You ready to get up?" Bill asked Chuck.

"Yeah."

The tone of Chuck's response showed he was also ready to give up."

"You going to give us any trouble?"

"No."

"See that you don't."

Bill clipped the last strand of barbed wire that kept Chuck down. Bill reached out and gave him a hand. Chuck stood up and stepped out of the barbed wire.

Chuck looked at Bill then at Doug. He decided that it was no use for him to try to escape.

"Hands behind you back." Bill said.

Chuck looked at Bill for a second before he turned his back to Bill and put his hands behind his back. Doug handed Bill his handcuffs. Bill cuffed him then led him to Doug's patrol car. He put Chuck in the back seat and shut the door.

"Let's get these two to Rapid City," Bill said.

Doug nodded then got in his patrol car. Bill got in his patrol car and headed to Rapid City with Doug right behind him.

CHAPTER THIRTEEN

When they arrived at the Sheriff's Office, the desk sergeant led Bill and Doug with their suspects down the hall to a room. In the room were Sean Carter, James Goodman, and Robert Hood. They were all sitting several feet apart with an officer between them. Standing at the door were two Air Policemen from the Air Force Base just watching them.

The officers were there to make sure the suspects didn't talk to each other. The suspects had been warned that talking would get them put in a cell. Bill noticed that all the suspects were handcuffed.

"The sheriff is talking to Captain Butler," the desk sergeant said. "Each one in this room will be gagged if he so much as thinks about talking at all. That includes asking a question of the officer next to them. I'll let the sheriff know you're here with two prisoners."

"Thanks, Sergeant."

Bill sat down and took a minute to look from one to the other. He was looking at them in an effort to help him decide which one he wanted to talk to first. It was easy to see that Chuck seemed to be interested in Robert. Bill wasn't sure if it was because he was afraid of what Robert might have to say, or if Robert would point a finger at him.

Cannon sat there looking at Chuck with squinted eyes. There was little doubt in Bill's mind that Cannon knew a lot more than he had told him. It seemed to Bill that Cannon might have had dealings with Chuck, or maybe it was because Cannon was not sure that Chuck would keep his mouth shut. From what Bill had heard about Chuck, Cannon might have reason to be worried.

Sean and James kept looking at each other. Bill got the feeling that they knew something, but he wasn't sure if they had anything to do with Parker's death.

Everyone turned and looked at the door when they heard it open. The sheriff was standing in the doorway looking around the room. He motioned for Bill to join him. Bill stood up and motioned for Doug to keep an eye on Chuck.

Bill left the room with the sheriff. He followed him part way down the hall. When the sheriff stopped, Bill stopped and looked at him.

"Did you have any trouble picking up those two?"

"Cannon didn't give us any trouble, but Chuck tried to run."

"Is that what caused all the tears in his shirt and pants?"

"Yes. When he ran, we chased him. He jumped a fence and landed in a pile of rolled up barbed wire. He got all tangled up in it."

The sheriff grinned at the mental picture he had of Chuck tangled up in barbed wire.

"Any serious injuries?"

"No. A few very minor puncture wounds. Most of them didn't even break the skin, but they were painful at the time."

"Okay. This was your idea, and you know something about all your suspects. That being the case, how do you want to move forward with this?"

"Before we get started, I think it would be a good idea if we get a search warrant to search Cannon's farm, the house, barn, every place on the property."

"I take it you have a good reason."

"Yes, sir. Cannon was in possession of a .38 caliber revolver. I have that gun now. I think it might be the .38 we've been looking for. I'd like the lab to examine it. If it is one of the guns used to kill Parker, I think a search warrant of Cannon's property is in order."

"I agree. I'll have the gun taken to the lab. If it comes back that it was used in the murder of Parker, I'm sure the judge will issue a search warrant. In the meantime, you can start your interviews."

"Yes, sir."

"Who do you want first?" the sheriff asked.

"I think it would be a good idea to start with the two Captain Butler brought over. I would like to question Sean Carter first. I think he might know something, but I don't think he is involved in the killing of Parker.

"Then I think James Goodman would be next. I sort of feel the same about him. I would like to ask them a few questions I didn't ask them the last time I talked to them."

"Okay. You start with Carter. We'll take him to the interrogation room."

"When I'm done with him, I would like to have him taken to another room. Don't take him back to the same room."

"Sounds good," the sheriff said. "I'll be watching while you question him. If you don't believe him, don't hesitate to pressure him for more information."

"Yes, sir."

"By the way, Captain Butler will be watching with me."

"Yes, sir. I figured he would be."

"I'll have Carter brought in. Give me a minute or so before you start questioning him."

Bill nodded, then turned and went into the interrogation room. He sat down at the table in the middle of the room to wait for his first suspect.

Bill looked around the room. Even though Bill had been in an interrogation room many times, it passed through his mind that the room was about as dull a place as he could think of at the moment. There was nothing in the room that could distract the prisoner from what was going on.

A couple of minutes later the door to the interrogation room opened. The sergeant had Sean Carter by the arm. He walked Sean to the table, took his handcuffs off and sat him down. The sergeant returned to the door, but didn't leave. He simply turned around and stood next to the door. It was obvious that he was there to make sure Sean didn't try to cause any problems for Bill, or try to escape.

"Hi, Sean. It's good to see you again. How have you been?"

"Okay, I guess," he replied suspiciously.

"Sean, do you know why you are here?"

"Because you think I had something to do with Parker's death?"

"How is it you know about Parker's death?"

"I didn't have anything to do with it."

"That's not what I asked. I asked how is it you know about his death?"

"I heard about it on the base."

"Are you sure that's where you heard about it?"

"Yes. That sort of thing gets around on the base, but I didn't have anything to do with it."

"Really?"

"I didn't have anything to do with it, I said!" he almost screamed.

"Tell me everything you can about the weekend that you, James, Chuck, and Robert went into the backcountry near Medicine Mountain. Start with Friday of that weekend. I want to know what you did and what you saw. I want to know everything. You understand?"

"I didn't see anything."

"Now, we know that isn't true, don't we?"

Sean looked at Bill. From the look on his face, Bill was sure that he knew something, but Sean didn't say anything.

"Okay, let's try this. When was the first time you were in the backcountry around Medicine Mountain on that weekend?"

"Sunday."

"Are you sure you were not up there on Friday or Saturday?"

Sean hesitated. He seemed far more nervous this time than when Bill questioned him at the Air Police Station on the Rapid City Air Force Base. Bill wasn't sure if it was because of where he was now, or because he knew something.

"I was only there on Sunday."

"On that Sunday, were you told something, or did you see something that you are afraid to tell me about?"

"No," he replied rather weakly. "I wasn't anywhere near Negro Creek."

"It's not going to help you to lie to me. I know you were there. I found your pocket knife on the bank of the creek, and you already told me you were at Negro Creek the first time we talked."

Suddenly, his eyes got big and his breath caught.

"You see, I know you were there. Lying to me is not going to help you one bit. It will only make things harder on you. It's time to get this off your chest before you get in so deep you can't talk your way out of it, and I can't help you."

Bill tipped back in his chair and looked at Sean. He was giving Sean time to think. Bill could see that Sean was trying to think of what he could say to get himself out of this jam he believed he was in.

"Okay, Sean. We know you were near where the body was found. We also know when you were there. What I want to know is what part did you play in Parker's death?"

"I had nothing to do with it. Honest, I didn't have anything to do with it. In fact, I was the one who called the Sheriff's Office to tell them about the body. At the time, I didn't know who it was, honest."

"Who else knew about the body?"

"At the time, I don't think anyone else knew about it."

"Did you tell anyone about it?"

"Yes."

"Who did you tell?"

"I told James. He didn't see it, but I told him about it. He wanted to go to the police, but I talked him out of it. We decided not to tell anyone about it so we wouldn't be suspected of killing the man."

"Did you see the body?"

"Yes," he admitted reluctantly.

"Did you tell any of the others?"

"No. I didn't tell anyone but James.

"Did James tell anyone?"

"I don't think so. We stayed together the rest of the time we were there."

"Why didn't you tell Chuck and Robert about the body you saw?"

"I was afraid to."

"Why where you afraid to tell them?"

"We had heard Robert talking to Chuck about a fight he had gotten into. We were afraid that the dead guy was the one he fought with, and we thought he might have killed him."

"Did you say anything to Chuck about it?

"No."

"Why?"

"Because Chuck can't keep his mouth shut."

"It seems I've heard that about him before."

"What?" Sean asked.

"Nothing. I think I'm done with you for now."

"Can I go?"

"Not yet. I have others to talk to."

Bill motioned the sergeant at the door that he could take Sean out. The sergeant walked over to Sean, had him stand up, put handcuffs on him, then took him out of the room.

"Give me a minute before you bring in James Goodman."

Bill followed the sergeant out of the interrogation room. He turned and walked down the hall to the room right next to the interrogation room. It was where Captain Butler and the sheriff had been watching and listening to what was going on and what was said in the interrogation room.

"How do you think it's going," the sheriff asked.

"I don't think he had anything to do with the murder. I'm not sure he actually knows who did kill Parker. I get the impression that he thinks Hood killed Parker, but I don't think he is sure of it."

"Do you think there is only one person involved," Captain Butler asked.

"No. I think there are two people involved. At the moment, I don't know for sure who they are."

"But you have an idea who killed him," the captain said.

"Yes, but I'm not a hundred percent sure, and I am not ready to say."

"Who's next?" the sheriff asked.

"James is next."

"Okay."

Bill turned and left the room. As he entered the interrogation room, he asked the sergeant to bring in James Goodman. The sergeant nodded then went down the hall to the waiting room, while Bill sat down.

The sergeant returned to the interrogation room with James. He led him into the room, took his handcuffs off and sat him down on a chair across the table from Bill. He then returned to his place next to the door.

"Hi, James. Do you prefer to be called James or Jim?"

"Everybody calls me, James," he said softly.

It was clear that James was scared to death. Bill doubted that James had ever been questioned by the police, other than when Bill had questioned him at the air base.

"Okay, James. You can relax. I just have a few questions to ask you."

"Am I being arrested," he asked, his voice showing just how afraid he was of just being there.

"No. Well, that is if I get answers to my questions. Are you ready to talk to me?"

"Yes, sir."

"Good. Tell me when were you in the backcountry near Medicine Mountain?"

"Just on the Sunday when I went with Sean, Chuck, and Robert."

"Were you ever in that area at any other time?"

"No."

"You've never been in that area around Medicine Mountain before?"

"Ah - - I was up there about a year and a half ago."

"Were you there alone that time?"

"No. I was with Sean."

"What were you doing that time?"

"We were exploring Medicine Mountain?"

"Had you ever panned for gold in Negro Creek before?"

"No."

"I understand that you and Sean found a body near the creek. Is that correct?"

"Well, - - no."

"No. You didn't find a body?"

"I didn't find the body. Sean found it and told me about it. I wanted him to report it to the Sheriff's office right away, but he didn't want to."

"Why didn't he want to report it?"

"He was afraid that the sheriff would think we killed him."

"Are you sure that was the reason?"

James looked at Bill. He was trying to figure out what to say, and what Sean might have said.

"No. I don't think he wanted to report it because he was afraid that if Robert or Chuck found out, they might not like it. Those two can be really mean if they don't like someone.

"Why would he think that?"

"Sean thought that one of them might have killed the guy."

"Why do you think Sean felt that way?"

"He told me that Robert got in a fight with some guy at a bar. He heard Robert talking to Chuck about the fight. He said he cut the guy pretty bad."

"So, you figured Robert had killed the guy. Is that right?"

"Yes."

"How did you get Sean to call the Sheriff's Office?"

"I told him if he called the Sheriff's Office and told them about where the body could be found without giving his name, no one would suspect us."

"So, he called the Sheriff's Office on Sunday evening?"

"Yes."

"Were you with him when he called the Sheriff's Office?"

"Yes."

"Do you know if Robert actually killed the man?"

"No. No, I don't."

"Do you think Sean knows if Robert actually killed the man?"

"No. Sean was pretty shaken up when he found the body."

Bill leaned back in his chair to think. He looked over at the sergeant standing by the door. The sergeant just shrugged his shoulders.

Bill could see that James was very nervous. Everything he said lined up with what Sean had said. He knew the two of them had had time to get their stories straight, but he couldn't help but think that the only thing they were guilty of was not telling the authorities about the body sooner, and not identifying themselves when they reported the body to the Sheriff's Office.

"Sergeant, you can take him out. I'm done with him for now."

"Okay. Who do you want next?"

"I think I would like Chuck Smart next. I would like to see if what he has to say matches up with what Hood told me. But give me a few minutes before you bring him in."

"Okay," the sergeant said, then handcuffed James and took him out of the room.

Bill sat down and looked at the only window in the interrogation room. He wasn't looking at anything, just thinking.

It wasn't but a minute before the door opened. Bill turned to see who was coming in. It was the sheriff and Captain Butler.

"Well, how do you think it went," the sheriff asked.

"Pretty much as I expected," Bill replied. "Really never thought that they had anything to do with the murder, but I was sure they, at the very least, knew something about it. What do you think about them, Sheriff?" Bill asked.

"I think you're right. I don't think they had anything to do with the murder."

"Captain?" Bill asked.

"I agree with both of you. I don't think they had anything to do with the murder either. Do you think you are going to need to talk to them again?" Captain Butler asked.

Bill looked at the sheriff before he answered, "I don't think so."

"May I take them back to the base?"

Bill looked at the sheriff before he answered. The sheriff simply nodded.

"I don't see why not," Bill said.

"In that case, I'll take them back to the base. I'll restrict them to the base for thirty days for failing to report a murder to the authorities in a timely manner. One, to teach them a lesson, and two, to keep them around if you should need to talk to them again."

“That sounds like a good idea. I’ll see you out. We don’t want the others to know they have been released,” the sheriff said.

The sheriff and Captain Butler left the interrogation room, leaving Bill to think.

Bill sat down. It was going to take a few minutes to get Sean and James out without the others seeing them leave.

It was only about ten minutes before the sergeant returned to the interrogation room. Bill turned and looked at him.

“You ready for the next guy,” the sergeant asked.

“I take it they got Sean and James out without the others seeing them?”

Yes. They took them out through the backdoor.

“Good. Bring in Chuck Smart, please.”

“Okay.”

The sergeant turned and left the interrogation room.

CHAPTER FOURTEEN

Bill thought about what he might get out of Chuck Smart. Chuck acted like he was pretty sure of himself, but Bill knew better. Behind that outer shell of self-confidence, there was a scared young man.

It was only a few minutes before the sergeant returned with Chuck. He took Chuck across the room, removed his handcuffs, then sat him down on a chair opposite Bill. The sergeant returned to the door and stood there watching Chuck.

Bill sat across the table from Chuck and just looked at Chuck without saying a word, or indicating that he was going to say anything. He was looking at Chuck with the hope that just sitting there in front of him would make him a little nervous. It took a couple of minutes before Chuck couldn't take the quiet any longer.

"Well, you got me here. Are you going to just sit there and look at me?"

"I was just trying to envision what you would look like in striped shirt and pants like the prisoners at the state penitentiary wear."

"You don't have anything on me that would send me to prison. All you have is me running from you."

"Oh, I forgot about that. We have you for resisting arrest, too."

"Big deal. I can beat that."

"You sure have a lot of confidence. What makes you think we don't have anything a lot more serious on you than you just resisting arrest?"

Chuck took a minute to think about what Bill had said. What do they know, was the question running through Chuck's mind at that moment?

"When you stopped by my house and told me to leave your mother alone, do you remember what I said to you?"

"I didn't pay any attention to you, or to what you said."

"That's not true. I know you were paying very close attention to me. I could read it on your face. You were scared half to death, just like you are now."

"I'm not afraid of you, or anybody."

Chuck was trying to show how sure he was that he could beat anything Bill might have on him. However, his body language was telling a completely different story.

"I think I know who you are afraid of. You're afraid of me, and you're afraid of Robert Hood. You also might be afraid of Martin Cannon."

Bill noticed the sudden, but very subtle change in the look in his eyes with the mention of Cannon's name. Bill had thought that if the murder of Parker was committed by two people, it might have been Hood and Cannon who had done it. Now, he wasn't so sure. He was beginning to think that it might have been Smart and Cannon.

"Okay, so you think you're a tough guy," Bill said. "I wonder how tough you will be when you're tossed in a real prison with real tough guys. Not with a bunch of kids who think they're tough, then run to mama when they get into real trouble.

"Let me tell you this. You are in real trouble and mama isn't going to get you out of it this time. The kind of trouble you're in is the kind that will put you in prison for a very, very long time."

Chuck just sat there looking at Bill. From the look on his face, he was scared to death that he might actually go to prison.

"It's time to get down to business. I want to know when you were in the backcountry? Namely, around Medicine Mountain, Copper Mountain and Negro Creek.

"Sunday."

"Are you sure you were there just on Sunday? I know you were off work from Friday to Sunday."

"I was only there on Sunday."

"No other time over that weekend?"

"NO!"

"Who were you with?"

"Robert Hood, Sean Carter. James Goodman, but you already know that."

"Were the four of you always together?"

"Yes."

"Now I know that's a lie. The four of you were not together all the time."

Bill sat there for a moment just looking at Chuck before he said anything more.

"You ready to tell me the truth, or do you need a little time to think about it. We have a very quiet place where you can be alone with your thoughts, and where you can sit, undisturbed, to think about your answers to my questions. It's called a jail cell."

"You can't just lock me up."

Bill turned and looked at the sergeant standing at the door.

"Sergeant, would you like to take Mr. Smart to one of the cells where he can be left alone to think. He might want to think about his future, or lack of it."

"Gladly," the sergeant said as he stepped toward Chuck.

"You can't do this?"

"Yes, we can. You are under arrest for resisting arrest. Sergeant, take him away."

The sergeant stepped up to Chuck, reached out and took him by the arm. He lifted Chuck out of the chair, turned him around and put handcuffs on him. He again took him by the arm and started for the door.

Just as the sergeant was about to take him out of the interrogation room, the door opened. Bill stood up and looked as Officer Thomas came into the room.

"You might want to wait a minute," Doug said. "I have the report on the .38 caliber revolver. It was definitely one of the guns that was used to shoot Franklin Parker."

"So, we have both guns that were used to kill Parker," Bill said, then turned and looked at Chuck.

Chuck looked at the paper that Doug had in his hand. He was feeling weak in the knees. He looked at Bill.

"Apparently, someone forgot to wipe the fingerprints off the gun," Doug said then looked at Chuck.

Bill took notice of Chuck's reaction to the news that someone forgot to wipe the fingerprints off the gun.

"Sergeant, take Chuck to a jail cell and make sure he is not disturbed. He wants a little time to think," Bill said.

The sergeant nodded, then led Chuck out of the interrogation room.

As soon as they were gone, Doug handed the report to Bill. Bill scanned the report, then looked up at Doug.

"This isn't a lab report. This is nothing more than your report of our activities in arresting Cannon and Smart."

"Oh, I must have gotten the wrong report. The lab report showed the gun had recently been cleaned and that there were no fingerprints on the gun. The lab report did show, however, that it was one of the guns used to kill Franklin Parker."

Bill looked at Doug for a minute, then began to smile.

"I'll say this much, it was sure a shock to Smart. He damn near fell over," Doug said.

"I think I'll let him think about it for a while," Bill said.

"I think that's a good idea," Doug said.

Just then the door to the interrogation room opened. The sheriff walked in.

"Doug, that was not the brightest thing you have ever done," the sheriff said. "But it sure gave Smart something to think about."

"First of all, can we keep Cannon overnight without charging him?" Bill asked.

"It's not a good idea in the eyes of the judge, but we can if we think he played a part in the murder of Parker."

"We got the .38 caliber gun from a desk at Cannon's farm," Bill reminded the sheriff.

"That should be reason enough to keep him. What's next?"

"What I would like to do is keep Cannon here while we let Smart sit in a jail cell for the night. I think Smart is about ready to break," Bill said.

"You might be right. I'll okay keeping Cannon overnight. In the meantime, I've got the search warrant from the judge you asked for. He was more than willing to sign it when we told him that one of the guns that was used to kill Parker was in the possession of Martin Cannon. You've got your search warrant to search Cannon's farm. What do you hope to find?"

"I hope to find that Cannon was at the murder site."

"How do you plan to do that?" the sheriff asked.

"I have castings of horses hoofprints I took very close to the murder site. I think one of his horses was there. Since he won't let anyone ride his horses, that would put him there, unless someone stole one of his horses.

"I also have castings of tire prints at the site. I want to see if they match any of his vehicles, primarily his pickup truck. The day I stopped in to see him, I noticed there was dried mud on his pickup that looked more like the dirt from along Negro Creek, than from the dirt found on most of the gravel roads, or in his driveway."

"We'll call it a day. You have your search warrant. You and Doug can go out to the Cannon farm and service the warrant first thing in the morning. The two of you can work out arrangements to meet. I want the two of you to serve it," the sheriff said.

"While we are there, I would like to find out if the sounds of the two shots could be heard at Cannon's farm," Bill said.

"You and Doug can work that out. You'll need a .45 and a .38."

"I have a .45 Colt like the one we have in the lab. Since it is the louder of the two, I don't think we will need a .38."

"I have a .38 revolver just like the one that was used to kill Parker. I'll bring it along so we can be one hundred percent sure our test is a good one," Doug said.

"Good idea. I think that's about it for today," the sheriff said. "I'll get Cannon and Hood locked up for the night. We'll start the interrogations again as soon as you get back. I want you to take your time and do a thorough search of the farm, even if it takes all day.

"You might want to question Mrs. Cannon. Do you think she will cooperate with you?" the sheriff added.

"She might. She was the one who told me the revolver was in a drawer in Martin's desk. She seemed pretty upset with him. She even told us that he was not to return to the farm, and made it clear that she actually owns the farm with her father."

"She might be able to verify where Martin was at the time of the shooting," the sheriff suggested.

"I'll question her about Martin's activities over the weekend that Parker was murdered," Bill said.

"Good," the sheriff said.

"I'll be out first thing in the morning," Doug said. "About seven?"

"I'll be ready," Bill said. "We can meet at the Hill City Café and have breakfast before we go out to the farm. It could prove to be a long day."

"Sounds good," Doug said.

"Okay, you guys are off duty. I'll see you back here after you have completed the search of Cannon's farm," the sheriff said. "Remember, do a good job even if it takes all day."

"Yes, sir," Bill said.

The sheriff turned and walked back to his office.

"I'll see you in the morning," Doug said.

"I'll meet you at the Hill City Café."

"Okay."

Bill left the Sheriff's Office and went out to his patrol car. He started it and headed for Hill City. On the drive home, his thoughts were on what he might find when they searched the Cannon farm.

It was almost six o'clock when Bill pulled into his driveway. It had been a long day. He went in the house and took a quick shower. He was pretty sure that Julie would be stopping by on her way to work.

Bill had just finished getting dressed when he heard a car pull into his driveway. He went to the backdoor and saw Julie getting out of her car.

She smiled at him when she saw him step out onto the pouch.

"Hi," Bill said. "Your timing was perfect. I just got dressed."

"When did you get home?"

"Just about an hour ago."

"Sounds like you had a long day."

"I did. Have you had something to eat?"

"Yes. I thought I should eat with grandfather to make sure he was getting a good meal. Have you eaten?"

"No. I'll get something after you leave for work."

Bill slipped his arm around her as they walked into the house.

"I'll fix you something. You can sit down and tell me about your day."

Bill sat down at the kitchen table while Julie started fixing dinner for him. He told her about his day while she fixed him dinner from some leftovers.

When she finished, she set his dinner on the table in front of him. After pouring a cup of coffee for each of them, she sat down across the table from him.

"It sounds like you are making progress on your investigation."

"That reminds me. Did I ever tell you the victim was shot and how many times?"

"I don't remember. You might have told me the victim was shot, but I don't think you told me how many times he was shot. Why?"

"The morning after I found the body, I ran into Martin Cannon. He wanted to talk to me about the murder. He told me that he heard two shots at his place. I didn't think he would have known that unless he was there. I didn't tell anyone he could have talked to that would have known how many times the victim had been shot."

"Well, I sure didn't say anything to him or anyone else."

"I know that. What I am saying is there was no way he could have known about the murder, or how many shots were fired unless he was there. The sound of the shots would not have carried to his farm."

"So, he had to have been there. Do you think he killed the man?" Julie asked.

"It sure is beginning to look that way."

Bill decided it was a good idea to drop the subject now. The conversation turned to more pleasant things while Bill finished his dinner. After he was done eating, they went into the living room and spent some time being close.

The time seemed to go by very fast. It was time for Julie to leave if she expected to get to work at the hospital on time.

Bill walked her out to her car. He took her in his arms, kissed her then opened her car door for her. Julie got in the car and looked up a Bill.

"Would you like me to stop by in the morning," Julie asked.

"I have to meet Deputy Doug Thomas at seven in the morning at the Hill City Café. We are going out to the Cannon Farm and serve a search warrant. We plan to have breakfast together, then serve the warrant. I will probably be gone by the time you could get here."

"Oh. In that case, would you give me a call when you get home?"

"Sure. It could be rather late."

"That's okay. Call me anyway."

"Okay."

Bill leaned down and kissed her, then closed the car door. He stepped back as she started her car. She smiled up at him briefly, then backed out of the driveway. Bill watched her as she drove away.

As soon as she was gone, Bill returned to the house. He cleaned up the kitchen, then listened to the radio for a little while before he turned in for the night.

CHAPTER FIFTEEN

Bill's alarm clock went off at six, giving him plenty of time to get a quick shower, shave, and get dressed in his uniform. At six forty-five, he left his house. He drove over to the Hill City Café where he was to meet Deputy Doug Thomas. He arrived just as Doug pulled up to the curb.

"Right on time. We'll have breakfast then head on out to the Cannon Farm," Bill said.

"Sounds good," Doug said as they entered the café.

Bill pointed to a booth. They sat down. It was only a few minutes before Sandy walked up to the booth and set a cup of black coffee in front of Bill.

"What can I get you to drink?" Sandy asked Doug.

"Black coffee, please."

Sandy left and returned shortly with a cup of black coffee for Doug. She handed menus to the two deputies, then waited for them to look them over.

"I'll have the breakfast special, eggs over easy," Bill said.

"Toast with apple butter?"

"Sure. And you sir, what would you like?"

"I guess I'll have the breakfast special, eggs over hard, and two pancakes."

"Anything else, gentlemen?"

"I think that will do," Bill said after looking at Doug to see if there was something he might want.

Sandy left and went to the kitchen with their orders.

"I take it you eat here a lot," Doug said.

"What makes you think that?"

"As soon as you sat down, she brought you a cup of coffee."

"I do eat here fairly often. Sandy and her husband own this café. She is also a fountain of information. She knows just about everyone in the area, and has a pretty good idea of what is going on here in Hill City, and in much of the area around here."

Doug looked around the café while they waited for their breakfast. He saw Rutledge sitting in the corner booth looking at them. He turned and looked at Bill.

"Is that Rutledge sitting over there?"

Bill looked over at Rutledge and nodded his head slightly. Rutledge nodded back.

"Yes, that's Rutledge."

"I thought he didn't like you?"

"I wouldn't say he likes me. Let's just say we get along better now. We had a talk the other day that smoothed over our relationship a bit. I certainly wouldn't say we are friends, though."

Just then Sandy came with their breakfasts. They thanked her, and went right to eating.

As soon as they finished eating, they paid for their breakfasts, then left the café. They walked out to their patrol cars. Bill stopped next to his patrol car.

"Doug, I think we need to take both cars out to Cannon's farm. I have no idea what we are in for out there. It might be best if we have both cars in case we have to haul a bunch of stuff back to the office.

"I've got the castings I took of a horse's hoof prints in the trunk. I want to check and see if they match one of Martin's horses."

"Okay, by me. You've got the search warrant, so I'll follow you."

Bill and Doug got in their patrol cars and headed out to Cannon's farm.

On the way out to the farm, Bill thought about how they would go about the search. He also thought about what they needed to watch for that might cause them trouble. Bill was hoping that Mrs. Cannon would not give them any trouble, or try to make the search harder for them than it needed to be. The search warrant was for any and all parts of the farm, including the entire house, barn, and any outbuildings on the property.

It was about eight-thirty when they arrived at the Cannon Farm. Bill drove into the drive and up to the house. He stopped close to the house and looked toward the front of the house. He saw the curtains in the kitchen window move slightly making it clear that someone was there.

Bill got out of his patrol car and looked toward Doug as he got out of his patrol car. Doug moved up close to Bill.

"It looks like Mrs. Cannon is home," Doug said.

"Yes. Well, I guess we best get this over with. You kind of hang back a little. I'll go knock on the door and present her with the search warrant. I hope this goes smoothly," Bill said.

"I hope so, too. Where are you planning on starting your search?"

"I think the house would be the best place to start. After we're done with the house, we'll have her remain in the house while we search the barn and tool shed, then I'll check the horse's hooves. By doing the house first, and keeping her in the house, she won't have a chance to hide anything."

"Sounds good to me. We might as well get started," Doug said.

Bill nodded in agreement. They had just started toward the house when Mrs. Cannon stepped out onto the porch.

"I think she has been expecting us," Doug said.

"It looks that way," Bill said. "Well, here goes."

Bill walked up to the porch and looked up at Mrs. Cannon. Doug was standing behind and slightly to Bill's right.

"Mrs. Cannon, I have a search warrant to search the entire property of your farm."

"I'm not surprised. I have been expecting you. Please come in. I will not get in your way. The only thing I would appreciate is that you try not to make too much of a mess of my house. I've heard that some of these searches often make a mess of the house."

"We will try not to make a mess, ma'am. We would appreciate it, if you would not get in our way, but stay close by should we need to ask you a question or two."

"Would it be okay if I just follow you around, then?"

"Yes. However, we do not wish to get in your way if you have something that you need to do."

"Where would you like to start?" she asked.

"Since the front door leads directly to the living room, we will start there."

Mrs. Cannon nodded that it would be fine with her. She turned around and went back into the house. Bill and Doug followed her in.

Once inside, Bill handed her the search warrant. She looked at it as if she didn't know what she was supposed to do with it.

"Do I need to sign this, or something?"

"No, ma'am. It is for you to read so you understand that we have legal authority to search your property," Bill said. "It also outlines what and where we can search."

"I know that you are looking for something that will prove Martin had something to do with the death of someone. Other than that, I have no idea what he has been up to."

"We are looking for anything that connects him to the murder of a young man, that is true. However, we are also looking for proof that, at the very least, he knows something about it."

"I have a question."

"Certainly. What is your question?" Bill asked.

"It's about the gun you took from his desk in the corner. Since you are here with a search warrant, I assume you have arrested him for some involvement in the murder. Have you had the gun tested?"

"That would be correct, and yes we have had the gun tested."

"Did it have anything to do with the murder of that young man?"

"Yes, ma'am, it did. It was one of the murder weapons."

She looked at Bill as if she knew it would, but hoped it wouldn't.

"Be sure you do a good search of his desk, and the tack room in the barn," she said.

"Yes, Ma'am."

Bill looked at her then at Doug. He wondered if she wanted them to find something that might get him out of her life, permanently.

She walked over to the corner of the living room, sat down on a wooden rocking chair and looked at Bill without further comment. Bill wasn't sure what was going on in her mind, but he remembered that she had told him not to bring Martin back to the farm, if he was released. She had also made a point of telling Bill that the farm belonged to her and her father, not to Martin.

Bill turned to Doug.

"Doug, start with the desk. When you are finish with it, search the rest of the house. I think I'll go out to the barn. It may save us some time."

"Sounds like a good idea."

Bill looked at Mrs. Cannon for a moment before he left the house. She was sitting in the rocker apparently reading the search warrant.

He left the house and started out toward the barn. He had no idea what he might find there. He wasn't sure if she was sending him on a wild goose chase, or if she knew there was something in the tack room that would make it easier for them to get him out of her life. Since he planned to check out the barn anyway, he might as well go ahead and do it now. He knew it could produce some damaging evidence that could put Martin in jail, or it could do nothing to further a case against him.

When Bill got to the barn, he pushed the big barn door open. He stepped inside, stopped, then began to look around.

There were twelve stalls, but there was only one stall with a horse in it. He walked up to the stall with the horse in it. After a quick look at the horse, he remembered that it was the horse Martin had indicated he had been working with when he heard the shots. Bill also remembered that Martin had made a point of telling him that it was his wife's horse.

When he was here the first time, there had been three horses in the corral that ran across the back of the barn. He didn't see them when he walked to the barn, and they were not in the barn. The question that came to his mind was where were the other two horses now?

Bill walked into the stall where the horse was standing. He reached out and ran his hand down the back of the horse while he looked it over. He also looked at the horse's hooves. The left front hoof looked like a horseshoe had been replaced recently. The fact that the other horses were gone and that the horseshoe on the one remaining horse had been replaced, meant that his cast was of little use to him now, since it was of the left front hoof of a horse.

After he checked the horse over, he was unable to find anything to indicate that the horse was sick or injured. Bill was curious as to why the horse was still in the barn on such a nice day. He was also interested in knowing where the other horses were that had been in the corral the first time he was at the Cannon farm.

He stepped out of the stall and looked down the inside of the barn. Bill found six stalls on one side and only four stalls on the other. Bill noticed that the side with the four stalls had a closed off area where the fifth and sixth stalls on that side should have been. That area of the barn was walled off into a room. His first thought was why did Martin need such a large tack room when they only had the one horse?

Bill walked to the closed off area and found the door had a heavy padlock on it. He figured that it was probably the tack room, but wondered why such a heavy lock? Was there something of real value in the tack room, or was it so no one could see what was in the room, or maybe both.

Since the tack room was locked, he decided that he would go up to the house and see if Mrs. Cannon had a key. As he walked toward the house, he thought about the heavy padlock. The thought that came to mind was he doubted that Mrs. Cannon would have a key. Martin probably didn't want his wife to be able to get in there. Bill had no reason to think that except that he got the impression that Mr. and Mrs. Cannon didn't seem to get long all that well. If Martin was hiding anything that he wanted to be sure that no one, including his wife, saw, the locked tack room would be the place. Remembering her comment about searching the tack room caused Bill to think that she might have some idea what was inside it, or at the very least, she had some idea that there might be something that Martin was hiding from her.

When Bill got to the house, he walked in the backdoor. He walked through the kitchen and dining room to the living room. He found Doug was still going through the desk. It looked like he was checking out every piece of paper he found.

"Doug, did you find any keys in the desk?"

"No. So far, I haven't found anything of interest except a few notes on a Sergeant Samuel Lawson. I have no idea what they have to do with anything, or who this Sergeant Lawson is."

"I know who Samuel Lawson is. He is Robert Hood's stepfather. We'll want to keep those notes. Maybe the sheriff can make sense of them."

"Okay," Doug said.

Bill looked around and saw Mrs. Cannon still sitting on the wooden rocking chair. She was slowly rocking back and forth while watching them. He walked over to her and looked down at her. She stopped rocking and looked up at Bill.

"Do you happen to have the keys to the padlock on the tack room in the barn?"

"No. As far as I know, Martin is the only one who has a key to that padlock."

"He didn't have any keys on him when we arrested him. Do you have any idea where he might have kept the key?"

"If he didn't want me to see what was in the tack room, he would not keep the keys in the house. It would be my guess it is hidden somewhere in the barn."

"What about his pickup? Would he keep them in his pickup?"

"He might, but probably not."

"What makes you say that?"

"The pickup is mine, but I sometimes let him use it."

"I see. Thank you."

Bill turned around.

"Doug, if you find anything more on Lawson, make sure you hang onto it."

Doug looked at Mrs. Cannon, then at Bill. He nodded his head that he understood.

"I'm going back to the barn."

"Okay," Doug replied.

Bill left the house and returned to the barn. He walked up to the tack room door and began looking around. There was no place on the front of the tack room to hid anything. He worked his way around to the side, but found no place to hid a key there. The other two walls were part of the corner of the barn.

While standing at the corner of the tack room, Bill looked around the barn. He was thinking about where he would hide a key here in the barn if he didn't want anyone to find it. His first thought was there had to be hundreds of places to hide something as small as a key.

Bill decided that he was going to have to look at every crack and crevice in the barn until he found the key. If he didn't find it, he would have to go into town and get a lock cutter and cut the lock off. He again looked around at the inside of the barn. There had to be thousands of places he could hide it. All he could think of was that it was going to take all day just to search the barn.

"You might as well get started," he said to himself.

Bill thought for a minute as he looked at the lock. "Where would I hide something as small as a key if I didn't want my wife to find it?" he asked himself out loud.

His answer was simple. He would hide it somewhere his wife was not likely to go. She would certainly spend some time on the floor of the barn since she had a horse. But would she go up into the loft? Bill looked around and noticed that there were several bales of hay in one of the stalls. With hay in the stall, she would probably not have a reason to go up in the barn's loft. He smiled to himself.

Bill went right to the ladder to the loft. He climbed up into the loft and then stood there looking around. The barn loft was about half full of bales of hay. He walked over to the area that would be just above the tack room. He looked around, looking for anything that didn't look right, a loose board, something out of place, a shelf that would be hard to see. He even pushed around some of the loose hay on the floor of the loft, looking for any place a key could be hidden.

At the point where a vertical support beam and the floor came together, Bill saw what looked like a loose board in the floor that was only about twelve inches long and six inches wide. It looked like all the boards on the floor except for two things. It did not appear to be nailed in place as it should have been, and it looked like it was much shorter than any of the other boards on the floor of the loft. It also looked as if it had just been simply set in place.

He knelt down close to the board and brushed it off. On closer examination of the board, there appeared to be a string that went down in the crack between the end of the board and the vertical beam.

Bill reached down, took hold of the string, and pulled the string up. The end of the board came up fairly easily. He lifted the board out of the floor and looked in the hole. It was actually like a small box built into the floor directly above the corner of the tack room.

Inside the box built in the floor, Bill found what appeared to be another small box. On a closer look, Bill found it was a small metal box. It looked like a tea box, a small painted square tin box that was used to store loose tea. Bill doubted that the box contained tea.

Bill took the tea box out of the hole and sat it on the loft floor. He opened the tea box and found ten rounds of .45 caliber ammunition. A look at the ends of the cartridges showed him that they were from the same lot of ammunition as the one shell casing he found at the murder site.

There was also a key ring with three keys on it in the tin box. When he removed the key ring, he noticed that there was a tag attached to each of the keys. The tag on one of the keys had the letters "TR" on it. From the look of the key, it was for a rather large padlock like the one on the tack room. The "TR" obvious meant the key was for the lock on the tack room.

The second key had a tag with the letters "GC" on it. Bill had no idea what the "GC" stood for. After examining the key, Bill thought it looked like a key that would fit a file cabinet lock. All he could think of was it had to be for something other than the lock on a file cabinet.

The third key on the ring had a tag with the letters "SSL" on it. That key was not for a padlock. Bill thought it might be a key to maybe a small metal lockbox. It was certainly not a key to any padlock Bill had ever seen.

While still kneeling next to the hiding place of the keys, Bill was looking at the key with the tag reading “SSL”. He spent about fifteen minutes trying to think of what SSL stood for. Unable to figure out what SSL stood for; Bill got up and went down from the loft to the tack room.

Bill took the key tagged “TR” for the tack room, fit it in the lock and unlocked the padlock. He stepped inside and looked around, but it was too dark to see anything clearly. There was a light hanging from the ceiling with a cord hanging from it. He pulled the cord and the room was instantly flooded with light.

He took a minute to look around the room. Along one wall was an Army cot with an old Army blanket on it. The cot was made up with a pillow under the blanket at one end. It didn’t look like the cot had been used for some time. At the head of the cot was a metal locker like those found in the Army barracks. It was about six feet tall and three feet wide. It had a padlock on it.

Bill made a mental note of the locker, then looked around the rest of the room.

It suddenly hit him what the SSL stood for. Seeing all the army items in the room, it reminded him that soldiers had a habit of putting their initials on things they owned. Was it possible that the SSL stood for Sergeant Samuel Lawson?

Bill remembered what Doug had told him. Doug had told him that he found some notes referring to, or about Sergeant Samuel Lawson.

A sudden thought came into Bill’s head. He started looking closely at the army blanket, cot and the back of the locker. Bill found “SSL” on each of the items, the blanket, cot, and locker. Bill’s first thought was, what was Sam Lawson’s things doing here?

Bill continued to look around the room. Along one wall, he noticed a dozen or so chairs were stacked in the corner.

They looked like they had been used recently because there was no dust on them. Bill looked at the dirt floor of the tack room. He could see neatly spaced circular indentions in the dirt floor. They formed a pattern. It occurred to him that the legs of the chairs in the corner could have made the indents in the dirt floor.

With closer examination of the dirt floor, and the examination of the chairs, it looked like the chairs had been set up in a pattern that looked like nine of the chairs had been set in three neat rows all facing the same way. There were four chairs set in front of them in a neat line. Those chairs were facing the other chairs. It looked like a meeting, or possibly several meetings had taken place in the tack room. All Bill could think of was that there were some sort of secret meetings going on in the tack room.

Bill decided that it would be a good idea to have pictures of this. He went out to his car, got his camera and took it back to the barn. He climbed up into the loft and took pictures of where he had found the keys. Bill then went into the tack room and took pictures of everything in the room.

As soon as he had finished taking the pictures, he took the key with the tag "GC" on it and tried it on the locked locker. The key fit the lock perfectly. He unlocked the locker and opened it. He immediately started taking pictures of the inside.

The locker contained half a dozen M1 Grand military rifles and seven .45 caliber Colt pistols like those used by the Army, along with four large ammunition canisters for both of the weapons.

There was also a wooden box in the bottom of the locker. Bill lifted the cover and found one dozen hand grenades. It suddenly came to him. The "GC" stood for "Gun Cabinet".

As Bill looked over what was in the cabinet, he wondered what Cannon was doing with all the weaponry, especially hand grenades which were illegal to have. He also wondered where did Martin get them. What did Lawson have to do with all this? Had Sergeant Lawson gotten them while he was in the Army? What did he plan to use them for?

Bill began to search everything in the cabinet and record it all in his pocket notebook. He wrote down all the serial numbers of the guns, the numbers off the ammunition canisters and the numbers on the box of hand grenades.

As he searched through the cabinet for anything that might shed light on what was going on here, he came upon a small notebook hidden behind the ammunition canisters. He noted that there were items written in the notebook that seemed to be in some sort of code or shorthand. Bill wasn't sure what it all meant, but he knew a guy who might have an idea or two about it.

Bill turned away from the gun cabinet and began taking pictures of the room and everything in it. As he was taking pictures of the inside of the tack room, he noticed a board that was about three feet by five feet in size. It didn't look like it was nailed to the wall, but simply hanging on the wall. He walked up to the board and tipped it up so he could see what was behind it. Behind the board was a three-foot by five-foot flag. It was a flag Bill had seen often during the war. It was a Nazi flag.

Bill's breath caught as it became clear that this was a meeting place for a pro-Nazis group of people. He took the board off the wall and took several pictures of it. He then replaced the board and took pictures of it to show how it was hidden from sight.

As soon as he was sure he had all the evidence photographed and logged in his pocket notebook, he walked out of the tack room. Bill locked the door to the tack room, then left the barn, taking the keys with him.

CHAPTER SIXTEEN

As Bill left the barn and walked toward the house, he glanced off across the field behind the barn. He stopped suddenly when he noticed there was someone sitting on a horse on the far side of the field. The horse was standing just inside the woods, but the color of the horse made it stand out against the dark brown and green of the forest.

The sun reflected off something. It seemed to be something up close to the man's face. About the only thing Bill could think of was the rider was probably a man, and he was using binoculars to watch the farm.

Bill was sure that whoever it was, he had probably been watching what was going on at the house and barn for awhile. There was little doubt that the man had seen Bill's patrol car. The patrol car was alongside of the house and would be clearly visible from where the man was sitting on the horse. Bill had no idea how long the man on the horse had been there, or what his interest was in what the sheriff's deputies were doing at the Cannon farm.

With what Bill had found in the barn, he thought it would be a good idea to get as much evidence out of the barn as possible, especially the weapons, and the hand grenades, and get the barn secured as quickly as possible.

When he got to the house, he went inside. Bill found Doug was still setting at the desk. He had been searching the desk when Bill went out to the barn. He noticed that Mrs. Cannon was no longer sitting on the rocking chair, but was now sitting on a straight back chair with her hands behind her back. Bill looked from Mrs. Cannon to Doug.

"Doug, what's going on here?"

"It seems Mrs. Cannon wants to throw out everything that belongs to her husband. She refused to stop when I told her to stop. I had to cuff her so she wouldn't destroy any evidence there might be here."

"I take it you found something interesting."

"I sure did. Based on what I found in this desk, Martin has been having some dealings with some pro-Nazis people on the east coast. When I told her about it, she came unglued and tried to throw everything belonging to Martin "out of her house", as she put it. I was able to keep her from destroying anything, but she wouldn't stop. I handcuffed her in the chair so she didn't destroy anything."

Bill turned and looked at Mrs. Cannon.

"What do you have to say for yourself?"

"I don't want any of that Nazi stuff in my house or on my property. My brother died at the Battle of the Bulge. He was killed by Nazi soldiers," she said as she began to cry.

"I'm sorry, but we can't find out who is involved and bring them to justice without evidence. We can't convict those involved if we don't have the evidence. Let us do our job and we will get all of this out of your house and off your property for good."

"I'm sorry," she said as she looked up at Bill.

"If I take the handcuffs off, will you promise not to interfere with us anymore?"

"Yes. I promise."

"Okay. I'll take the handcuffs off. If you interfere with us again, I will have you cuffed again, then have you taken into Rapid City where you will be locked up until we finish our investigation. Is that clear?"

"Yes. I'm sorry."

"Doug, if she gives you any trouble at all, put your handcuffs back on her and call for an officer to come and get her," Bill said more to get her to cooperate with them than to make it an order.

"Yes, sir," Doug said with a slight grin.

Bill looked at Mrs. Cannon, then at Doug. He motioned for Doug to step away from the desk.

“I need to talk to you for a moment,” Bill whispered.

Bill moved over to the door that led into the kitchen. As soon as Doug moved over next to Bill, but where he could still keep an eye on Mrs. Cannon, he looked at Bill.

“I think we might have a problem. I don’t want her to hear me.”

“Okay. What kind of a problem?”

“We have someone watching us from across the field behind the barn. It looks like he has been there for awhile. I think the sheriff should know. I’m going out to the patrol car and call in.”

“What do you want me to do?”

“Keep doing what you were doing. I’ll let you know what the sheriff says.”

“Okay.”

Doug returned to the desk while he waited for Bill to call the sheriff.

Bill turned and went out of the house to his patrol car. He placed a call to dispatch.

“Car eight to Dispatch.”

“Dispatch, go ahead car eight.”

“I need to talk to the sheriff. It’s rather important.”

“I’ll patch you through.”

There was silence for a moment before the sheriff came on.

“How is it going out there?”

“We have found a ton of evidence that there is a pro-Nazi cell operating from the Cannon ranch. Could you send someone out here with a truck as quickly as possible to get it?”

“Yes. I take it there is a lot of stuff if you want a truck.”

“That would be correct.”

“Do you have it secured?”

“As best we can at the moment. I saw someone in the woods behind the barn. It looked like he has been watching us. I can see him from here. I don't know if it means anything, but it could be a serious problem for us."

"I'll get someone out there to help as soon as I can."

"Thanks. I think it would be a good idea if you contact Sergeant David Johnson at the Army Ordnance Depot. We found ammunition, rifles, pistols and hand grenades in the barn. All of them Army issue."

"I'll contact Johnson, and I'll be out there with a couple of deputies to help you secure the place as soon as I can."

"Doug and I are going to do our best to protect the evidence until you get here. Just so you know, I have taken pictures of all of it.

"Do you think you will have a problem?"

"We might. I only saw one person across the field from the barn. If he is a member of the pro-Nazi group that had been meeting here, we could have a serious problem. I'm sure they would rather burn the barn down than let us get our hands on what is in it. It might be possible for him to get enough of the members together in a short time to try to destroy the evidence."

"I'll get a couple of units out there as fast as I can. Do what you can to protect what evidence you can, including the barn."

"Yes, sir. Out." Bill said.

Bill got out of his patrol car and walked around to the back. He opened the trunk and got his rifle out and loaded it. He also got the shotgun out of his patrol car along with a box of shells for each weapon. He went to Doug's car and got a rifle out of the trunk for Doug. Bill then went back to the house.

When he walked in the door with the guns in his hands, Doug turned and looked at him.

"Is the sheriff getting us some help?"

"He is going to call up anyone in the area. He is also on his way out here."

"It will take him over an hour to get here. The sheriff wants us to protect our evidence, including the barn. He is sending out reinforcements as quickly as he can."

"What can I do to help?" Mrs. Cannon asked, having overheard Bill.

"You can stay here in the house."

"Doug, go out to the barn and take up a position where you have a good field of view of the area behind and to the northside of the barn. Call out if you see anyone coming this way. Take your rifle. Don't hesitate to use it to protect the barn. I'll keep an eye out the front of the house, the south facing side of the barn, and the area around the house in case they come at us from across the road."

"Got it," Doug said, then took the rifle and an extra box of ammo. He went out the backdoor of the house.

"You said you could see the horse. What color was it?" Mrs. Cannon asked.

"Yes, I could see it. It looked like kind of a light gray horse, maybe a dapple gray. It stood out against the dark green of the forest. Do you know who owns such a horse?"

"The horse could be one that Martin had here for about two or three months."

"Did the horse belong to Martin?"

"No. I think Martin was just boarding it for one of his friends for a short time."

"Do you know the name of Martin's friend?"

"Not really. All I know is I overheard Martin call his 'friend', sergeant. I wouldn't know that if I hadn't overheard it by accident."

"Why do you say that?"

"He never introduced the men who came here to me. He always said it wasn't important for me to know their names. That's when I knew something was going on out in the barn. I didn't know what, but it was something. Now I know what it was."

"You said he called him, 'sergeant'?"

"Yes."

"Did you hear him call him anything else?"

"No. He never called any of the men by their names. Most of the time, I just saw them drive into the yard and park near the barn. They never came to the house. Martin had told me that I was not to come out to the barn when he was having his friends over for a "little get together" as he called it.

"He told me one time that they were just getting together to play cards and didn't want to be bothered. I got the feeling that it was something more than playing cards."

"Thanks. I want you to go upstairs and keep watch out of the upstairs window in front. I don't want you to do anything other than call me if you see anyone, even if it is just a vehicle that drives by. Do you understand. I even want to know if it is a sheriff's patrol car."

"Yes," Mrs. Cannon said then left and went upstairs.

As soon as Mrs. Cannon went upstairs, Bill moved over to the side of the house that allowed him to see the wooded area across the drive and the front of the barn. He knew it would take the sheriff a little over an hour to get there from Rapid City. Bill had no idea how long it would take for any of the other deputies to get there. He knew it would depend on where they were when they got the call to come to his aid.

Time passed slowly for Bill and Doug as they waited for what, they didn't know. Bill wasn't sure if the man on the horse was a threat to them or not. Just to be on the safe side, he would consider the man on the horse to be a threat to them. In that way, they would be ready for whatever happened.

Bill's attention was drawn to a voice from upstairs where Mrs. Cannon was supposed to be watching the road.

"Deputy Sparks, there are two cars coming down the road."

"Can you tell who it is?"

"No, not yet, but they are driving very fast."

"Keep watching them. Let me know if they look like they are slowing down as if they plan to turn in your driveway."

"They are just about to come over the hill."

Mrs. Cannon's voice showed that she was nervous about what might happen.

"They are slowing down. Oh, it looks like two sheriff's cars."

Bill let out a sigh of relief. It looked like reinforcements had arrived. He moved away from his location and went to the front door of the house. He stood just inside the house while the two patrol cars turned into the drive. As soon as they stopped in front of the house, Bill stepped out on the porch.

"It's good to see you guys."

"The sheriff called us and told us to get over here as fast as we can. He said you needed help. What's up. He didn't tell us anything more than that." Steve Branson said.

"We found a pro-Nazi cell here. There was someone across the field watching us. We have a ton of evidence that gives us the names of some of them who are involved."

Bill was interrupted by Harold Raines. Bill looked at Harold and saw he was looking across the field at the woods with binoculars.

"Bill, there's now at least six men on horses across the field. I can't be sure that there are not more because they are hard to see in the woods. From what I can see, they are well armed," Harold said while still looking across the field.

"Grab a rifle and go out and help Doug," Bill said to Steve. "And Steve, take your patrol car into the barn so you have a radio available in case you need it."

"Harold, grab your rifle, you come with me into the house.

Harold grabbed a rifle from his patrol car while Steve got in his patrol car and drove it into the barn. Soon, both deputies were in their assigned positions. Steve to help Doug, and Harold to help Bill.

As soon as Harold was in the house, Bill told him where he wanted him.

"Mrs. Cannon?"

"Yes."

"Keep an eye on the area in front of the house and along the road. We could come under attack at any time now."

Bill had Harold cover the drive, the wooded area on the other side of the drive, and the front of the barn. Bill moved to the kitchen in the back of the house. From there he could see where the men on horses had gathered together. He thought about how many chairs were in the tack room and how they had been set up. There was a total of thirteen chairs. There were six men on horses across the field. That meant there were at least six, possibly seven pro-Nazi members whose whereabouts were unknown. The question that came to Bill's mind was, where were they?

Since the six across the field had not done anything, so far. Why were they waiting? It was Bill's guess that they were waiting for more of the members to get there, or to give the rest of their men time to get around to the other side of the farm.

"Mrs. Cannon, have you seen any activity out front or across the road?"

There was a moment of silence before she responded.

"I don't see anyone, or any movement across the road."

"Thanks. Harold, keep an eye open. I'm going to call the sheriff."

"Okay. Be careful."

Bill went out to his patrol car. He placed a call to dispatch.

"Car eight to Dispatch."

"Go ahead eight?"

"We have at least six men gathering on the far side of the field behind Cannon's barn. I understand there are more officers and possibly some soldiers coming this way. Call the sheriff and see if he could have some officers or soldiers move in behind those across the field from us. We think there are as many as thirteen members of this group. So far, they have not made a move against us. We think they might be waiting for the rest of them, or they are waiting for the others to get into position to attack us from the front of the house while they attack us from the barn side."

"When the sheriff called Sergeant Johnson and told him what you had, he indicated that he would bring reinforcements. I will contact him and see if he can get some of his soldiers around behind them."

"Thanks, eight out."

Bill quickly returned to the house and took up his position. It was once again time to wait to see what was going to happen. Bill was sure they were ready for an attack, at least as ready as they could be considering how few there were to protect the evidence they had found.

CHAPTER SEVENTEEN

Time passed slowly as Bill and his fellow officers waited to see what was going to happen. It seemed that even the trees were waiting for something to happened. There was no breeze to cause the branches to sway, and not a bird could be heard singing in the trees or in the meadow, and not a single blade of grass was moving. Everything was still. The quiet was almost deafening.

Suddenly, Bill saw Steve running across the drive toward the house. He could see that Steve was holding something close to his body. It wasn't until he got closer to the house that Bill realized that Steve had a walky-talky. Steve was holding it so it would be almost impossible for anyone on the other side of the field to see what he had, even with binoculars. As soon as he was in the house, the handed a walky-talky to Bill.

"I found this in a box in the loft of the barn. There were two in the box, but there had to have been four in the box at some time. The men across the field have one of them, and someone on the other side of the road has the other one, and we have two.

"We have been able to listen in on them and on what they are planning on doing. I turned it on and could hear one of them talking on it. I don't know who they are by name, but they are planning somcthing. It's not clear what.

"So far, they haven't said anything very interesting, yet. At least nothing about what they planned to do. If we don't press the 'talk' button and just listen so they don't know we have these walky-talkies, we might get some information on when and how they plan to attack us. That information could be a lot of help to us in holding them off until reinforcements arrive," Steve said excitedly.

"It sure could," Bill agreed.

"I better get back to the barn. I'll leave this one with you. So far, they haven't said anything that would give us some idea of what they plan to do, but I think that their main objective will be the barn."

"I'm sure you're right." Bill said. "Most of the hard evidence is in that barn."

Steve nodded in agreement, then turned and returned to the barn.

Bill returned to his position with the walky-talky in hand, then turned it on. He set the walky-talky, on the floor next to the window, then sat down so he could see what was going on outside. It was time to wait and see what was going to happen.

Time passed slowly. Bill could not see any movement in the trees across the road in front of the farm. There was little talking on the walky-talkies for at least twenty to thirty minutes. If the men in the woods across the field from the barn had one of the walky-talkies, where was the person who had the other? He was probably across the road getting ready to attack from both sides at the same time.

Bill listened carefully to what little chatter was coming across on the walky-talky. There was nothing said between the two talking that would give him some idea what they were going to do, or where the others were. He was only guessing that the others were across the road in front of the farm. Suddenly, something was said that caught Bill's attention.

"S-1 to C-1," came over the walky-talky.

"C-1 to S-1, go ahead."

"We are in position. I cannot see anyone looking our way. If they are in the house, they are keeping back from the windows. They are probably watching you."

"We know there are at least four deputies and Mrs. Cannon in the area. Two deputies in the barn, and two in the house. Mrs. Cannon is probably in the house. I don't think that she will be a problem, but she will have to be eliminated. She knows too much. I want no one left alive. We will have to burn the barn and the house to the ground to make sure there is no evidence of our activities left here. Do you understand?"

"Yes, sir. I understand."

"This is war. This is no longer a game. This is what we have been training for. Take no prisoners. Are you ready?" C-1 asked.

"Yes, sir. We are ready."

"We are ready here. Commence operation, NOW," came the command from C-1.

Almost immediately after the command to commence the operation had been given, Steve saw six men on horses come out of the woods and quickly began to spread out in a long line.

As soon as they were spread out, the man on the grey horse raised his hand and looked down the line, first to his left then to his right. Apparently satisfied they were ready, he dropped his hand and yelled.

"Charge."

The line of horsemen began to charge across the field toward the barn. Steve and Doug were ready for their attack. They held their fire.

Suddenly, there were shots being fired from the house. Steve and Doug held their ground. They waited until the horsemen were almost halfway across the field before they opened fire on the horsemen. In the first volley of shots, Steve and Doug dropped two riders off their horses. On the second volley, they took two more riders to the ground, one of them being the leader. The other two quickly turned and headed back to the woods as quickly as possible, but only one of them made it into the woods.

Meanwhile, five men came across the road from the woods and started to work their way toward the house. Bill and Harold opened fire on them but with the heavy cover of trees they only got one.

The men from the woods managed to work their way toward the barn under the cover of trees and farm equipment. Bill saw that one of them had made it fairly close to the barn. It looked like he was lighting a rag stuffed in the neck of a glass bottle filled with a pale-yellow liquid. Bill took careful aim at the man with the glass bottle. Just as he was getting ready to throw it at the barn, Bill pulled the trigger on his rifle. The slug from his rifle hit the glass bottle. When the bottle broke, it splashed the liquid from the bottle all over. The liquid quickly burst into flames.

A good deal of the liquid splashed on the man, setting his shirt and pants on fire. The man dropped to the ground and rolled around to put out the fire on his clothes. He screamed in pain as he tried to put out the flames. He was able to get the fire out, but not before he had some serious burns.

Harold had continued to shoot at the attackers killing one and wounding another. The wounded one and the last one retreated back across the road and into the woods.

The shooting had just ended when an army truck came over the hill. It stopped near the gate to the Cannon farm. Five well-armed soldiers jumped out of the back of the truck and quickly took control of those in the area. With armed soldiers facing them, the two men who had retreated into the woods were quickly captured. They surrendered without further resistance.

All the men, except the one who escaped across the field were rounded up and brought to the farm. The six that died in the attack were laid down in a stall in the barn.

Three were treated for their wounds by an Army Medic who was with the soldiers. Once they were taken care of, they were put in a stall in the barn with the one who had run but got caught. They were under guard by two of the soldiers.

As soon as everything had settled down, Sergeant Dave Johnson drove the Army truck up to the barn. He stepped out of the truck and looked around. He turned his attention toward the house just as Bill stepped outside.

"Thanks for the help," Bill said.

"You're welcome. It's good to see you again. I hear you have some Army Ordnance for me to pick up.

"Yes. It's in the barn. It is possible evidence in a murder case, so I'll need it secured," Bill said.

"I'll make sure it is secure until you tell me that it can be put into our inventory."

"Fair enough."

Just as they turned to go to the barn, they heard several shots fired from across the field. Immediately, everyone ducked for cover and pointed their weapons in the direction that the sound of the shots had come from. It was only a moment or two before a man stepped out of the woods with his hands on his head. He was quickly followed by a sheriff's deputy.

"It looks like the one we thought got away, didn't get all that far." Doug said as he walked up to Bill and Dave.

"I think that is all of them, that's eleven," Steve said with a big grin.

"I'm not so sure," Bill said.

"What makes you think we didn't get all of them?" Sheriff Henderson asked as he walked up behind Bill and the others.

Bill turned around and saw the sheriff.

"Sir, it's good to see you."

"Good to see you and the others still in one piece. What's this about you thinking we didn't get all of them?" the sheriff asked.

"There is a possibility that we didn't get two of them."

"What makes you think that?"

"Well, sir. The floor of the tack room showed that chairs had been set up in an obvious pattern. The tack room, where they apparently held their meetings, has a dirt floor. It showed four chairs were set in a neat row in front of a flag that is hidden behind a board on the wall. Those four chairs faced so the flag would be behind them. In front of the row of four chairs, were three more rows of three chairs. Those chairs were facing the four chairs in front of the flag.

"From the looks of the impressions from the legs of the chairs, they were all used. That would indicate that thirteen people had been meeting there," Bill explained. "Since the chairs had been stored in a corner of the tack room, that would indicate that there had been thirteen people at the last meeting.

"There were only eleven Nazis involved in the shootout here," Doug said with a worried look on his face.

"That's right," Bill said.

"Are you sure?" the sheriff said.

"Yes sir."

"Okay, how many do we have here now?" the sheriff asked.

"We have eleven. Six dead, three injured and two captured in good condition. Of the three injured, two have none life-threatening injuries. One is in serious condition with multiple serious burns. Then there are the two who surrendered. That's eleven," Bill said.

"Let's say you are right. Do you have any idea who the last two are?" the sheriff asked.

"I have a pretty good idea who one of them is, that would be Martin Cannon. He was not here because he is in jail."

"What about the other one?"

"At this time, I don't know who it is. However, I have someone in mind who just might have an idea who it is."

"You mind telling me who that might be?" the sheriff asked.

"Sergeant Samuel Lawson."

“You got to be kidding. He is a decorated soldier from the war. He fought against the Nazis.”

“I didn’t say he is involved with this pro-Nazi group, although it is possible. I would like to know how his cot, his blanket, his locker, and his key to the locker with a tag that had ‘SSL’ on it got into the barn. I think ‘SSL’ stands for Sergeant Samuel Lawson. Those in the Military put their name or initials on almost everything they owned so they could identify who it belonged to. Some noncoms also used the rank before their initials. All those items had his initials on them. By the way, the guns and ammo we found were in the locker that had his initials on it.”

The look on the sheriff’s face told Bill that he was having a hard time believing that Sam Lawson could have anything to do with such an organization.

“Okay, how do you plan on finding out if he is involved?”

“I plan to ask him?” Bill said.

“That’s your plan?” the sheriff said.

“Yes, sir. I plan to ask him how his property ended up in the possession of one Martin Cannon.”

“I take it by that you do not plan to tell him that his property was used by a pro-Nazi organization?”

“No, sir. I’m not going to tell him anymore than what I have to. Where I go from there will depend on what he says and what kind of reaction I get from him.”

Sheriff Henderson just stood there looking at Bill for a moment. It was obvious he was thinking. Bill’s plan didn’t sound like much of a plan, but at the moment he couldn’t think of anything else.

“Didn’t you already talk to him a few days ago?” the sheriff asked.

“Yes, sir. I talked to him about his stepson.”

“That would be Robert Hood, right?”

“Yes, sir.”

“How did he react when you talked to him?”

"He was cordial. I wouldn't say he was friendly, but he did answer my questions. It was clear he didn't think much of his stepson. He said he was a thief and was no good. He told me that Robert stole money from him.

"However, when I interviewed Robert, he said he didn't steal anything. He also said his stepfather didn't believe him."

"Who do you believe?"

"I don't know. Robert seemed to be cooperative, and seemed to be telling the truth, but he could be just a good liar. I do know that Mrs. Lawson has been helping her son. The day that I arrested Robert, I saw his mother leaving the cabin where Robert was hiding. At the time I arrested Robert, he was putting groceries away. She was helping her son hide out by supplying him with food."

The sheriff looked down at the ground for a moment. It was clear that he was thinking. When he looked up, he looked at Bill.

"Okay. You can question him, but remember, he is a decorated war hero who fought against the Nazis. You show him the respect he deserves, unless he is uncooperative."

"Yes, sir. I have no intentions of causing him any embarrassment unless I have no choice."

"Good. You should probably get over to his place before he gets wind of what happened here. I'll see to it that everything here is covered," the sheriff said.

"Thank you," Bill said.

Bill immediately went to his patrol car. He put his rifle and shotgun in the car, then left the Cannon farm. He headed for the Lawson's farm.

CHAPTER EIGHTTEEN

It was mid-afternoon when Bill pulled into the drive to Lawson's farm. He drove up to the house and stopped. Bill took a minute to look up at the house before he opened the door of his patrol car. He couldn't help but think that there were some serious problems in that house. What kind of problems, he didn't know, but what he did know was Sam's wife was doing things to help her son behind his back.

As Bill stepped out of his patrol car, he saw Sam Lawson step out on the porch. Bill couldn't tell from the look on Sam's face what he might be thinking.

"Deputy Sparks, what brings you out here this afternoon. Are you still looking for Robert?"

"No, sir. I know where Robert is."

"I take it from your statement that you have him in custody."

"That would be correct."

"Then, what is it I can do for you?"

"I would like to ask you a few questions, if you don't mind."

"I don't mind. Come on in. The coffee pot is on. We can talk at the kitchen table."

"Thank you."

Bill followed Sam into the house. As he passed by the door to what looked like a sewing room, he saw Mrs. Lawson looking at him. He nodded to her, but she didn't respond. She didn't smile, but simple looked at him. Bill couldn't tell what was going through her mind, and wasn't sure he wanted to know. He continued to follow Sam to the kitchen.

Once in the kitchen, Sam motioned for Bill to sit down at the table. Bill pulled out a chair and sat down, all the time watching Sam as he poured coffee into mugs.

"How do you like your coffee," Sam asked.

"Black's fine."

Sam set two mugs of coffee on the table, then pulled out a chair and sat down.

"Okay, what do you want to know?"

"Your stepson tells me that you didn't believe him when he told you that he didn't steal your seed money. Is that true?"

"Is what true, that he told me he didn't steal the seed money, or that I didn't believe him?"

"Actually both."

"Yes, he did tell me that he didn't steal the money, and yes, I didn't believe him."

"Since we're on the subject of stealing, has he taken anything else that belonged to you?"

"I'm not sure if he stole some of my things or not, but I had some of my personal things taken from the loft of the old barn just behind the house."

"What sort of things?"

"There was a locker that was given to me by an officer. He gave it to me when we were discharged from the Army. It was for saving his life, he said. I think it had actually been his locker at one time."

"Did it have your initials on it, or something that would show it was your locker?

"Yes, as a matter of fact it did. What's this all about?"

"I was just interested in if there had been something on it to identify it. Was there anything else?"

"Yes. There was an army blanket and cot that I stored in it. It wasn't any secret that I had the locker. The keys to it were in the lock. There wasn't anything of any real value in it."

"Do you have any idea when the locker and its contents were taken?"

"No. I'm not sure. It could have been almost anytime. I don't go up in the loft of that barn very often. Most of my hay is stored in the larger barn over by the corral."

"When did you discover they were missing?" Bill asked.

"Shortly after I ran Robert off the farm. Maybe a week or two after that. I figured he took them to wherever he was hiding. I would have given them to him, if he had asked."

Sam's last comment struck Bill as strange. He wondered why he would give them to Robert if he told him he would shoot him for trespassing if he ever came back to the farm?

"Do you know where his hiding place is?" Bill asked.

"No, but I think it is somewhere around Medicine Mountain or Copper Mountain. I think he was hiding in one of the deserted cabins somewhere around there. I understand there are several deserted cabins in those mountains."

"What makes you think he might be hiding around there?"

"I overheard my wife talking to her sister on the phone. From what she said, it sounded like Robert found a place near the old Copper Mountain Quarry."

Bill got the impression that Sam knew his wife was helping Robert.

"Have you ever attempted to find him and talk to him?"

"No. I doubt he would want to hear from me. He hates me, but then I guess I can't blame him too much for that," Sam said.

"What makes you say that?"

"Well, I lost my temper when I told him I would shoot him if he ever showed his face on this farm. I guess the missing money was the last straw. He had been a failure at almost everything he had done. But I wouldn't shoot him. What I should have done was help him rather than toss him out," Sam said.

From the way Sam talked, Bill got the impression that he really was sorry he hadn't tried harder to get along with Robert, and maybe help him in some way.

"I've been thinking a lot about Robert since you were here last," Sam said.

"Oh. How do you think you could have helped him?" Bill asked.

"I don't know. Maybe I could have asked him to help me here on the farm and taught him how to work a farm and care for the animals. Even pay him for the work he did to give him some incentive to do a good job," Sam said.

"Maybe if I had taken the time to teach him how to farm, then somewhere down the line he could get a place of his own if he has a mind to. That way he wouldn't have to work for someone else."

"I can see where that might have helped him. But he is an adult, and is responsible for his actions."

"That's true, but I still could have tried harder to help him. I don't know if it would do any good, but I should have tried."

Bill sat there and sipped on his coffee while looking at Sam. He thought about what Sam said. Maybe it wasn't too late for him to help Robert.

"Have you talked to Robert since your fight with him?"

"No, of course not."

"Don't you think it would be a good idea if you talk to him?"

"Why. What's it going to change?"

"Maybe nothing, but maybe something for the good of both of you."

Sam looked at Bill. He wasn't sure what was going on in Bill's head.

"What are you saying?"

"I'm saying that Robert may be charged with the murder of an airman over near Negro Creek. I don't think he did it.

But he is going to need someone who believes in him. Someone in his corner. Someone like you."

"If you don't think he killed the man, why is he in jail?"

"Because I think he might run if I let him loose. I need time to find out if he is telling me the truth or not."

"What do you think I can do for him?"

"You can let him know that he is not alone, that you will help him any way you can. You might even think about telling him what you just told me about helping him learn to farm."

"I doubt he will even talk to me," Sam said with a hint of sadness in his voice.

"You will never know if you don't at least try to talk to him."

Sam sat there looking at Bill. It was easy for Bill to see that he was mulling it over in his mind.

"Okay. I'll talk to him. Can you arrange it?" Sam asked.

"Yes. I'll make the arrangements for you to see him. I will make sure that what the two of you talk about is private, just between the two of you."

"When will I be able to talk to him?"

"How about tomorrow at the county jail. I'll call you as soon as I can get it arranged," Bill said with smile.

Bill could see that Sam was thinking about it already. He decided it was time for him to leave. Bill stood up.

"I'll be in touch," Bill said.

Sam just nodded, then Bill turned and left the house. He left Sam sitting at the kitchen table. He was sure Sam had a lot to think about.

As Bill walked out to his patrol car, he was thinking about what might happen when Sam and his stepson meet. He wondered if Robert would even talk to his stepfather. Bill had no idea what the outcome of such a meeting would be, but it probably wouldn't make things any worse. But on the other hand, it just might improve their relationship.

Bill got in his patrol car and started it. He took one more look toward the house before he put the car in gear and drove out onto the road in front of the Lawson farm.

As Bill drove toward Hill City, he took a look at his watch. It was too late to drive back to Rapid City and report to the sheriff his conversation with Sam Lawson.

Something said during his conversation convinced Bill that Sam was not a part of the pro-Nazi group who had been meeting at the Cannon farm. Yet, he was still convinced that there was someone else involved, that there were thirteen meeting in the tack room only days before he arrested Martin.

He began to review in his mind what he had seen in the tack room. There had been four chairs in a row with the backs of the chairs toward the wall where the Nazi flag was hidden behind a board. Then there were three rows of three chairs, a total of nine chairs, each chair facing the row of four chairs. That made thirteen chairs in all. The legs of all the chairs sunk deep enough in the dirt floor to indicate that all the chairs had been used. There were also the footprints in front of each chair.

With eleven pro-Nazis dead or in custody from the attack at the Cannon farm, that left two unaccounted for. Since the meeting had been held at the Cannon Farm, it only figured that one of them was probably Martin Cannon who was in jail, that left one unaccounted for. Who was the one unaccounted for if it wasn't Sam Lawson? That was the question that was running through Bill's mind.

Suddenly, Bill slammed on the brakes and quickly turned around. He headed back toward the Cannon farm.

It took Bill about forty-minutes to get back to the farm. He drove in and went directly to the barn. Parking in front of the barn, he got out of his patrol car and almost ran into the barn. He ran to the tack room door, reached out and opened the door. He walked in and turned on the overhead light. The first thing he noticed was the tack room was empty of the weapons and any other evidence.

Bill began examining the area where the chairs had been, hoping that the boot prints where the marks of the chairs' legs had been had not been destroyed by those who had come in to get the weapons and other evidence. With all the traffic in and out of the tack room during the fight to keep the evidence safe, and during the removal of evidence, he would be lucky to find any good boot prints.

With his flashlight held at an angle, he was able to make out most of the boot prints where people had sat on the chairs. A few of the boot prints had survived the removal of evidence.

However, there was one lone boot print that had survived and was clear enough to make a casting of it. It was of a riding boot, a boot with a smooth leather sole and a fairly high heel. It was unlike all the rest of the boot prints. The rest were work boots, or work boots like military men might have worn. There was one other thing that made the riding boot print different. It was smaller than the others. That was at least partly due to the fact that riding boots were often narrower and often had more pointed toes than work boots, because they had to fit in stirrups from a saddle, often quickly. But this boot print was very small almost like a woman's cowboy boot.

Bill went to his patrol car and got out the kit used to make casts of tire tracks from the trunk. When he returned to the barn to make a cast of the cowboy boot print, he found it had been brushed over making it useless.

Bill quickly drew his gun as he looked around. He didn't see anyone, and he didn't hear anyone. In the short time it had taken him to get his kit out of the trunk of his patrol car and return to the barn to make the cast, someone had come in the barn and brushed out the boot print. That meant they couldn't be far away.

Bill quickly checked each stall, then climbed into the loft. Whoever had brushed out the boot prints was not in the barn. Since he had gone out and came back in the front of the barn, it was most likely that whoever brushed out the boot prints had probably been in the barn and saw Bill looking at the boot prints. That person brushed out the boot print, then went out the back of the barn.

Bill walked out the back of the barn checking for any new tracks. He saw none. It was easy to see that a person could quickly disappear into the woods and be gone from the area in a matter of seconds without being seen, and without leaving a boot print.

As Bill slipped his gun back in his holster, he took a minute to look down at the ground. There were a lot of boot prints from all the people who had gone in and out of the barn. None of them looked like the riding boot print he had seen in the tack room.

He stood there looking around. Bill wasn't looking at anything, he was just thinking. If the riding boot print was so small, was it possible that it was a woman who made the riding boot print?

That thought caused Bill to look toward the house. Was it possible that Mrs. Cannon was one of the pro-Nazis? He knew it would not be the first time he had run into a woman that worked for a pro-Nazi group. He also knew that the women who were Nazis could be just as violent and as determined as the men.

Bill quickly turned and headed for the house. When he got to the house he didn't bother to knock. He simply opened the door and looked for Mrs. Cannon. He found her in the kitchen. He glanced at her feet. She was wearing slippers. His attention was quickly drawn to her face when she spoke.

"Is there something I can do for you, Officer Sparks?"

"Yes. Do you own a pair of cowboy boots?"

"Yes, of course. Why?"

"Could I see them?"

"Certainly. There is a pair of the cowboy boots I use when I work around the barn on the back porch. I also have a dress pair in my closet upstairs in the bedroom."

"Show me."

Mrs. Cannon looked at him for a moment, then started for the back porch. Bill followed her to the back porch. Once on the porch he could see a pair of cowboy boots in a tray just inside the door. The boots were dirty and scuffed, obviously used for working around the farm. From the look of them they had been in the boot tray for some time. They also looked larger than the ones that made the boot print in the tack room.

She looked at Bill and said, "Are you satisfied?"

"Yes. These are not the boots I saw prints of in the tack room. These are bigger."

"You saw prints from cowboy boots that are smaller than my boots?"

"Yes. Do you know of anyone who has been here that has smaller feet than you?"

She looked at him while she thought about what he had asked.

"You found prints from cowboy boots in the tack room that are smaller than mine?"

"Yes. Well, actually, they looked more like riding boots, or woman's cowboy boots. Why? Have you seen a woman out there?"

"No, but I saw a man out there who wasn't even as tall as I am."

"When was this?"

"It was the last time Martin had one of his so-called 'meetings' out in the barn. He might have had small feet. Frankly, I didn't notice his feet."

"How tall was he, do you think?" Bill asked.

"I only saw him once, and that was out by the barn. Since I saw him walking close to Martin, I would guess he was at least a foot shorter than Martin. That would make him about four ten, or four eleven. He was certainly not any taller than five feet tall," Mrs. Cannon said.

"Other than being short, was there anything else outstanding about him?"

"No, I don't think, wait. He seemed pretty sure of himself. The way he talked to Martin as they walked from that man's car to the barn, I got the feeling that he was in charge, of what I didn't know."

"What gave you that idea?"

"I'm not sure because I couldn't hear them talking, but I was sure that Martin was replying to him by what looked like, 'yes, sir' and 'no sir'."

"You mean something like the way an enlisted man in the Army might reply to, say, an officer?" Bill suggested.

"Yeah. Just like that," she said.

Bill wasn't sure he should believe her. He had gotten the feeling that she just might do almost anything to make sure that Martin could not come back to the farm. But on the other hand, he couldn't simply dismiss what he had been told.

Maybe it was time to talk to one of the injured attackers. Maybe one of them could shed some light on who the little guy might be, if there was such a man.

It was time for Bill to head on home. He could write up his report and take it into the Sheriff's Office in the morning. He wanted to talk to Robert while he was there. Bill got in his patrol car and headed back to Hill City.

It was well after seven when Bill drove into his driveway. It had been a long day and he was tired and hungry. He locked up his car and went to the house. When he opened the backdoor to the kitchen, the first thing he noticed was the smell of something cooking in his kitchen. He smiled to himself.

"Hi. It looks like you have had a hard day," Julie said.

"I have," he said

Bill took her in his arms and pulled her close. He kissed her. She leaned back and looked up at him.

"Has it been a rough day?"

"That would be an understatement."

"Why don't you take a shower, then we'll have dinner."

"That's a good idea. I'll be just a few minutes."

As soon as Bill finished showering, he got dressed in jeans and a comfortable shirt. He walked out to the kitchen and found a dinner of baked chicken with potatoes and corn on a plate. Julie was just serving up a glass of milk.

"Sit down," she said.

Bill sat down and looked at the meal then looked across the table at Julie.

"I'm sorry that I got home so late, but I had something that came to mind that I needed to check out as soon as possible."

"It's all right. I know this investigation has been difficult. Right now, you need to eat."

Bill smiled at her then began to eat. Not much was said while they ate dinner.

As soon as they were done eating, they cleaned up the kitchen together. There was enough left over for Bill to have another meal of chicken.

They had just finished taking care of the kitchen when Julie turned and looked at him. He was hanging up the dish towel. He turned and looked at her.

"I wish I could stay longer, but I have to go to work."

"I'm sorry I didn't get home sooner."

"It's all right. I at least got to have dinner with you. You look tired."

"I am."

"You get some rest. I'll stop by in the morning."

"I'd like that."

Bill reached out, took her in his arms and kissed her. He slowly let go of her after a long kiss.

"I would like to stay, but I have to go or I'll be late. Besides, you need to get some rest."

Bill didn't say anything. He knew she was right. He slipped his arm around behind her and led her to the door.

Bill followed her out to her car and opened the car door for her. She got in then turned and looked up at him. She smiled.

"I love you," she said.

"I love you, too. Drive careful."

"I will."

Bill closed the car door and stepped back. He watched her as she started the car, then backed out of the drive and drove away.

As soon as Julie was out of sight, Bill went back in the house. He was tired, and he didn't feel like listening to the radio, so he went to bed.

CHAPTER NINETEEN

Bill was up in plenty of time to fix a good breakfast for Julie. He knew she would be stopping by about eight. He got dressed in his uniform so he was ready to go to work as soon as they had finished breakfast.

It was just a couple of minutes before eight when she drove into the driveway. Bill waited for her on the porch.

As soon as she was on the porch, he put his arm around and led her into the kitchen. He gave her a kiss, then pulled out a chair for her to sit on.

"How did your night shift go?" Bill asked as he dished up a healthy portion of scrambled eggs and ham.

"It went well. It wasn't very busy. We did have a man come in with an accidental gunshot wound to his leg. It wasn't very serious. I cleaned the wound and put a dressing on it. The injury didn't require hospitalizing him."

"Did he give you a reason for the accident?"

"He said it was stupid, and that he knew better than to wipe down his hunting rifle before he checked to make sure it was empty. He also said he was getting it ready for deer hunting season," Julie said with a slight chuckle.

"What did you find so funny," Bill asked.

"First of all, he didn't look the type to be a hunter."

"What do you mean?"

"He was fifty-three years old, he was overweight, and he didn't look like he was physically fit enough to be tramping around in the woods. He was also less than five feet tall. He just didn't look like someone who could get a dead deer out of the woods by himself."

Bill took notice of Julie's description of the man. He fit pretty close to what Mrs. Cannon had told him yesterday.

"Did you get a name for this guy?"

"Sure. I needed it for our records."

"Do you remember his name?"

"Yes. It was hard to forget. The name he gave me was Raymond Tallman. I thought it was a funny name for someone like him since he was so short."

"My guess would be that it was not his real name."

"What makes you say that?" she asked.

"He just might be the man I'm looking for. Did he wear cowboy boots?"

"I guess you could call them cowboy boots, but they were more like riding boots with high heels. How did you know that?"

"Where was the injury on the leg?"

"It was just below his left knee. Why?"

"Was the gunshot wound a new wound? Like one that happened that day, or was it one that could have happened a day or two ago?"

"It didn't look very serious. He said he did it yesterday, but decided that he should have it looked at so it wouldn't get infected," Julie said. "What's going on here? Why your interest in Mr. Tallman?"

"I think Mr. Tallman was shot at the Cannon Farm yesterday afternoon."

"How is it that you know where he was shot?"

"There was a little skirmish out at the Cannon Farm yesterday. We got all of those involved except one. I think he just might be the one who got away."

"You mean you were in a gunfight and you didn't tell me about it?"

Bill was surprised by her sudden reaction. He could see the anger in her eyes. He was thinking that he probably should have told her about it last night, but he didn't because he didn't think it was a big deal since none of the deputies were injured, and it lasted less than twenty minutes.

"It wasn't any big deal. None of us were hurt. I can't really tell you all about it at this time. We are still investigating it, and still looking for one of them. We don't want it to get around. If it does, it will only make it harder for us to find the one that got away."

Julie just looked at Bill. She didn't know what to say.

"Honey, please don't say anything to anyone about this. There might be others, we just don't know. This little guy is the only one I think might have gotten away because no one saw him in the actual skirmish."

"I'm sorry. I have to go," Julie said suddenly. "Grandpa is expecting me to fix him breakfast."

Julie got up and started for the door. Bill knew that he had upset her. He didn't intend to upset her, but he had.

"Julie, please try to understand. It's not easy to talk to you about what I do and everything I get involved in."

Julie stopped and turned around. She looked at him for a minute, she took a deep breath and let it out slowly.

"I'm sorry. I should know that these things happen in your line of work, but I need to know about them."

"Why? So you can worry about me?"

She looked at him for a moment, then walked back to him and put her hands on his shoulders. She looked up at him, then raised up on her tiptoes and kissed him lightly.

"No, because I love you," she said.

"I love you, too."

Julie let go of him, turned around and walked to her car. She got in and started it, then looked at Bill. She smiled, then drove away.

Bill just stood there and watched her leave. He wasn't sure what had just happened. He didn't want to lose her.

As soon as she was out of sight, he turned and went back into the house. He wasn't sure if she would want to see him again. He wanted to go after her, but decided against it. He would give her time to think about it. He hoped he had not lost her.

It was time to head into Rapid City and have a talk with the sheriff. He needed to report the information that he learned from Julie. He also needed to set up a time when Sam Lawson could talk to his stepson, Robert Hood. He had no idea what might come of that, but he hoped it would work out okay for both of them. Bill got in his patrol car and headed for Rapid City.

Bill arrived at the county building where the Sheriff's Office is located at about half past nine. He had just walked into the building when the desk sergeant called to him.

"Bill, the sheriff wants to talk to you. He tried to get hold of you before you left Hill City, but he didn't get an answer."

"I must have just missed him."

"He told me to tell you to go on in his office."

Bill nodded toward the desk sergeant, then walked down the hall to the sheriff's office. He knocked on the door and was told to enter.

"I was hoping that you would come in this morning," the sheriff said.

"The desk sergeant told me you wanted to see me."

"Yes. How did it go with Sam Lawson?"

"I think it went well. He was cooperative, answered my questions, and didn't seem to have any idea how his personal things got in Cannon's barn."

"Did you tell him about what had been going on in that barn, you know, the pro-Nazi group meetings held there?"

"No. I didn't think it was necessary. We did talk about his stepson, Robert, though."

"What about him?"

"Lawson seemed genuinely concerned about him. He said he was sorry for running Robert off his farm, and wished that he had helped him rather than run him off. He said he lost his temper. Lawson wants to come here and have a talk with his stepson in the hope of mending their relationship, and maybe help him in some way."

"Do you think he should see his stepson?"

"I think it would be a good idea. At least here, Robert couldn't get up and leave. Giving Lawson the opportunity to sit down and talk with Robert might not improve their relationship, but it certainly won't hurt it any."

"I'll have to agree with you on that. It might even help us a little."

"It might," Bill agreed. "I would like to call Lawson and tell him that he can come in and talk to his stepson."

"Okay. Are you planning on being here while Lawson is here?"

"Yes, but I will not be where I can hear what they are saying to each other."

"Okay, give him a call. By the way, I take it you don't think Lawson had anything to do with the pro-Nazi group?"

"No, I don't think so. He seemed to answer my questions without any hesitation. And his answers seemed logical. He did say he thought that Robert might have taken his personal things from the barn to use in his hiding place, but couldn't say that for sure. He indicated that he had no idea when they were taken from his barn. I was a little surprised when he said that he would have given the things to Robert if he had simply asked.

"I have something else to talk to you about," Bill added.

"Okay. Call Lawson, then we'll talk. I have a call I need to make, too. We can talk after that."

Bill nodded, stood up and went out to the officers' desks. He sat down at one of the desks and placed a call to Lawson. Sam Lawson told Bill that he would come in to talk to Robert right away.

After the call to Lawson, Bill went to where the holding cells were located. He walked up to the one Robert Hood was in. Robert looked up at Bill, but didn't get up or say anything.

"Robert, you're going to have company in about an hour or so."

"I don't want my mother to see me in here."

"It's not your mother. It's your stepfather."

"I don't want to talk to him. I don't even want to see him," he said sharply.

"Robert, I'm going to say this just once, so you better pay close attention. Your stepfather wants to help you. He wants to give you a second chance, and he wants to apologize for running you off and not listening to you. I suggest you don't make the same mistake. You need to listen to him. And if you have two brain cells in that head of yours, you will listen to him."

Bill looked at Robert for a moment, then turned and left Robert to think about it. He returned to the officers' area and sat down. He had only been there for a couple of minutes when Doug walked in.

"Say, Doug. What did you do with all that stuff you found in Martin Cannon's desk?"

"It's in the box on my desk. I haven't had a chance to sort it out and catalog it. I figured you would want to go over it with me."

"I would. Do you have time to do it now?"

"Sure. Can you tell me what you are looking for?"

"I'm looking for a man named Raymond Tallman."

"I've seen that name somewhere," Doug said.

Doug opened the box on his desk and began going through the papers in the box. He pulled out a small notebook from under some papers and began thumbing through it.

"I think this is where a saw the name of Tallman."

Doug thumbed through several of the pages before he stopped and began to skim through each page. He suddenly stopped, turned toward Bill and smiled.

"Here it is. Raymond Tallman, Colonel Raymond Tallman."

Doug handed the notebook to Bill.

Bill looked at the notebook and began to read it. As he read it, he began to smile.

"I think I know who this Raymond Tallman really is," Bill said.

"Who is he?"

"I saw him at a distance in Hill City. I saw him carrying a box into one of Hill City's gift stores. I think it's called 'Western Collectables'. It's a place that has the usual tourist type items, but it also has antiques and collectable items."

"Yeah, I've seen him. He doesn't look like the usual pro-Nazi type."

"That's just it. He would never be taken for a person who belonged to any military type organization. It's the perfect cover," Bill said.

"The business would be the perfect place, too. He could get shipments of just about anything in boxes and crates, and it would seem normal to anyone who might be watching him. He sure doesn't look like the type to be a member of a military organization," Doug said. "He can't be more than about five feet tall, if that."

"Maybe he doesn't look like the type, but from the looks of the information in this little notebook, he is actually the leader of this pro-Nazi group."

"I've been in his store. I don't think his name is Tallman," Doug said.

"I've only seen him once or twice, and that was at a distance. I've never been in his store. Do you remember what his name is?"

"I'm not sure. It seems to me it was something like, Ray Smith, or something like that," Doug said.

"It shouldn't be too hard to find out what his name is, or at least the one he is using.

"What do we do now?"

"We study this notebook. We need to know as much about the organization as we can."

"Then what?" Doug asked.

"Then we talk to the sheriff and see if he thinks we have enough to get an arrest warrant and a search warrant of his store."

Bill pulled out a chair and started going through the notebook. He was surprised at what he found. First of all, he was able to figure out what plans they were working on, that being an attack on the ammunition depot at the Air Force base. Either to blow it up or to steal any explosive ordnance they could get their hands on.

Secondly, to attack the Sheriff's Office to cause as much damage and confusion as possible. As well as, drastically reduce the number of officers with the goal of making the Sheriff's Office ineffective.

Bill also figured out why Franklin Parker was killed and who had killed him. Notes in the notebook indicate that Franklin Parker had been a member of the pro-Nazi group. He had probably stolen something of value from the pro-Nazi group. Since Parker had been found with three gold coins where he had been murdered, it was probably what he had stolen. It looked as if the gold coins were going to be used to buy more weapons in order to carry out their plans, but without the gold coins they would not be able to purchase the weapons needed to carry out their plans.

"I would say that the notebook will probably get us warrants on all of them," Bill said.

"Just how many warrants do we need? Other than the ones we already have in custody." Doug asked.

"In the notebook is a list of the members of the pro-Nazi group who live in the area. After eliminating those from the list who died in the attack at the Cannon Farm, and those who were captured alive and are still in custody, there are six of them who live in the Rapid City area.

"Four of the six listed in the notebook live in Rapid City. They actually live at the Rapid City Air Force Base as Airmen. The three airmen listed were William Smith, Peter Kinsley and Harold Riemann. Franklin Parker was the fourth one. He was the murder victim that started this investigation. That makes three of them still at the air base. There are also two who do not live on the base, William Hill and Billy Hill. They are brothers, and live together in a small apartment in north Rapid City. So that makes a total of five arrest warrants we need.

"Sean Carter and James Goodman were not listed in the notebook," Bill added.

"There were three listed in Hill City. Martin Cannon, Chuck Smart and Raymond Tallman. Chuck Smart and Martin Cannon are currently in custody. Raymond Tallman, or Ray Smith, is listed as living in Hill City. So that's one we need to arrest there.

"Robert Hood's name was not one of those listed in the notebook. I think we need to get in touch with Captain Butler at the air base and have him arrest Smith, Kinsley, and Riemann. They apparently were not with those who attacked us at Cannon's Farm," Bill said.

"Do you think we have enough information for an arrest?" Doug asked.

"I think so. Either way, it's time to talk to the sheriff and see what he thinks."

Bill stood up and headed for the sheriff's office with the small notebook in his hand. Doug followed along behind him. When they got to the door to the sheriff's office, Bill reached out and knocked.

"Come in," the sheriff said.

Bill went in first with Doug right behind him.

"Excuse us, sir, but are you done with your call?"

"Yes. What's up? You look like you have something important."

"We do."

"Okay. Have a seat."

Bill and Doug sat down in front of the sheriff's desk.

"We would like you to look at some of the evidence we have gathered from Martin Cannon's house. Actually, Doug found it while searching the house."

"Okay. I take it this has something to do with the raid on the Cannon Farm?"

"Yes, but it is more than that. We think we have found some additional members of the pro-Nazi group operating out of the Cannon Farm, or at least under the same leadership, namely Tallman. We also have information on what their plans are," Bill said.

"Okay. Let's take a look at it."

Bill handed the notebook to the sheriff, then gave the sheriff a little time to look it over. After a few minutes, he looked up at Bill and Doug.

"Tell me what you think this is all about?" the sheriff asked.

Bill took several minutes to explain what evidence they had and how it laid out.

"The pro-Nazi group was meeting at the Cannon farm, Martin Cannon being one of them. The little guy who owns the Western Collectables store in Hill City is the leader of this pro-Nazi group."

Bill went on to explain the rest. As soon as they were finished explaining what they thought was going on, they sat back and waited for the sheriff to comment.

The sheriff studied the small notebook for several minutes. He looked up at Bill and Doug and smiled.

"You've done a good job. I think you have enough to get arrest warrants for all those involved, including those who survived the attack at Cannon's Farm. I'll make a call to the judge and get your arrest warrants," Sheriff Henderson said.

"Bill, I want you to give a call to Captain Butler and have him arrest Smith, Kinsley and Riemann, and hold them until we can get out there to serve the arrest warrants on them. I'll get a couple of officers to go to the air base and serve the warrants on those men. I'll also ask the state police to pick up the Hill brothers. I should have the arrest warrant for Tallman by the time you have talked to Captain Butler.

"As soon as you are done making the arrangements with Captain Butler, go to Hill City and pickup Tallman, or whatever name he goes by.

"Take Doug with you to arrest this Tallman fella. Being the leader, he may want to resist being arrested, so be careful."

"Yes sir."

Bill and Doug left the sheriff's office. They stopped at the desk where Bill called Captain Butler. It didn't take very long before Captain Butler was on the phone.

"Good afternoon, Bill. What can I do for you?"

"Good afternoon, Mike. I need a little help. We had a skirmish with a pro-Nazi group in the backcountry yesterday."

"I heard about that."

"We managed to get hold of a notebook which has the names of members of the group. Four of them are or were airmen stationed at your base."

"You're kidding."

"I'm afraid not. We are getting arrest warrants for them as we speak. I would like you to take them into custody and hold them until our deputies can come and serve the arrest warrants."

"Are you sure of your information?"

"Absolutely, sir. We are in the process of getting the arrest warrants for several others as well. In fact, a couple of them are currently in custody now. They were picked up and were here yesterday as part of the investigation into the murder of Franklin J. Parker."

"How is the murder of Franklin Parker connected to the pro-Nazi group?"

"Franklin Parker was one of the pro-Nazis in this group. We believe he was murdered because he stole some German gold coins from the pro-Nazi group."

"What are the names of the ones you want?" Mike asked.

"William Smith, Peter Kinsley and Harold Riemann."

"Two of the three work in weapon ordnance," Mike said.

"I'm glad we found out about them before they could do any harm."

"So am I. It sounds like your murder investigation got to be a lot more than a simple murder case," Captain Butler said.

"It sure did, but there's no such thing as a 'simply murder case'. By the way, part of the plans we found involved your air base."

"How so?"

"They were planning to steal explosives from the base."

There was complete silence on the line. Bill gave Mike time to let what he said soak in.

"I'll have them waiting in my office all cuffed and ready for transport to your jail. I might add, after you are done with them, our justice system might like to have them."

"I'll remember that. Thanks, Mike. I'm sorry it turned out this way."

"Bill, I can assure you that I am not. You may very well have prevented the theft of some very deadly material from this base, and possibly saved some lives. It also makes me want to take a hard look at how we protect weapons and explosives here. Thanks."

"Some time ago, I promised you that I would fill you in on my investigation when it is over. I'll be stopping by one of these days. We can sit down with a cup of coffee and have that talk."

"I look forward to it. By the way, will you be coming to get them?"

"No. I will be going after the leader of the group in Hill City."

"Okay. Tell the sheriff, I look forward to turning them over to him."

"I will. Talk to you later."

"Be safe. Goodbye,"

Bill hung up the phone just as Sheriff Henderson came out of his office.

"Did Captain Butler agree to help us by turning the three airmen over to us."

"Yes, sir. He said he would have them in cuffs and waiting for you to send the deputies to pick them up at his office."

"Good. You will have your warrants in the next fifteen to twenty minutes."

"Thank you, sir.

Bill looked at Doug and smiled. It was time to wait, and a time to prepare. Bill reviewed the store where Tallman was likely to be with Doug since Bill had never been in the store. He was sure that Tallman, or Smith, would not like the idea of being arrested. He would know that he had a lot to lose, possibly his life.

It was about two-fifteen in the afternoon when Bill and Doug received the arrest warrant for one Ray Smith, aka Raymond Tallman, from the sheriff. They immediately went to Bill's patrol car and headed for Hill City.

CHAPTER TWENTY

It was a little past four in the afternoon when Bill and Doug arrived at the Hill City limits. They had it all planned out. Bill would drop Doug off about a block from the Western Collectables store. He would then wait until Doug had time to get to the back of the store.

As soon as he was sure that Doug was ready to cover the back of the store, Bill would pull up in front of the store and casually walk into the store and look around as if looking for something to buy. He wouldn't make a move toward Tallman until he was sure Tallman was the only one in the store. He didn't want any customers in the store when they arrested Tallman. If Tallman tried to resist arrest, Bill didn't want any bystanders around who might get in the way or get hurt.

When it was time for Bill to move in, he drove up in front of the Western Collectables store. He parked right in front of the store, and casually walked inside.

"May I help you, officer." Mr. Tallman asked, his voice sounding pleasant.

"I'm just looking for something for my girlfriend. It's her birthday, and I want something different, you know. Not the usual thing guys give their girls. But I don't want something really strange, either. I do want it to be something special."

"I understand. Does she like antiques?"

"Yes, as a matter of fact she does like antiques, especially antique jewelry."

"I have some very nice pieces right over here."

As Tallman turned his back on Bill, Bill made sure there was no one else in the store.

"Over here, I have some ----. What the hell?"

Bill grabbed Tillman from behind and pushed him over a table that had a lot of tourist gifts on it. He pulled Tallman's arms around behind his back and quickly put handcuffs on him while pinning him down over the table.

"Doug, I got him."

Doug came in from the backroom. He saw that Bill had Tallman in handcuffs, and had control of the situation.

Bill stood Tallman up, then searched him for any weapons before he turned him around.

"What the hell do you think you're doing?"

"Doug, lock the front door and put up the closed sign."

"You can't bust in here and lock up my store," Tallman protested.

Doug immediately went to the front door and secured it. He then put the closed sign on the door.

"The place is secured. I locked the backdoor."

"Good."

"What the hell do you think you're doing. I'll have your ass for this," Tallman yelled.

"You are under arrest. This is an arrest warrant for Raymond Tallman, or should I say, Colonel Raymond Tallman," Bill said as he stuffed the warrant in Tallman's pocket. "It's also a search warrant for your store, and any living quarters you might have here, or elsewhere."

"My name is not Raymond Tallman. It's Ray, or Raymond Smith."

"Oh, I'm sorry. I forgot to tell you. The arrest warrant is also for Ray Smith."

Tallman just looked at Bill. He wasn't sure what was going to happen to him.

"What am I being charged with. Did I sell an antique locket to some old lady who said it was stolen from her?"

"No. It's nothing that simple. It's a lot more serious than that. It's for the murder of Franklin J. Parker. Well, that is for now. There are likely several other charges to follow. Some of them just might be Federal charges."

"I didn't kill anyone."

"Doug, take him to the backroom and stay with him. I'm going to look around out here."

"Okay. He has an office in the back."

"Just watch him for now. We'll search his office later."

"Come on, buster," Doug said as he took Tallman by the arm. He almost had to drag him to the backroom of the store.

"You can't do this. You can't search my store," Tallman protested.

"That is where you are wrong. Like I said, the arrest warrant has a search warrant attached to it," Bill reminded him.

As soon as Doug had Tallman in the backroom, Bill started looking around the store. He wasn't sure what he was looking for, but he was sure he would know it when he saw it. Actually, Bill did know what he was looking for. He was looking for something that would confirm that Tallman, aka Smith, was involved with the pro-Nazi group.

The first place he searched was the shelves and drawers under the counter. He didn't find anything there of importance. There were just the things that would be under any counter in a store like this.

After searching under the counter, he stood up and looked around the store. There were a number of items in the front part of the store where something that would connect him to the pro-Nazi group could be hidden.

Thinking about it, Bill decided that it would be stupid to keep anything like that where people might come in and accidently find it while looking around the store for something to buy. Bill didn't think Tallman was stupid.

Bill decided that his time would be better spent looking in the backroom and in Tallman's office. He could always come back later and look again in the front of the store.

Bill went into the backroom. Doug was sitting on a chair watching Tallman, while Tallman was sitting on another chair in a corner.

"Didn't find anything, did you?" Tallman said with a look of superiority.

"If it will make you feel better, no, I didn't find anything. I'm not done looking."

Bill's last comment seemed to wipe the stupid grin off Tallman's face. Bill motioned for Doug to come with him. Bill moved across the room from Tallman. Doug joined him while still keeping an eye on Tallman.

"What's up," Doug whispered.

"I want you to keep a close watch on his reactions as I look around. If you see a reaction like he might not want me looking there, give me a little nod. If he looks worried, I'm probably getting close to something he doesn't want me to find."

"Got it," Doug said.

Doug returned to where he had been sitting. It was off to the side where he could keep an eye on Tallman without him realizing it.

As soon as Doug was seated, Bill began to look around the backroom. The first place he started was a tall cabinet next to the door that led into the front of the store. The cabinet did not have a lock on it.

Bill opened the cabinet and began going through it. The cabinet was filled with office supplies such as paper, receipt books, and other supplies. Bill looked over at Doug. He shook his head.

Bill saw a large old fashion steamer trunk in the corner. It was almost hidden by a heavy curtain, but the curtain had not been closed tight enough to completely hide it. Bill slowly pulled back the curtain so he could get a good look at it. He turned and looked at Doug. Doug nodded his head slightly. Bill looked at Tallman. He could see the worried look in his eyes.

"What's in the trunk?" Bill asked.

"Nothing that you would want," Tallman said sharply.

Bill turned and looked at the trunk for a couple of seconds. There was a heavy padlock on the trunk. He turned and looked at Tallman. He could see the sweat on his upper lip. It was obvious that he did not want Bill opening the trunk.

"I'd like the key to this trunk," Bill said.

"You can't open that. It's my private things and you can't even look at them without my permission."

"Okay. You don't want to give me the key, that's your choice. Doug, bust it open."

"You can't do that."

"Doug, bust it open."

Doug moved up to the trunk, took his gun out of his holster, pointed it at the lock, then slowly pulled back the hammer.

"NO. The key is in the center drawer of the desk over there," Tallman said.

Tallman nodded his head toward a roll-top desk in the corner of the room. Doug walked over to the desk, then reached out and pulled open the center drawer. In the front of the drawer were several keys on a key chain. Doug handed the key ring to Bill.

Bill took the keys, then went over to the trunk.

"Which key is it?" Bill asked.

"I'm not going to help you search my store."

Bill smiled then knelt down in front of the trunk. He took the key that looked like it might fit the lock and inserted it in the lock and turned it. The lock popped open. Bill removed the lock, then opened the trunk.

Inside the trunk was a tray that could be lifted out. The tray had several compartments. Bill found two pair of black shoes that were polished to a bright shine. In a larger compartment was a pair of dress boots, also polished to a bright shine. The thing was, Bill had seen boots just like them. They were high top boots like he had seen German officers wearing while he was in Europe. He also found sox and two pair of black gloves in the smaller compartments.

Once he had seen all there was of interest in the compartments, Bill lifted the tray out and set it on the floor. There was a white cloth covering whatever was in the bottom of the trunk. He removed the cloth. He had a pretty good idea what he would find. He was not disappointed.

Inside the trunk were two complete uniforms of a German Colonel. On the jacket were an array of metals, including a black Maltese Cross. Bill had no trouble recognizing the uniforms. He had seen enough of them while in Germany during the war. Bill pulled the jacket out of the trunk and held it up. He quickly noticed a name tag above the left side pocket. It read, “Colonel Raymond C. Tallman”.

“It looks like we have caught us a real live German Colonel. This looks like it would fit him just fine,” Bill said to Doug as he held up the jacket.

Bill turned back to the trunk and began rummaging through it. He found a small leather pouch. When he lifted it up, it felt heavy. When he started to open it, Tallman yelled at him.

“That’s mine. You have no right to open it.”

Bill just looked at him for a second or two, then opened the leather pouch. He turned it over in his hand. Six solid gold coins fell out into his hand. The coins were just like the ones he picked up where Franklin Parker’s body was found.

“Well, I’ll be darned,” Doug said.

“This is interesting,” Bill said.

Bill looked at Tallman. There was little doubt that Tallman was angry.

“How many of these are there?” Bill asked.

“I’ll not tell you.”

"Well, let's see. There was six here, and I already have three. I should say that the sheriff has three. That makes nine. How many are there?"

"Where did he get coins like that?" Doug asked.

"These are very special coins," Bill said. "They were made and given to several people to help them escape from Germany in nineteen-thirty-six, or there about. The German officers got them by taking them from those trying to escape Germany. Then they would kill them and keep the coins for themselves."

"What do you want to do?" Doug asked.

Bill looked at Tallman. He could see the look of fear on his face.

"Doug, keep an eye on him. I'm going out to my patrol car and talk to the sheriff."

"No problem. If anyone tries to help him escape, I'll just shoot him first."

Bill didn't say anything. He turned and went to his patrol car. He sat down and called in.

"Car eight to dispatch."

"Go ahead, eight."

"Can you patch me through to the sheriff?"

"He is standing right here. He's been worried about you."

"What's going on out there?" the sheriff asked.

"We have Raymond Tallman in custody. By the way, I think his real name might be Colonel Raymond C. Tallman.

"Really," the sheriff said.

"We started our search of the place. We found a real German uniform that would fit him. I also found six more gold coins."

"Has he been cooperative?"

"No, not one bit. He has been very uncooperative."

"Okay. I'm going to send two deputies out there to bring Tallman in here where we can lock him up. I want you and Doug to stay there and secure the store. We have no idea what he might have in that place."

"Yes, sir."

"Over," the sheriff said.

"Over."

Bill hung up his mic, then returned to the store. Once inside the store, he told Doug what was going on.

Bill went to the back of the store to make sure that the backdoor was secure so no one could come in. After making sure the front door was also secure, he took up a position where he could see anyone who might try to come into the store. Bill sat down on a chair and watched out the front window, while Doug sat close to Tallman and watched the backdoor. It was a time to wait.

It took almost an hour before two Pennington County patrol cars pulled up in front of the Western Collectables store. Sheriff Henderson got out of one, and two deputies got out of the other. They walked up to the door and knocked. Bill saw who it was, then opened the door.

"Doug has Tallman in the backroom." Bill said.

"Good."

The sheriff walked to the backroom of the store. The first thing he saw was Doug sitting next to a little man. The little man was in handcuffs.

"Doug, I want you to go with Kenton and take Tallman to jail. I want him put in a secure cell, alone. I don't want anyone, and I mean anyone, talking to him or getting anywhere near him until I've had a chance to talk to him."

"Yes, sir."

Doug stood up and grabbed Tallman by the arm. He started out the door with Kenton on the other side of Tallman. The two officers put Tallman in a patrol car, then left Hill City for the county jail in Rapid City.

Meanwhile, the sheriff, Bill and Officer Wilson searched the store. They loaded the trunk, along with a number of papers they found in a box hidden way back in the bottom of a closet, into the sheriff's patrol car.

Sheriff Henderson, Officer Wilson and Bill searched the rest of the store and the living quarters in the back of the store. In the living quarters, they found two Nazi flags, a box containing German combat metals, and a list of contacts in other parts of the country. When they were finished, they had loaded all the additional evidence they had found into the sheriff's patrol car. Confident that they had gotten all the evidence that was in the store and the living quarters, the sheriff locked up the store and put a sign on the door that told the world the Western Collectables store was permanently closed.

Bill and Wilson stood outside next to the car. They were keeping an eye out for anyone who might want to interfere with them, and possibly try to get the evidence from them.

Sheriff Henderson looked around then turned toward Bill.

"It's been a long day for you. I don't see any reason for you to come all the way to Rapid City just to turn around and come back. Wilson and I can get all this stuff to Rapid City. We'll have help getting it locked up at the office. Tomorrow, I'll have help logging it all in. Why don't you go home and get some rest?"

"Thank you, sir. Do you want me to come in in the morning?"

"It's been a long day, why don't you come in, oh say, eleven o'clock. We should have all the evidence logged in by then. I'll buy lunch and we'll go over the evidence and see what we have on this Tallman fella."

"Yes, sir," Bill said.

"I'll see you tomorrow about eleven."

"Yes, sir."

Bill walked over to his patrol car. He stood by it and watched as Wilson and the sheriff got in his patrol car. Bill got in his patrol car.

As soon as the sheriff's patrol car started to move, Bill followed them to the edge of town. He pulled off to the side and watched them until they were out of sight. Not seeing anyone following them, Bill turned around and went home.

Just as he was about to turn into his driveway, he noticed Julie's car was parked there. He had not expected to see her tonight. After yesterday, he wasn't sure she wanted to see him again.

Bill parked his patrol car at the end of the drive next to the garage. He got out and walked toward his house. Just as he was stepping up on the porch, Julie opened the door and looked at him.

"I wasn't expecting to see you here," Bill said.

"Do you want me to leave?"

"No, of course not. I just didn't expect to see you."

"Bill, I'm so sorry about how I acted."

"It's okay."

"No, it's not okay. You were just trying to protect me from worrying about you. I understand that. And I reacted poorly. I'm sorry."

"I should have trusted that you would understand what I do, and there is a certain amount a risk in it.

"I will try to understand better. I don't want to lose you. I love you," she said.

"I love you, too."

Julie stepped up to him, reached out and put her hands on his shoulders then raised up on her tiptoes and kissed him.

Bill wrapped her in his arms and kissed her back, holding her close to him. After a long and passionate kiss, Bill leaned back and looked into her eyes.

"Are you going to be late for work?" he asked.

"I'm off tonight."

"How long had you planned to stay here?"

"Until you got home," she admitted.

"It's kind of late."

"I know. Have you eaten?"

"No."

"I'll fix you something while you take a shower, or," she said with a grin.

"Or what?" he said playfully.

"Or, we'll eat and then we can take a shower together. I'll wear one of your shirts to bed, if you like."

"I like the second choice best."

"So do I," she said with a grin.

Bill took her hand and led her into the house. Julie fixed a light dinner for the two of them. After eating, they took a shower together, then went to bed. They didn't go to sleep right away, but they did fall asleep in each other's arms.

CHAPTER TWENTY-ONE

It was almost nine o'clock when Bill woke. Julie was curled up beside him. She opened her eyes and smiled at him.

"You ready to get up?" Julie asked.

"I need to get up pretty soon. I have to meet with Sheriff Henderson at eleven."

"Will you be gone all day?"

"I don't know, but it could take all afternoon. I have to turn in my report of what happened yesterday. I don't know for sure, but I might have to help with the evidence we got from the Western Collectables store last night."

"Do you want me to wait here for you?"

"What about your - - - - -,"

Bill was interrupted by his phone ringing. He got out of bed and hurried to his phone. He picked up the receiver.

"Hello."

"Bill, I'm glad I caught you. This is Sheriff Henderson."

"Yes, sir. Is there a problem?"

"No. I just wanted you to know that you will not have to come into the office."

"I need to submit my report on last night."

"Write it up and bring it in tomorrow."

"Has something changed?"

"As a matter of fact, yes. A lot has changed. The FBI has taken over."

"Why?"

"It seems you have uncovered just one cell of a larger pro-Nazi Organization. The information we got by arresting Colonel Raymond Tallman has produced names, addresses, phone numbers, and locations of several other cells around a five-state area. The FBI is on their way here to pick up those we have in custody and the evidence to charge them under federal laws.

"That's great," Bill said. "It saves us a lot of work."

"In this case, we've done all the work, now we can forget it."

"Will they be charging whoever it was who killed Parker?"

"According to the FBI agent that will handle the case, Tallman gave the order to kill him, and Martin carried it out with the help of Chuck Smart. And yes, that will be an extra charge of murder against those three.

"Since it is over for us, I thought you might like to have the day off."

"Thank you. I wouldn't mind having the day off."

"The lead FBI investigator is very pleased with what you have done. He asked me to convey to you his most heartfelt thanks. He also said that with the evidence you uncovered, he didn't think any of them would go free."

"You tell him 'thank you' from me?"

"I will. I wanted you to know the outcome of your hard work."

"Thank you. I would like to know one other thing?" Bill asked.

"What's that?"

"How did things work out between Robert Hood and Sam Lawson?"

"Sam visited with Robert for a little over two hours in the privacy of one of the interrogation rooms. When they came out, they were still talking to each other. I released Robert, and dropped all charges. Robert told me that he was returning to his stepfather's farm to learn how to run a farm.

"Sam told me that he was going to help teach Robert to farm. He also said the farm next to his was for sale. He plans to buy it and put it in Robert's name, then they will work both farms together."

"Wow, that's a whole lot more than I expected to happen."

"Yes, it is. Well, you enjoy the day off. I see your schedule has you off for a couple of days in just another day. Why don't you take two days off and add them to your regular days off? You have been working a lot of overtime. It will be payment for some of your overtime. I don't want to see you here until you are regularly scheduled to be here."

"Thank you, sir."

"You're welcome," Sheriff Henderson said, then hung up.

Bill hung up the phone and looked toward his bedroom. Julie was standing in the door looking at him. He smiled at her.

"Would you like to go back to bed?"

She smiled at him as he walked toward her.

"What happened?"

"I have four days off."

"What happened?"

"I'll tell you later," he said as he turned her around and walked her back into the bedroom.

EPILOGUE

It was several months later when Sheriff Henderson ~~eived the results of the trials of those involved in pro-Nazi vities in the Black Hills and surrounding states. All were victed of Federal crimes. Tallman, Chuck Smart and rtin Cannon were also convicted of the murder of nklin Parker. They were all sent to a Federal Prison ere Tallman, Smart and Cannon are to be hung for ırdering Parker.

A letter from the FBI thanking the Sheriff's Department, d the individuals who made the capture of those involved the pro-Nazi organization possible.

The gold coins were sent back to the sheriff. The sheriff ave them to Bill to take to Dieter Schmidt. He figured that)ieter was really the rightful owner of the gold coins.

Bill and Julie paid a visit to Dieter Schmidt and his wife. Bill told them about the investigation and capture of those involved. Since there was no one who could be identified as the people who had originally had the gold coins, they were given to Dieter Schmidt. They were given to him because it was his father who made the gold coins.

Mr. Schmidt gave the gold coins to a military museum in Washington D. C. as part of a display of World War II items. The display included a picture of Dieter's father and mother, along with a write-up about the gold coins and Dieter's father's part in helping the men escape Germany.

Bill also went out to the Rapid City Air Force Base to visit with Captain Butler. They had a nice talk over a cold beer at the officer's club while Bill told the captain the whole story as he had promised he would after it was all over.

Made in the USA
Monee, IL
20 January 2024

51517457R00140